DRAGON ATTACK

A bellow shook Beartooth's Camp, and there was Riversong, vast and copper-green in the shimmering sunlight, flying straight towards them from the east. Bellchime's body trembled, and a breeze began blowing at his back as the warriors raised their spearthrowers.

Now! Riversong swooped down to shoot a blast of flame at the tents and goblin warriors, the warriors let fly a volley of spears, and a sudden hurricane wind swept the flames back into Riversong's face, knocking over one of the burning tents and throwing a few goblins off their feet. Riversong scooped his wings forward to let the blast of wind sweep him upward and back, over most of the confusion of spears and fire. Many of the spearshafts burned up, and a few spearheads clattered uselessly against the dragon's tail.

Bellchime's body shook again . . .

DRAGONBOUND

CARL MILLER

ACE BOOKS, NEW YORK

This book is an Ace original edition,
and has never been previously published.

DRAGONBOUND

An Ace Book/published by arrangement with
the author

PRINTING HISTORY
Ace edition/December 1988

ISBN: 0-441-16626-1

Ace Books are published by The Berkley Publishing Group,
200 Madison Avenue, New York, New York 10016.
The name "ACE" and the "A" logo are trademarks belonging to Charter
Communications, Inc.

PRINTED IN THE UNITED STATES OF AMERICA

10 9 8 7 6 5 4 3 2 1

for Jeani Callan
Alison Jones
Kayanne Pickens

CONTENTS

EAST OF THE SEA

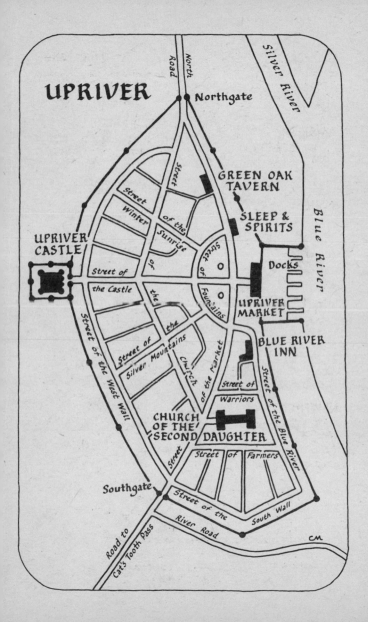

DRAGONBOUND

1

THE DREAMSENDING

1.

"Years and years ago," the storyteller began, and Periwinkle sighed, twisting her straight black hair. What a dull way to begin a tale of Mugwort the Dragon! Old Froth knew all the stories, but he was a bore to listen to.

"Excuse me," Periwinkle said, and withdrew from the circle of older children and young adults seated by the hearth. Her shadow moved across the castle tower's stone wall, which was hung with tapestries; her footsteps tapped lightly on the oaken floor. Her mother, the warrior Black Rose, still seated at the table finishing a late meal, stopped her before she reached the stairs.

"You should hear Froth's story," she said. "A warrior must know all the stories."

"I still remember that story as Bellchime told it, five winters ago. His words brought Mugwort back to life. Froth's words make a dragon dull."

"Bellchime is gone. Froth is your storyteller."

Even in the firelight Periwinkle could see the gray in Black Rose's hair. She treats me like a child to deny her own age, Periwinkle thought, but there was no arguing with Black Rose when she used that tone of voice.

"I will listen to Froth," said Periwinkle.

She moved back to the circle and sat down next to her younger brother, Mandrake. She stared at the sputtering logs on the hearth and thought of dragon-fire.

"Mugwort startled awake, uncurled the vast length of his body, crawled out of the great tower, and leapt into the air. His wings shadowed the forest; his scales held the luster of the moon."

Periwinkle blinked. Those were Bellchime's words, not Froth's, and that was Bellchime's voice. Bellchime sat in front of the fire, his hair dark and curly, his beard framing his smile. She sat facing him alone.

"I must talk with you," he said.

What Periwinkle wanted to do was kiss him, take him upstairs to her room, and lay with him in her bed, their naked bodies pressed together and his hands caressing her breasts.

He said, "I love you, but you must know the truth. I am dragonbound. I am not a black wizard or a dragon's slave, even though it has been four years, but I need help."

She was too shocked to know how to respond for a moment, but then asked, "What can I do?"

Someone was shaking Periwinkle's shoulder.

"Wake up," whispered Mandrake.

Froth stopped his monotone account of Mugwort the Dragon's devastation of Turtleport in mid-sentence. "This is more than rudeness," he said. His squinting sharp eyes and his warty beardless face made him look almost like a goblin. Periwinkle shuddered. "What did you dream?" he asked her.

"I do not remember," she lied. She looked over at the table and saw that it was cleared and her mother gone to bed. How long had she been sleeping?

"You lie," said Froth.

"I may be a woman of only fifteen summers, but I am the warrior Tarragon's daughter. Who are you to ask me what I dream?"

"Froth the Storyteller at your service, my lady."

Periwinkle smiled sarcastically. Froth was more than the dull storyteller she had been forced to listen to the past four winters. He was a man of power.

"I believe I already know what you dreamed," Froth continued, confirming her opinion. "A certain handsome young storyteller told you he is dragonbound, did he not? For four years I have tried to find this man, but he is too powerful, too well hidden. He truly is dragonbound, and you should know what that means."

"You mean we have to kill him and his dragon?" asked Barleycorn, the weaponmaker's son.

"No!" cried Periwinkle.

"What is Bellchime the Storyteller to a warrior's daughter?" asked Froth, who knew the answer. "He has come many times before into your dreams, to enchant you. You would not be so much in love with an eleven-year-old's memory of a good storyteller."

"You think I love a storyteller?" asked Periwinkle, regaining her composure. Froth was right. Her dreams of Bellchime were messages, which meant she knew where he was; she knew he needed her help; she knew he loved her.

"He is no mere storyteller now, but a wizard," said Froth. "You must consider your father's farmholders and the danger they face. A dragon learns from the person it binds, and these are the lands Bellchime knows best. Or if Bellchime prevails, think of the power he will be unable to control. Need I remind you of what the wizard Bracken did to the Isle of Hod with his weathershaping?"

"Spare me," said Periwinkle. "You who know so much about me must know I despise your storytelling."

Mandrake and another older boy laughed.

"I make no romance out of Mugwort," Froth said coldly, glaring at them all. "Those who admire dragons are those the dragons choose."

"How does a dragon choose the person it binds?" asked Barleycorn. "Tell us a story about that."

"Bellchime said they found their partners by hearing them think," said Mandrake.

"Their slaves," corrected Froth.

Periwinkle shuddered again. She had to slip away now, out of the circle and out of the castle, or Froth would find his way into her dreams tonight and learn where Bellchime was. If only Bellchime had told her sooner that he was dragonbound! She was a warrior's daughter, well trained. She could kill the vile thing and set him free. Now she understood why Bellchime had never returned to her, except in dreams. She would have to go to him.

"Years and years ago," said Froth, "Mugwort the Dragon came out of the sea and swam up the Bigfish River. No one knows where or on what night he crawled out of the water and crawled through the woods to the cottage of Auroch the Witch."

"Auroch was a healer, not a witch," said Periwinkle.

"She was a witch and Mugwort made her worse. He climbed onto her bed, a cold wet thing, and when she opened her eyes to see what was on top of her, she saw the dragon's eyes and was bound with dragon-laughter in her mind. She was an old, old woman, but as the dragon emptied her mind over the years, she became younger. Now I ask you, Tarragon's daughter who knows all, from what sort of woman but a witch could a young dragon learn such a spell?"

"There are some who say that Auroch once had a family, a husband and son, who died years before. They say she was lonely, that her misplaced love for the dragon made her seem years younger," Periwinkle replied.

"One does not love a dragon," said Froth. "One serves or fights a dragon. Auroch became younger. The dragon's skin and body dried as he grew, until he was strong enough and hot enough to fly."

"How big was he then?" asked Barleycorn.

"A dragon is usually about the length of a human's arm when it leaves the sea. I saw one such dragon strangled in a fishnet in Rockport. A dragon takes at least five years to grow large enough to be independent, and by that time it is bigger than a horse."

"What happens if the person the dragon binds is killed before then?" asked Jasper, the boy sitting next to Barleycorn.

"If the dragon is not killed also, it will bind another person. Often a dragon will kill its own slave and find a more suitable one."

Periwinkle saw her chance, slipped out of the circle, ran lightly to the tower stairs, and climbed quietly, past her mother's room, to her own room on the top floor. There she opened her chest, took out her leather fighting clothes and heaviest winter fur, her knife, her bow and quiver, her hidden supply of dried fruit and hard cheese, and the pouch of freedomwort roots that her mother had given her. She took off her dress, put on the leather jacket and pants, and packed the supplies, forcing herself to be calm, to remember everything she would need.

Meanwhile, Froth was still talking to Jasper and Barleycorn about Mugwort the Dragon and Auroch the Witch. He looked at the fascinated younger children, at Mandrake staring at his feet, and saw that Periwinkle was gone.

"Blood!" said Froth. "Mandrake, where is your sister?"

"She left."

"That dragonbound Bellchime cursed her! Where is your mother?"

Mandrake had never seen Froth so angry, still he could not resist saying, "Mother went to bed. Periwinkle probably was bored and did the same."

"Periwinkle will try to leave the castle," said Froth. "Please tell your mother and the night guard."

"I will go," said Mandrake, and ran to the stairs.

"Storytime is over for tonight," Froth told the others, who said goodnight and walked to the stairs and hallways, except for Eastwood and Stonewater, a boy and girl from the farmhold surrounding the castle, who fumbled with their wool cloaks.

Mandrake hesitated halfway up the stairs to his mother's room. If Bellchime really was dragonbound, why had his parents kept it secret from him? If Froth knew, they must know. Mandrake remembered liking Bellchime's stories, and remembered his voice and friendly face. He could not imagine such a man becoming like Auroch the Witch, muttering curses and choking to death in her own vomit. Instead of going to Mother's room, he climbed the last flight of stairs. Periwinkle's door was closed. He knocked.

"Periwinkle," he called. "Periwinkle, if you do not answer me I will wake Mother."

"What do you want?" asked Periwinkle.

"Let me in."

"I am in bed, I am trying to sleep, I want no more of that goblin-storyteller's nonsense, good night."

Mandrake sighed. There were many things he needed to talk about with his older sister, but there was no use when she was in *that* mood. At least Froth was wrong about her wanting to run away.

Periwinkle listened carefully to Mandrake's steps going downstairs, waited till she heard him pass Black Rose's room, waited till she heard another door creak open, opened and closed her own door at the same moment, tiptoed quickly down the stairs, and opened the outside door as quietly as she could. It was snowing in the courtyard. She pulled the hood of her fur over her head and walked to the stables, because if she ran, her footprints would look different from the others.

2.

"Did you rouse your mother?" Froth asked Mandrake.

"I went to Periwinkle's room. She is in bed, just as I said she would be."

"Did you see her yourself?"

"She said she wanted no more of your nonsense."

Froth sighed. "I wish it was nonsense. Dreams like the one your sister had while we were sitting here are dangerous. That dream was a sending from Bellchime meant for her mind only, but I heard some of it. He has wooed her, even made love with her, in her dreams, and now he summons her. She might have decided to leave this castle right now in the dark and snow on a mad quest to save Bellchime from his own dragon—as if that could be done."

"How do you know all this?"

"I am a wizard," said Froth. "Knowing things is my concern."

Mandrake looked at Froth the Storyteller's coarse features, trying to see Froth the Wizard. Was this another secret Froth shared with Mother and Father? He had to talk to Periwinkle. He could not trust anyone else.

"Yes, I am a wizard," Froth repeated. "I took Bellchime's place as storyteller to find him."

"And if you find him, what will you do?"

"What do you think I will do?"

"You will try to kill him," Mandrake said sullenly.

"Bellchime and his dragon are a danger to us all. Would you have the fields burnt, the farmholders devoured—"

"I know the stories," Mandrake interrupted. "You are a grown man; you say you are a wizard. I am still a boy, if a warrior's son. Is it not wrong to kill a man for something he has not yet done?"

Froth was silenced by this remark.

"Good night, wizard," said Mandrake. "I am going to bed."

"Good night, warrior."

The fire burned low. Froth stood up and walked over to the woodpile to get another log, wishing Tarragon had left more servants behind when he left for Slot's Castle. He threw the log onto the fire and poked the embers with the rod. Flames rose, warming his hands and face.

The boy was right in a way, he thought. To these inlanders who had no personal experience with dragons, Bellchime had done nothing to deserve death.

Froth looked into the fire, straightened his spine, and began breathing more slowly, deeply. He would be a tree, an oak tree, in Periwinkle's dream tonight; he would hear what Bellchime said to her. Part of Froth's mind melted in the fire, searching for Periwinkle's dream. His deep roots drew water from the earth, his branches spread wide, his leaves were countless. Periwinkle was not there. Froth sent, but she did not dream about a tree. The tree melted in the flames. An animal might be better, one that could fit into any dreamscape. The liquid part of his mind contracted, shaping a common fly, small, shiny, restless, buzzing. Where was Periwinkle? She did not dream about a fly. Froth let the fly expand and melt in the flames and opened his eyes. Periwinkle was not asleep. What was she doing if not sleeping?

Froth got up and hurried to the tower stairs, then down the steps to the courtyard door. He opened the door and looked out. Only vaguely could he see the other towers and the great hall through the falling snow. He saw three sets of footprints: Eastwood, Stonewater—and Periwinkle.

He heard steps behind him.

"She is gone," said Mandrake. "I broke into her room."

"I know," said Froth. "Wake your mother."

"We have to follow her trail before it gets buried."

"A few minutes will not matter now, and your mother must know. Wake her."

"Will you come with me?" asked Mandrake. "I do not want to try explaining this to her."

Froth puffed hard as he followed the slender boy up the spiral to her bedroom door.

"Mother!" called Mandrake, knocking a certain way.

"What is it?" she asked.

"Periwinkle has left the castle. Froth says Bellchime is cursing her."

"Is Froth with you now?" she asked.

"I am here," said Froth. "Your daughter fell asleep when you sent her back to the story circle, and Bellchime came to her in a dream, summoning her. She left the circle again—"

A woman dressed in leather jacket and pants, holding a dagger, opened the door. "Why would my daughter tell you about such a dream if she meant to act on it?" she asked coldly.

"She—she did not tell me."

"You are a wizard, then. You intercepted the sending. Why did you not stop her?"

"My lady," stammered Froth, "your daughter despises me. I could not order her to stay. When she left the circle, I sent Mandrake to wake you."

"What did you do, Mandrake?" asked Black Rose, and the boy shuddered.

"He said he talked to Periwinkle," said Froth.

"Let Mandrake speak for himself."

"Mother, I could not believe Froth. Is Bellchime really dragon-bound? I talked to Periwinkle and she said it was nonsense. Then Froth told me he was a wizard. Did you know this?"

"Your son despises me also," muttered Froth.

"Perhaps I despise you, myself," said Black Rose. "You who warned us so persuasively about the dangers of Bellchime's powers told us nothing about your own."

"Periwinkle and I were not even told Bellchime has powers," interrupted Mandrake.

"If I had powers to match Bellchime's, I would not need to earn my living storytelling," said Froth.

"Nor would you have been captured by goblins last summer while searching for Bellchime," said Black Rose, "unless you were plotting with them. Some say you resemble a goblin."

"Who? Your daughter? I may not have told you everything about myself, but I told no lies. I was trying to find and kill Bellchime and his dragon."

"That is Tarragon's duty and mine. We want no further incidents with the goblins. We must keep our hunting rights."

"Your duty to kill Bellchime?" pleaded Mandrake. "What has he done?"

"A warrior cannot wait for the enemy to strike first," said Black Rose.

"But how do you know he is our enemy?" asked Mandrake.

"Your sister runs through the snow in the middle of the night at the summons of a dragonbound man," said Froth, "and you wonder if this man is your enemy?"

"Maybe he loves her," said Mandrake.

"If he loved your sister, he would come for her in person. He would not bewitch her to come to him."

"Periwinkle is almost sixteen," said Black Rose, "and if she is going to this man, she has chosen to go. A warrior takes responsibility for her actions."

"She is no warrior till she passes her test, and less mature for her age than you think," Froth said. "We should pursue her and bring her back."

"If we want to find Bellchime and the dragon, we should let her lead us to them," said Black Rose. "I will send Heroncry on her trail. Mandrake, go rouse him."

Mandrake started down the tower stairs.

"Wait!" called Black Rose. "We will all go together. I do not want either you or Froth running through the woods chasing Periwinkle. She knows how to avoid goblins. You do not, and obviously Froth does not, either."

Froth muttered under his breath while they descended, "She knows where Bellchime is. We could make her tell us."

"No," Black Rose said firmly. "I would not compel my daughter to come back or to give us information she wishes to keep secret. I should have told her the truth about Bellchime as soon as I myself was convinced. Now, it will be very hard to deal with him and his dragon without making her hate all of us." Black Rose opened the outside door. "I want to go across the courtyard."

Snow fell thinner than before, but Froth could no longer see the footprints.

"Her trail leads to the stable," said Black Rose, pointing. They did not follow it, but hurried through the snow to the great hall. The great hall was unlit and unheated, unused since Tarragon and his retinue went to Slot's Castle. The three entered an adjacent tower, walked up another spire of stairs and down a hallway.

"Heroncry!" called Black Rose, knocking a pattern on his door. "Heroncry, wake up!"

"Of all times," said a woman's voice.

"I am not asleep," said Heroncry. "Be with you in a bloody moment. This better be important." Heroncry mumbled something and the woman mumbled something back.

Heroncry opened the door, a tall thin man with a gray mustache, wrapped in a fur robe. "What is it?" he asked.

"My daughter left the castle and I want you to follow her. She is going to meet the dragonbound Bellchime. Find Bellchime and kill the dragon."

"You!" said Heroncry, staring down at Froth. "You stirred this up somehow."

"My lord, I did not," stammered Froth. "Bellchime came to Periwinkle in a dream, when she fell asleep while I was relating the history of Mugwort."

"I should not wonder at that," said Heroncry.

"Anyway, I intercepted the dream and learned—"

"You are a bloody wizard! I know your plan! Let her slip out of the castle to lead us to Bellchime. Typical wizard's trick. Let the dragon grow up, I say. We have men and women here stout enough to kill it when it attacks—"

Suddenly Heroncry found himself peering from behind some trees at a burning house on the edge of what looked like a seaport. A dragon held the burnt body of a woman in its forepaws like an otter holding a fish, and bit it in two.

You think you are my enemy, said the dragon's voice in his mind, *but I fear no one*. The dragon ate the other half of the burnt woman.

Heroncry stared wide-eyed at Froth.

"An angry man is vulnerable to suggestion," said Froth.

"What did I see?"

"You saw the dragon Riversong eating my wife in the ruins of Moonport twenty years ago," said Froth. "You were angry, and I showed you my own anger. You heard a dragon's voice. Would you have such a thing attack Tarragon's Keep?"

"Certainly Bellchime's dragon is much smaller," said Heroncry.

"Yes, and it knows how to hide very well," said Froth. "You know. You have tried to find it yourself."

Heroncry nodded.

"It can go on hiding for years until it is that large and powerful," said Froth. "Which no doubt is Riversong's story. No one saw that dragon until it was huge, and no one knows who it bound as a dragonling. But I swear I did not let Periwinkle slip out of the castle. Even now, I would rather have her brought back here. She could tell us where Bellchime is."

"I told you I will not have my daughter treated as a child," Black Rose said to Froth. "Young as she is, she is a warrior. But her actions may threaten this castle and keep, so she must be followed."

"You are too bloody proper," said Heroncry. "Let me bring her back, let this wizard go into her mind a little to find out where

Bellchime is hiding, then go with four or five warriors and kill the dragon easily."

"That is how I would do it," said Froth.

"Are you saying you fear to face this dragon alone?" Black Rose asked Heroncry.

"It would be about four years past binding age?" Heroncry asked Froth.

"About that. Probably smaller than a horse and not yet breathing fire, but very intelligent, very perceptive. Small dragons are as good at evading warriors as large ones are at eating them."

"Then I should be able to kill it," said Heroncry. "I will bring arrows to wound it and a sword to finish the job, food for about two weeks, trinkets to bribe the goblins. I will be right back."

Heroncry closed the door and moved things around inside, mumbled something to the woman.

"You are going to hunt what?" she said.

Heroncry mumbled some more.

"Blood! I am glad I am not a warrior. Make sure you get paid well this time."

"Hmmph," said Heroncry. In a moment he opened the door, wearing a fur tunic, leather pants, a pack and quiver, and a medium-length sword in his belt.

"You will be amply rewarded," said Black Rose.

"Tush," he said in a low voice. "I was the last time, but do not tell her that. And do not tell my wife I was with her if she comes back from Slot's Keep while I am gone."

"You think she does not know?" said Black Rose.

"I know what she is doing in Slot's Castle also, and it is not visiting her sister."

"Why did you marry the wrong woman?" asked Mandrake.

"Not your concern," said Heroncry.

"Mandrake, it is not your place to tease a warrior," said Black Rose.

"I was not teasing," Mandrake said sullenly. "I do not know why you teach me that warriors should behave one way and then get angry when I ask them why they behave differently."

"It is not your concern," repeated Heroncry. He looked at Froth. "I want this wizard to come with me."

"You want Froth?" asked Mandrake.

"Yes," said Heroncry, who then asked Black Rose exactly what she wanted him to do.

"Kill the dragon, kill Bellchime," said Black Rose.

"No!" said Mandrake.

"He must, and you know why he must," said Froth.

"A dragon is one thing, but it is wrong to kill Bellchime."

"With the dragon dead, Bellchime will either be a mindless idiot, or a wizard mad with powers he cannot control."

"And Periwinkle? What if the dragon binds her?" asked Mandrake.

"She would not be bound to it long enough for its death to damage her mind," said Froth.

"Let us go," said Heroncry, and the two men walked briskly down the hallway to the tower stairs.

2

THROUGH THE
SNOWY WOODS

3.

"I have ridden you before," Periwinkle said soothingly to her mother's great red war-horse. "I have many miles to ride, and you are the only horse who can get me out of the keep."

Restless and ready for a long ride, the horse nodded his head and whinnied softly while Periwinkle put the saddle on his back, the harness over his head. Unlatching the stall, she led him out and closed the stall again. The horse snorted when he felt and smelled the cold snowy air come in through the opening stable door. She led him out into the courtyard, closed the stable door, and climbed on his back.

As she expected, the castle gate was still open, but the gate to the keep surrounding the castle was always barred and guarded. In this heavy snow Periwinkle hoped to pass for Black Rose, and if she were lucky, no one would discover she was missing till morning.

Wisps of smoke rose from the chimneys of the half-timber farmhouses in the center of the keep. She turned left at the first crossroad and rode around the foot of Castle Hill toward the keep's west wall. Three sides of the high stone wall of Tarragon's Keep stood atop cliffs, where the Indigo River flowed from the west into a great bend of the Moonstone River. But the west side faced slowly rising land, so this wall was double, and here was the only gate.

The horse, enjoying the exercise and excited by the novelty of this ride through the storm, neighed loudly when they stopped at the foot of the gate-tower.

"Raise the bars!" Periwinkle shouted in a deliberately hoarse voice. "Black Rose wishes to pass!"

"By what code will I know your return?" a voice from the tower yelled in reply.

"Mugwort the Dragon has destroyed Turtleport!" shouted Periwinkle.

"Ho, ho!" shouted the guard, and the ropes and pulleys groaned while the bars went up. Periwinkle rode beneath the great arch of the gate and across the yard.

"Raise the bars!" she shouted at the outer gate. "Black Rose wishes to pass!

"What will be your code?" the outer guard called back.

"May a mountain mammoth knock down your tower!" yelled Periwinkle.

"Good one!" he shouted and raised the bars.

Periwinkle rode through the outer gate and up the road, hardly believing she had gotten out so easily. Beyond the side road going south to Hammer's Keep, the forest loomed pale and vague. Her road twisted uphill through the trees. She urged the horse on, fearing that someone from the castle would follow soon. Spruce boughs heavy with snow passed low overhead.

This seemed as good a place as any to leave the road and get lost in the woods. No goblins would be lurking on the trails to waylay hunters or travelers in this storm, and she could find the ridge between her father's keep and Slot's as easily off the road as on it. Branches slapped her face at first, but soon she was inside the grove, and the horse found a trail that went north and down, toward the Indigo River.

"No," said Periwinkle. "We want to go between the river and the road. This way. Here is a trail."

In a few minutes she was back on the road.

Her first impulse was to run her mother's horse as fast as he would go, but then she gave thought to the miles she had to ride, and urged him to run only where the road was level, which was seldom. Snow fell lighter an hour later as she reached a grove of elms she remembered from two summers ago, when she had ridden with Heroncry to Slot's Keep. The traceries of the branches arched high over the road, fading into the pale gloom. She began to see animal tracks, two-toed prints of a deer walking up the road, three-toed prints of a unicorn crossing north.

On impulse she urged the horse onto the unicorn's trail. Though even the largest unicorn is smaller than a horse, her mount had no trouble following the path. She looked west through the trees where the ground rose slowly toward the ridge; downhill toward the river she judged to be northeast. She would climb the ridge, and from the ridge see Blue Dragonstone Mountain, or at least the clouds surrounding it, and somewhere behind the mountain was Oak Lake, where Bellchime was. In waking life she knew Oak Lake only from her father's descriptions of goblins camped there, but the mountain she had seen from the road.

The silence of the snow was broken by a loud "hoo-hoo!" but Periwinkle did not see an owl. The path wound around the side of a hill, over a frozen streamlet. Snowfall stopped, and treeshadows sharpened as clouds thinned over the moon. Perwinkle looked up at the moon through swirling marble clouds and around at the snowy woods and felt more intensely alive than ever before.

4.

Meanwhile, Heroncry and Froth were having difficulty persuading the keep's inner gate-guard to raise the bars.

"Quit the bloody nonsense and let us pass! We have orders from Black Rose herself!" shouted Heroncry.

"You cannot leave the keep while Black Rose is away!" bellowed the guard. "Those are my orders from Tarragon!"

"That was Periwinkle riding Black Rose's horse!" shouted Heroncry. "If we lose her trail because of this delay, you will lose your job—or your head!"

"I know my job better than you, Heroncry!" snapped the guard. "Black Rose is out, and you must stay in, unless I hear otherwise from Black Rose herself!"

"Maybe I can reason with the fool," Froth muttered.

"I have never yet met a reasonable guard," said Heroncry.

Froth said nothing to the guard, but got a small purse out of his pocket and raised it high. In a few moments a light appeared in the peephole of the tower door.

"What do you offer me?" asked a hushed voice.

"Five silver pieces," said Froth and showed him what looked like five silver treemarks from Upriver.

"I will say Forest and Froth asked to be let out," said the guard, opening the tower door to receive the coins.

"Raise the bars first," said Froth.

"Two coins now, three after I raise the bars, and if you cheat me, I will signal the outer guard."

"Done," said Froth, handing him two coins.

The guard raised the bars, walked down the stairway, and got his other three coins from Froth.

"A pretty price you paid to get us through that gate," Heroncry said to Froth when they passed beyond the arch.

"Not really," said Froth. "I only gave him five pennies with a bit of suggestion, and let his greed do the rest. I have not done that trick in years."

"I hope your pennies will stay treemarks until we pass the outer gate."

"They will," said Froth. "Let me do the shouting this time."
They stopped at the outer gate.

"Raise the bars!" yelled Froth. "Froth and Forest wish to pass!"

"Let Forest speak!" shouted the guard.

"Go ahead," Froth mumbled. "He will hear Forest's voice and see Forest's horse, I think."

"Forest and Froth wish to pass!" shouted Heroncry.

"Not Forest, but Heroncry!" bellowed the guard. "Why do you lie?"

"He saw us before I spoke to him," muttered Froth.

"You are a poor excuse for a wizard," said Heroncry. "Now what do we do? I know this man, and he will not be bribed."

"Would the truth work?"

"No, I am not Forest," shouted Heroncry, "and the woman you let out last hour is not Black Rose!"

"Who is she then?" asked the guard.

"Periwinkle!" shouted Heroncry. "We have orders from Black Rose to follow her!"

After a long pause the guard shouted back, "What will be your code?"

"Five pennies is a fair price!" shouted Heroncry.

"Ho!" said the guard and raised the bars.

"We forgot to leave a code at the inner gate," Froth said while they rode out.

"Blood," said Heroncry. "By the time we get back even the guard we cheated will be glad to see us!"

"I see her trail," said Froth.

"None too clear, even though the snow has stopped," Heroncry said. "Hard to see in the forest. Somewhere she will leave the road and we may keep trotting and wipe out her traces before we realize she no longer is ahead of us."

"If we stop and look too often, we will lose her," said Froth. "She must be at least an hour ahead of us."

"We are following her, not chasing her," said Heroncry.

They passed the road to Hammer's Keep, rode into the woods, and lost the trail in a dense spruce grove.

"Just as you said, and sooner than you expected," said Froth.

"Yes. Hmm," said Heroncry, turning his horse. He rode slowly back, looking more at the trees than the ground. "See that?" he asked. "Snow knocked off the spruce boughs."

"Lead on," said Froth.

Heroncry muttered as the branches slapped him.

5.

Periwinkle was still following the unicorn's tracks, but the way had become difficult, a steep slope with thorn bushes. She was about to backtrack, find some other path, when she heard a snort, and branches snap. For a moment, frozen in the brush above her, was a huge buck silver unicorn almost as large as her horse, the spire of his horn as long as her arm, his mane more brilliant than snow.

Swift as the wind he charged; the horse bucked and leapt to one side; Periwinkle held on, barely. The unicorn turned and looked back at her from far below and whinnied loudly.

Already he was trotting back toward her. Periwinkle notched an arrow into her bow and aimed. The unicorn dodged to one side just as the arrow flew past him, then ran away from her, still uphill. She urged her horse to run uphill, away from the unicorn, and by luck the horse found an easy path through the trees. She glanced back and saw the unicorn already above her, standing still.

She stopped her horse, notched another arrow, but the unicorn did not charge or move closer. She walked her horse a few paces up the trail, and the unicorn neighed, bowing and raising his head. She rode the horse farther, and kept going, and saw the unicorn turn away and walk back to his thicket.

"Good boy!" Periwinkle said to the horse, hugging his neck.

6.

"Bet you five bewitched pennies this leads right back to the road," Heroncry said, back in the spruce grove.

"She knows we are following her," muttered Froth.

"Impressive," said Heroncry when they reached the road. "Not good enough to lose us, but impressive all the same."

7.

Ahead of her, Periwinkle heard the rushing headwaters of the Indigo River, a dark stream some twenty feet wide, with snow-covered boulders between its rapids, and icicles under its banks. The path wound up the near side for half a mile, to the river's source, the two huge springs of Indigo. Periwinkle stopped her horse to look at this river erupting from the ground, but what caught her eye was a carved totem of the Fangtooth Cat Clan, planted in the middle of the trail where it crossed above the springs. She was on a goblin trail, and not far from a guarded camp or cave, probably a cave. She rode up to the totem to look at it more closely.

A half-sized distortion of a fangtooth cat's head on a stick, it was painted in bright colors lost in the shadowed moonlight and decorated with long feathers. No tracks surrounded it; it had been planted before the most recent snow. The goblins believed strange things about these totems, Froth had said. Fierce spirit animals would help them kill any enemy who dared pass such a mark. Froth never clearly said whether he believed this or not.

Periwinkle had no wish to fight goblins now, with or without fierce spirit-beasts, so she shot an arrow into the snow at the base of the totem-stick, meaning that she would kill any goblin who followed her trail, and rode her horse off the goblin-path and uphill away from the roar of Indigo Springs.

This direction, however, was too steep for the horse, and he was forced to pick his way around the hill back down to the path. She stopped him. Ahead of her was no goblin camp or cave, but a small wooden hut in a fenced clearing, such as a human hermit might build. The windows were dark but smoke curled out of the chimney. Before Periwinkle saw the sleeping wolf on the doorstep, it smelled her and howled.

"Bite your tongue, wolf! What is it this time?" croaked a voice from inside.

"A stranger who would talk to you!" Periwinkle called.

"No one comes to talk to old Gar. Gar has no friends, no people."

"Perhaps I will be your friend," said Periwinkle.

"Do not say that to Gar before you see him."

A light went on inside the hut, the door opened, and the wolf jumped up on the figure who hobbled out, licking his face. He was short, squat, and wrapped in ragged leather.

"Get down!" he snarled at the wolf, then looked at Periwinkle on her tall horse outside his fence and asked, "What are you?"

"Lost," she answered.

"I can see that," he snapped. "Bring your horse in the yard and come inside and old Gar will set your directions right."

"My horse fears your wolf."

"Ah—yes," rumbled Gar. "Wolf's killing days are over, but Gar will keep her in the house. Come in."

Periwinkle led her horse through the gate, tied him up, set her pack beside the door, went inside, and got her first good look at Gar. He was almost bald, his brow was heavy, his ears pointed, and he had a short gray beard. He in turn stared back at her with piercing translucent blue eyes.

"You are either a young human warrior or a witch," he said.

"You are partly goblin."

"Goblins call Gar half-human; humans call Gar half-goblin; Gar just calls himself Gar and wants you to do the same."

"I beg your pardon, Gar," she said. "I am called Periwinkle."

"A strange name for one so far from the sea. Take off your furs and sit by the fire; warm your feet. Gar may live alone, but he knows how to treat his guests."

Gar's voice was hoarse and gravelly, but his words seemed kind, so she did as he told her, and set her bow and quiver by the hearth. The wolf was stretched out asleep by the fire.

"Fine weapons you have," said Gar. "These are marks of Stonewort's Keep, are they not?"

"Black Rose, Stonewort's daughter, and her husband Tarragon rule the keep now. Stonewort died when I was small, nine or ten winters ago."

"Dead nine or ten winters," repeated Gar.

"Did you know him?" asked Periwinkle.

"Gar knows no one, and no one knows Gar. Gar has no people."

Periwinkle saw his eyes watering, as though he wanted to cry. Her gray eyes earnestly met his.

"But Gar has the best place to live now," he continued. "Indigo Springs is a power spot. Many animals live here: unicorn, elk, wolf, fangcat, deer, spirit animals, too. Gar does not need the human-people of his father or the goblin-people of his mother. No one looks Gar in the eye with love, no young war-woman of Stonewort's Keep. What are you?"

"As you say, a young war-woman from Tarragon's Keep. You told me not to offer you friendship before I saw what you were, so I offer it to you now, if you can accept it."

"People say that to Gar before, always when they need something. When Gar gives it, they turn away from him and scorn him. So now, when people come to Gar, he gives what he can, asks for nothing. Gar dishonors both father and mother by being born, people tell him, but you, young war-woman, look Gar in the eye, see Gar's beautiful eyes. Gar knows he has beautiful eyes, if all else about him looks ugly."

He smiled at her; about half his teeth were missing.

"Let us trade," said Periwinkle. "If you do something to help me, I will do something for you, not necessarily anything you ask for, but something agreeable to both of us."

"So what can Gar do for Periwinkle?"

"I am on a quest," she began, and stopped. "A friend urgently requested my help," she began again, and stopped again. She knew Bellchime was dragonbound, knew he needed her help, knew he was at Oak Lake, but she did not know what he wanted her to do when she got there, and did not know how much of this she should tell Gar.

"There is much you would hide about your quest," he said. "That is fine with Gar. Gar would rather you keep secrets than lie to him."

"I have told nobody where I am going or why. I left the keep after dark."

Gar became more intent; the corners of his mouth stretched into an expression neither smile nor frown; but he said nothing.

"One man guessed I might try to do what I am trying to do. He may follow me or cause someone else to follow me." Periwinkle's eyes met Gar's. "I must go to Oak Lake, and the less trail I leave, the better."

Gar's eyes opened wide, then narrowed to a squint. "Gar thought as much," he rumbled. "What friend will you meet at Oak Lake? Some young goblin lad? One thing Gar will not do is help you become mother to another like Gar."

"Who I become mother to is not your concern," Periwinkle said. "Stop regretting your own life."

"How dare you say that to Gar?" he barked.

"You have a beautiful place to live, a power spot nearby, a hut that is snug and tight—"

Gar pressed his lips together and scowled. "You do not know what being alone is like."

"Maybe not," said Periwinkle.

The wolf stretched her forepaws and yawned, then sat up beside Gar and sniffed his hands.

"Gar is alone. Wolf does not talk." He scratched Wolf behind her ears.

"I am sorry, Gar. I do not understand you, and I wish I had more time. I am not going to Oak Lake to meet a goblin, but a human man, some say a wizard. Tell me at least the best way to the ridgecrest."

"Go around Gar's fence to point nearest chimney, take lower fork when the trail branches the first time."

"Thank you," said Periwinkle. "Now what can I do for you?"

"Gar wishes he had more time to consider this, but he knows you are in a hurry. Gar wonders why the goblins at Oak Lake who used to hate humans so much would let one live with them. Gar's mother came from that camp."

"My great-grandfather Tipspear used to stick goblin heads on poles outside the keep, I am told. My mother and father honor treaties with goblins. Times have changed."

"You are Stonewort's granddaughter."

Periwinkle sighed. "Yes."

"Times have changed when a descendent of Stonewort offers Gar friendship."

"I speak only for myself, Gar, not for the keep."

"Gar knows that. He will do something more for you. If others come this way, he will confuse them. Who will come? Turner? Greenspear?"

"Turner is an old man and Greenspear is dead. If a warrior comes, it will probably be Forest or Heroncry."

"Gar does not know these war-men. Who is the man who guessed your purpose?"

"You probably do not know him either. His name is Froth the Storyteller, but I think he is a wizard."

"Froth!" cackled Gar, doubling up with laughter. "Gar has met him. He came to Indigo Springs last summer, Gar's last visitor before you. Foolish, arrogant man, obsessed with finding—" Gar paused for a moment and looked at Periwinkle's face intently, "—finding a wizard who he claimed was bewitched by a dragon. This is the same wizard who waits for you at Oak Lake, is he not? What can you possibly do to help such a man?"

"I only know that he believes I can help him."

"Gar sees you have pride and confidence, and you think you love this wizard. Maybe you succeed and maybe you fail. Humans tell wild stories, make dragons more powerful than spirit-beasts. Gar hopes these stories are not true. Gar wants you to succeed. You are gentle; you try to understand old Gar. Froth has sharp eyes and a harsh voice, scorns Gar when Gar cannot help him. Gar would love to confuse Froth. And in return—" he paused, thinking. "Could you give Gar a human knife, or a crystal, or that food Gar's father called 'cheese' before the goblins killed him?"

"I will give you some cheese now, and those other things next time I see you, if I have them by then."

Periwinkle wrapped her fur around her, picked up her bow, went outside, and gave Gar some cheese from her pack. Gar said farewell to her and watched her mount the horse and ride away.

"Get up, lazy thing!" he said to the wolf. "Back outside for you." She whimpered and ran to the door with her tail between her legs. Gar shut the door. He could not resist nibbling a few bites of cheese before putting it away and going to bed.

Gar had no idea how much sleep he would get before less friendly guests arrived, so he lay down on his straw bed and pulled his only fur over himself. He would be ready for them—ah, yes—the way he had been ready for the band of goblins that had driven him out of the cave he used to live in. He would dream the Great Mother Cat, the fierce spirit who was his own mother's first ancestor. She would possess him and give his mouth the power to tell the right truth and the right lies to accomplish his ends.

8.

Heroncry and Froth rode the miles of moonlit road, heard an owl and a distant wolf, saw tracks of two deer and a great elk.

"Wish we were hunting," said Heroncry. "A choice feast that elk would make, a fine fur also. Try trailing a great elk sometime. They leave a hard trail, hard for even a wolf or a fanged cat to follow."

Not too much farther on, they saw Periwinkle's horsetracks leave the road where an exceptionally large unicorn had crossed earlier.

"Are you certain it is a unicorn?" asked Froth.

"We will have to ride single-file and should be quiet," Heroncry said, ignoring Froth's question. "Do not call out unless it is important."

They urged their horses off the road onto the unicorn's path, and for a long time followed the prints of horse and unicorn. Abruptly Heroncry stopped his horse and motioned Froth to ride up beside him.

"Both Periwinkle and the unicorn left the path here," he said in a low voice. "This may be another trick, and a dangerous one, too."

"What do you mean?" asked Froth.

"Unicorns are not all shy and flighty, especially the bigger ones, and this one is huge."

"You think she doubled back down to this path farther on?"

Heroncry frowned. "Possibly." He reached for his bow and an arrow. "Wait here."

Something crashed through the trees and before Heroncry could notch his arrow, the unicorn was upon them, charging Froth's horse. The horse bucked and leapt to one side, snapping the reins out of Froth's hands and tumbling him backwards onto the snow. Heroncry's arrow flew in front of the unicorn, for he stopped in mid-gallop. Froth's horse took off ahead down the main path. The unicorn leapt to one side to dodge another arrow and ran uphill. Then all fell silent.

Heroncry held his horse tightly with his legs, looking uphill for any sign of the unicorn. A minute passed, and another minute. Still nothing.

"Guess he is gone," said Heroncry. "Never saw anything dodge arrows like that one." He looked at the snow where Froth had landed.

"I am up here," said Froth, sitting on a large limb of an old oak.

Heroncry laughed. "You climb well for a man your age."

"I am not that much older than you."

"Stay there. I will get your horse."

Heroncry rode down the path. Froth sat uncomfortably in the tree for what seemed a long time, but finally Heroncry returned, leading the other horse.

"Went all the way down to the river," he said, while Froth fumbled his way out of the tree.

"The path meets one going up this bank of the river, does it not?" asked Froth. "I was here last summer. Have you ever seen the springs?"

"No," said Heroncry.

"They are incredible. The whole river gushes out of holes in the dragonstone. I talked to a hermit who lives in a hut just beyond the springs. I think he told the goblins I was prowling round. He is half a goblin himself."

"Not many of those ever born," said Heroncry. "Old Greenspear knew one once. He lived in a cave between the Copper and Moonstone Rivers, till the goblins drove him out. He must be dead now; he was old even then. Gar was his name."

"Unless there are two half-goblins named Gar, he is not dead. Gar lives in that hut. He is very old. I tried befriending him but got disgusted with his fits of emotion. I think he is feebleminded."

"Hard, being an outcast all his life," said Heroncry. "But who can trust a halfbreed? No natural allegiance."

"Exactly," said Froth.

"However," said Heroncry, "Periwinklc did not go that way."

"You did not see her trail at the river? You mean we must face that unicorn again?"

"Yes, if he is still here."

"Blood," said Froth.

Heroncry got bow and arrow ready, and walked his horse

uphill, where the snow was much trampled by horse and unicorn. One set of horse-prints went up another path.

Froth reluctantly urged his horse to follow Heroncry.

"Come on," Heroncry called, then swore under his breath when a silver streak crashed through the web of moonlight uphill from him. The unicorn came to the path and stood facing him.

"I do not want to fight you," said Heroncry. "Please let us pass."

The unicorn threw his head back and whinnied loudly. Froth rode his horse into the woods above the path while Heroncry's horse stepped forward. The unicorn lowered his head and charged down the path at Heroncry, passing beneath Froth. Heroncry's horse dodged behind a tree, then galloped up the path. Froth's horse fell in behind Heroncry's, and both riders slowed their mounts to a walk when sounds of the unicorn crashing through brush faded behind them.

"Good trick," said Heroncry. "If we were hunting him, we would never get him now. Bad luck to kill a unicorn anyway."

"You say that because you missed him twice," said Froth.

They rode in single file as before. Fingers of cloud reached for the moon when they heard the sound of the Indigo River ahead, and closed the sky by the time they reached the springs. Heroncry stopped his horse and motioned Froth to ride up next to him, and spoke in the softest voice that could be heard over the roaring water.

"Is that Gar's totem?" he asked, pointing at the Fangtooth Cat symbol.

"He had no totem last summer," said Froth. "I do not think an outcast like Gar is entitled to use any totem."

"Periwinkle shot an arrow at it and left the path again."

"I can see that as well as you."

"Seems each time we follow her detour, we end up on the same trail we started. Let us go look at this Gar's hut."

"You challenge the totem?" asked Froth. "I think that this time Periwinkle changed direction to avoid trouble. We do not know if Gar still lives there."

"Bad time of year to move at his age," said Heroncry with a wink. "I would not be much of a warrior if I did not challenge a few totems, now would I?"

9.

When the wolf howled, Gar remembered nothing of his dream but a voice like Periwinkle's asking him the way to Cricket Swamp.

Gar lit his only lamp and opened the door, but saw no horses or riders outside the fence. The moon was almost hidden, and Wolf was snarling.

"Gar knows you are out there," he croaked. "Come finish your business and let old Gar have his sleep."

Two fur-wrapped men on horses appeared at the gate.

"That is better. Tie your horses and come in. Gar knows you follow young war-woman with long black hair. This night is too cold for Gar's old bones." He closed the door and waited.

"Is this a trap?" asked Froth.

"Not many goblins could hide in a hut that size," said Heroncry.

"What about the woods?"

"You go in and talk to him. I will watch the horses. Try to find out where Periwinkle is trying to go."

Froth got off his horse, opened the gate, and walked up to the door. The wolf paced around him but did not growl. She was obviously old.

"Take off your fur, sit down," said Gar when Froth stepped inside. "Gar recognizes Froth, but who is the other man?"

"His name is Heroncry."

"Just as the war-woman said, Froth and Heroncry. Gar does not want to be involved. Gar has no friends, no people. You want war-woman, you follow her trail. Gar cannot betray his guests."

"Not like you betrayed me to the goblins," said Froth.

"Gar did no such thing!" he barked. "If goblins found you, they did it on their own. Goblins hate Gar more than you do. They do not ask Gar for anything."

"Look me in the eye and say that," said Froth.

"Gar will not look Froth in the eye. Gar knows that Froth is a wizard."

Froth reached into a pocket and brought out a moonstone crystal. "Yes, I am a wizard, and I offer you a wizard's gift," he said, and when Gar looked at the stone, Froth's eye met a reflection of Gar's eye, and Froth heard Periwinkle's voice in Gar's mind asking the way to Cricket Swamp.

Suddenly, Froth found himself standing in a blizzard, and a fanged cat jumped on him, tearing his clothing and scratching him cruelly with her claws.

"Thank you," said Gar to Froth, who was rolling on the floor howling. "Gar has always wanted to have a crystal."

Heroncry thrust open the door, drawing his sword. "Move and I kill you!" he bellowed.

"Gar did nothing to Froth," he croaked. "Froth tried to rape Gar's mind and met the spirit fangcat who lives there."

Froth stopped rolling and lay panting on the floor, unable to speak.

"Froth also accused Gar of betraying him to goblins. Gar did no such thing! Gar has no people, only spirit-beasts. Gar cannot afford enemies. Gar does not betray Froth to goblins, does not betray young war-woman to Froth."

"You have an armed enemy in your bloody house right now unless you break this spell," snapped Heroncry.

"Gar made no spell, Gar can break no spell."

"Make your spirit-beast let him go."

"She already has let him go," said Gar. "Look, the wizard sleeps."

Heroncry lowered his sword, put it back in its scabbard. "Back away from him; sit on the bed," he ordered, then raised Froth's heavy shoulders and shook him. Froth mumbled a few inaudible words but would not wake up. Heroncry slapped Froth's face, but he only snorted. "Why will he not wake up?" Heroncry asked Gar, but Gar was asleep himself on the straw bed. Heroncry tried twice more to rouse Froth before falling asleep himself.

—3—

BELLCHIME'S DRAGON

10.

Looking north along the ridgecrest from the back of her mother's red war-horse, Periwinkle saw the great cone of Blue Dragonstone Mountain touch the clouds that stretched fingers to cover the moon. Froth once told Mandrake that long ago this mountain breathed fire like a dragon, and the fire changed into dragonstone when it cooled, but Periwinkle did not believe this. He also said the ridge had many caves, which goblins camped in while hunting mountain mammoth. Periwinkle did believe in caves, and intended to shelter in one before dawn.

"This is my warrior's test," she told herself when she became hungry and tired. Her endurance, her resourcefulness, her sense of what was right, she would prove in the next few days. She was a warrior now.

Snow fell lightly, then stopped again. The ridge became sharp and rocky, but her horse found footing. She came to a broad saddle sparsely covered with trees, then found easier riding on a mammoth trail curving below the ridgecrest. Here in a dragonstone outcrop was her cave, with an opening wide enough for her horse to crouch into.

"Is it safe?" she asked him. "You smell no bear or fangcat?"

The horse seemed willing to rest in the entrance, so she walked inside and curled up to sleep in her fur, without eating any of the cheese she had promised herself for hours.

In a dream, mile after mile she was still riding, unable to evade the warriors on horseback who followed her, unable to remember where she was going or why. The warriors somehow changed to a fangtooth cat. The cat sang to her.

When she startled awake, the cave was black and silent but for the wind and the breathing of her horse. She felt panic, felt abandoned because Bellchime had not entered her dream.

Into dark sleep she drifted awhile, then rode into the goblin camp at Oak Lake, determined not to fear the dozens of goblins seated around the fire, though their faces were painted like skulls. They would not answer when she asked where Bellchime was. She held back her tears but still they laughed at her. They began a chant she did not understand. The snow fell so deep that it buried them and put out their fire.

She was naked in a milky nothingness, warm like steam from a cauldron of soup, and trying to run from a voice telling her to kill Bellchime, but her feet touched nothing. She called Bellchime, and heard his voice answer. She was treading water in a summer pool and he was standing on the gravel beach. He took his clothing off and dove in, swam to her.

"Do not awaken," he said. "You are dreaming. Tell me where you went to sleep."

"In a cave," she said absent-mindedly and kissed him, felt his body's warmth through the cool water.

"Which cave?" he asked, as though in a hurry for this information.

"I was at Indigo Springs," Periwinkle tried to remember. "I was on the ridge, tired, and the cave had no bears. I am being followed."

Before she could kiss him again, Bellchime turned his head to look at the shore, where his dragon crouched, ready to spring. Its sudden bellowing lunge into flight toward them awoke Periwinkle.

In the cold cave's dim morning, she shuddered, then felt a tension in her throat release itself. Bellchime had reached her, and would meet her somewhere farther up the ridge with his dragon. She was not sure what she would do then. For now, she would eat cheese and fruit to ease her hunger, and she would chew some freedomwort root.

"Chew a piece of root the size of your smallest fingernail," her mother had told her on her twelfth birthday. "Chew it thoroughly for several minutes, then spit out the pulp, and no matter how many times you make love, you will bleed at the end of your month."

Black Rose had also told her how to recognize the plant in the forest, but she had enough here for more than a year. The juices were incredibly bitter, but she kept chewing.

11.

Back at Gar's hut, Heroncry had managed to awaken Froth long before dawn, and after riding the weary miles of a partial night's sleep, they now looked at Black Rose's reddish horse in front of a shallow cave, glowing brilliantly in the morning sunlight.

"This is not the way to Cricket Swamp!" said Froth.

"Footprints tell truth better than goblins, even goblins put under spells."

"Gar is a stronger wizard than I am."

"And Periwinkle may have lied to him about her destination," added Heroncry. "Let us see if the night wore any sense into her. Periwinkle!" he shouted.

Periwinkle stepped around the horse, blinked at the bright sun on snow, and saw two men on horseback down the ridge, Froth and Heroncry. They were treating her as an equal, calling her that way, so she would wait.

"You followed me," she said when they rode up.

"For the safety of Tarragon's Keep, we had to," said Heroncry.

"You do not know what you are doing," said Froth.

"I admit that, but neither do you. You have orders to kill, do you not? I am free to act as I judge right."

"So am I," said Heroncry. "I am a warrior, same as you."

"Bellchime asks for my help. I must talk to him about it. I think he wants to control his dragon by binding us both to it. I do not think I want this." She looked at the two men's faces. Froth seemed very disturbed, but everything about dragons disturbed Froth.

"Bellchime is already a lost man," said Froth. "We do not want to lose you."

"A person who can love is not lost," said Periwinkle.

"You think he loves you," said Froth. "Bellchime may even believe this himself, but the dragon will turn you against each other. I know. A dragon made me kill my master."

Periwinkle looked at Froth's face without understanding.

"You were an apprentice wizard?" asked Heroncry.

"My master was named Taproot. We lived in a shack near an abandoned mine west of Cat's Tooth Pass, in the Silver Mountains, where unknown to me he had a dragonling chained up in one of the pits. I dreamed a voice in my mind told me to kill Taproot, then I dreamed I killed him. Taproot intercepted this sending from his dragonling, the same way I intercepted the message Bellchime sent you yesterday," Froth said to Periwinkle.

"He asked about my dream, asked if I wanted power, told me about the dragonling, told me we must master it together before it mastered us. I said he was already in its power, but he denied this."

Froth took a deep breath before continuing. "I feared he would kill me first, and he was raising a dragon, a crime punishable by death on the coast where I grew up, so I muttered a spell to make a knife look like the stirring spoon, and stabbed him to death when he came to the hearth to sample the soup. He died unable to mutter a curse, but bloodied my clothes. I changed, packed my belongings, and threw burning logs on the straw beds. No book or herb of such a wizard did I want! The shack went up in flames. In my mind, the dragon rejoiced, saying, *Set me free and I will love you,* wanting to empty my mind. *I will sing to you. Come set me free,* it said, and I followed its gurgling sobs to the pit. It could not have been more than five feet long, its wings mere buds. I looked at the misshapen monstrosity in the pit, trying not to hear the soft voice in my mind asking, *Why do you want to kill me?* I threw a rock that broke its leg. *I did not kill your wife,* it said. My next rock smashed its skull."

Periwinkle's gray eyes found Froth's. "A hard story, well told, and I thank you for it," she said. "Last night I dreamed the dragon's voice said, *Kill Bellchime,* but I will not kill Bellchime. You and your master struggled for power long before you knew about his dragon. Two such people cannot long rule anything together."

Froth was unable to speak, unable to believe Periwinkle's decision.

"You think two lovers do not strive for power over each other?" asked Heroncry.

"I know you at least strive for power with your wife and both your mistresses," said Periwinkle, "but it is not so with everyone."

"Show me respect," said Heroncry, wondering how Periwinkle could know about his second mistress.

"I am sorry," said Periwinkle. "I do respect you."

"And I you, more is the curse. Black Rose was right, Froth. Periwinkle will make her own bloody decisions and we cannot interfere unless it threatens the keep."

"I must ride alone. You may follow, out of bowrange."

After Periwinkle repacked her things and rode her mother's horse up the ridge, Froth said to Heroncry, "She does not know the power, the deceit."

12.

Periwinkle met the power not long before noon, over a field of gravel with patches of snow, and it was beautiful, Bellchime riding a young she-dragon the color of distant mountains, twisting and turning in the sky. The dragon flapped and folded her ribbed wings to land on the ridgecrest a courtyard's space away from Periwinkle.

"Leave your horse to the men who follow you!" shouted Bellchime. "Come ride with me!"

Periwinkle hesitated a moment before dismounting, then found herself running, with her pack, across the gravel to Bellchime. With wings folded, the dragon looked no bigger than Black Rose's horse, though the neck and tail made her longer.

"Do I know you?" asked Periwinkle, looking up at the man on the dragon's shoulder, who was dressed in leather pants and a fur-lined hooded jacket. His face looked much more rugged than the man she remembered.

"You have changed far more than I," he said.

The dragon, which had been making a low rumble like a gigantic purring keepcat, opened her mouth and bellowed. Black Rose's horse lost nerve and took flight.

"She senses an enemy approach," said Bellchime. "Hurry!"

"Help me up," said Periwinkle. The scales were warm and dry, and vibrated with the dragon's purring.

"Her name is Distance," said Bellchime. "Hold on tight."

Periwinkle felt the muscles roll beneath her when Distance

flapped her wings. The ground fell away, tipped and tilted. A strong wind blew in her face and her stomach jumped, while rock formations and forests patched with snow unrolled beneath the dragon's neck and legs. Distance bellowed again and flew over the ridge. Blue Dragonstone Mountain on the right gleamed white with snow. Periwinkle wanted to talk to Bellchime but the wind was too loud.

"Where are we going?" she tried to shout.

Bellchime shouted back something that may have been, "Hold tight!"

13.

Echoing down the ridge came a screeching roar.

"The dragon bellows," said Froth.

"Sounds a bloody lot bigger than you said it would be," said Heroncry, notching an arrow in his bow.

"Look," Froth cried. Galloping toward them without Periwinkle was Black Rose's horse, and something like an eagle soared in the distance, with two bumps on its neck. Froth rode toward the red horse, shouting "Stop!"

"Blood on the earth, she is riding it with him!" said Heroncry.

"You warriors and your honor, calling that girl a woman!" said Froth. "It was only the best of luck that kept her horse from stumbling and breaking a leg."

"Seems to be flying round the mountain to the north side," Heroncry said. "Oak Lake country is sacred to goblins and forbidden to our sort. A full day's ride from here at least."

"What now?"

"If we go to Oak Lake, we risk starting a war, but if the goblins allow a dragon there, they may be planning war themselves. Looks like we may be the first humans except Bellchime to see Oak Lake since Stonewort's campaign. Interested?"

The dragon's dwindling form became obscure.

"My heart tells me that we have already lost this hunt," said Froth. "It flies, we walk, and they know about us."

"We may learn something about them," said Heroncry.

14.

The wind blew cold on Periwinkle's face, snatching strands of hair from her hood, while the snowy trees unrolled beneath the dragon's neck and forelegs. The sun over her shoulder made the snowy cone of Blue Dragonstone Mountain, close to the east, a brilliant white.

Without warning the trees lunged upward, separating into cones of dark green and white. Bellchime shouted something and slapped the dragon's neck, but Distance ignored him, and both humans on her shoulder winced at the force of her anger. The ground twisted crazily when Distance veered between the treetops toward a brown animal, probably a doe. With a sudden jolt, her jaws snapped the doe's neck, but when she seized the bleeding carcass in her claws and tried to rise again, the weight was too much, and she landed awkwardly with a hard bump. Periwinkle fell off on her back in a snowbank, momentarily stunned. Bellchime was also thrown off, and covered with blood. Distance was greedily tearing large red chunks of meat off the deer's hind legs, slurping blood and crunching bones.

"Are you all right?" asked Periwinkle, helping Bellchime to his feet. Apparently the blood was the doe's.

"I will be," said Bellchime. "She is hard to control."

Someday this will be you, said the dragon's angry inner voice. *This human girl is useless. She knows nothing.*

"Never underestimate a warrior, Distance," said Periwinkle, reaching for her bow and two arrows where they had fallen on the snow. Bellchime jumped on her and knocked her to the ground. She seized his head by the hair.

"I came here to love you, not to fight you!" she shouted.

"Kill Distance and you kill me!" said Bellchime, his face warped with pain.

"If we will ever be lovers, we must trust each other," she said quietly, forcing him to look deeply into her eyes. "Do I look at Bellchime or Distance?" she asked.

"Attack Distance and you also find her here; otherwise, Bellchime."

"Froth was right about you; you are a lost man."

"Find me," he whispered, tears forming in his eyes.

"Release me and I will," said Periwinkle. He got off her; she sat up looking at him. "Look in my eyes, Bellchime. I am the child who loved your wisdom, who loved the clever way you told the old tales. I am the woman whose dreams you explored, who has come not at your summons but at your request, for no better reason than love. Do you wish to be a dragon's dinner, or do you wish to kiss these lips?" Bellchime reached to pull her back to him, but she said, "I cannot find you if you hold me. Remember my dreams. I will kiss you soon, and more, after I am through with your dragon."

She picked up her bow and arrows again and walked over to the dragon gutting the deer. Bellchime fell to a shuddering fit, at war with himself.

"Stay where you are, dragon," said Periwinkle, taking aim at her.

Do not kill me and I will love you.

"The way you love Bellchime?" she asked, pointing to the man trembling impotently on the snowbank.

He is a mere wizard. You are a strong warrior.

"You said otherwise a few moments ago."

I was wrong. You have more power over the wizard than I have.

Periwinkle kept close watch on every muscle of the dragon's scaly body, remembering not to be distracted for an instant by any of her clever words.

You admire me, said Distance.

"You are beautiful," said Periwinkle. "You try to bind me. Your eyes search for mine. Do you dare gaze into my eyes after seeing what I did to Bellchime?"

Periwinkle did not want to kill this thing, but wanted to ride through the sky on her shoulders again. With a confidence that surprised her, she looked into the deep green pools of the dragon's eyes, into the widening pupils. The dragon was walking closer to her, but she lowered her bow, knowing that she did not need it.

A new world was opening inside her, and she took deep breaths to make room. Here were all the chests of gems, hoards of gold, the great cities in flame.

Something inside her did not resist this flow of thought, but deflected and changed it, to the dreaming time, the timeless time, the small web-footed creature with undeveloped wings swimming the surface of a summer sea, searching for the mouth of a river, feeling an aching loneliness for something else that thought.

"Periwinkle," said Bellchime.

There stood the man she must kill, the man who betrayed her—but these were not her own thoughts.

"Distance, he betrays neither of us," she said. "I will not kill him for you, nor do I want you filling my mind with blood and death the moment you think I am distracted."

"Periwinkle, what have you done?"

"I am dragonbound," she said and smiled. "I decided not to kill her. I feel fine, and you look much better."

"I think you have found me," he said very soberly.

"Then do not be so grim about it. Come, let us cut some venison off this carcass for ourselves." She drew a knife. "I think Distance has eaten her fill."

"She eats more each time," said Bellchime.

"Is there shelter for us nearby?"

"We are less than an hour from the den."

Periwinkle wrapped the meat in some skin and put it in her pack. "This will make a mess, but I see no other way," she said.

"We are already a mess," said Bellchime, and she laughed. Distance was rubbing her scales on the snow to clean herself.

Bellchime mounted first, then Periwinkle with her bow and pack. Trees tilted past them and fell below. The wind on Periwinkle's face was colder than before, with the sun fading into a high mist, but the dragon's body warmed her. Around Blue Dragonstone Mountain they flew. Oak Lake was one of two patches of frozen white in the bare trees far down the mountain, but they did not go that way. A lower cone stood on the slope of the main mountain, and near the summit of this, halfway up a cliff, was a cave much larger than the one she had slept in the night before. Steam seemed to drift from its mouth. The dragon folded her ribbed wings, swooped right into the misty dimness and landed; no ledge stood in front.

"It is warm here," Periwinkle said, dismounting and taking off her fur.

"I hope no goblins saw us. We do not normally go out by day, even though they are probably still far below, in their winter camps."

Bellchime dismounted, walked into the darkness, and snapped his sparker several times before he was able to light a tallow candle on a rock. Periwinkle followed him around a bend, where she saw a straw mattress, a few unusually small books, some cooking utensils and other tools, and a stool.

"Sit down," he said. "I will cook the deer." He got the pieces of meat from her pack, impaled them on a skewer, and took them down a long tunnel. While he was gone, Distance crawled into the room and lay down, filling most of the bare floor space. "It will cook fast," Bellchime said, returning. "The steam vent is very hot."

"When Froth said this mountain breathed fire like a dragon, I did not believe him."

"Froth is a man who knows many things. We who nest with a dragon are the fools," Bellchime said, nodding at Distance. "But I do have my plans."

I will not kill Riversong, said Distance. *If such a mighty one exists, I will mate him when I reach my majesty.*

Periwinkle turned to Bellchime's face with mixed admiration and disbelief. "Bellchime the Storyteller kills Riversong, mightiest dragon of the age, with his own dragon Distance, and frees the coast," she said. "A fool's plan, indeed! Would you then become king? What human could wield so much power and remain human?"

"A wizard might."

"Name me one wizard who has ever done this."

"Wintercress."

"He was son of the Moon and could change himself into a wolf, according to the stories. Name someone real."

"You are no one to scoff at Wintercress being son of the Moon," said Bellchime. "You yourself are a daughter of the Great Mother Fangcat, though I cannot imagine how you became this."

Periwinkle was puzzled. "What do you mean? I did dream about a fangtooth cat last night after I left Gar's hut, but so what?"

"Gar did this for you? He is a powerful shaman."

"He is? He seemed like a halfbreed outcast."

"He is also that," said Bellchime.

"He never told me that he knew you."

"Did he say he did not know me?"

"No."

"He knows much more than he seems to know," said Bellchime. "He knew how to make the Great Mother Fangcat hide most of his thoughts and feelings from Distance, which made her dislike him. This spirit is in you also. She helps you soften the dragon's hold on my mind, and keeps the dragon's hold on your own mind gentle."

"How is the venison doing?" asked Periwinkle.

Bellchime walked down the tunnel, returned with the meat, and cut portions.

"It tastes good," said Periwinkle.

"I misjudged Gar badly," said Bellchime. "I thought I had found a friend and teacher, and told him about my hidden cave near Oak Lake. A few days after I returned to that cave, one of the goblins from Stormbringer's Camp found it, and then a messenger came, giving me the usual four days to leave. Each time before, when this happened, I just left and found another home in some other goblin camp's territory, but this time it was the dead of winter, and I was angry, because I thought Gar had betrayed me."

"He would not do that," Periwinkle said firmly.

"I know that, now. I misjudged him. I was furious about everything, and somehow Distance's power came through my anger to swirl the winds into a storm that blew down half the tents of Stormbringer's Camp. I could sense my own fury in the storm raging outside the cave, but it was beyond my control. Tomcod, the shaman, knew that I had made the storm, and came to my cave himself as soon as it slackened, offering me a truce."

Bellchime looked into Periwinkle's eyes and said, "I am so afraid of what I may become."

Periwinkle said, "Gar told me that he hoped humans were wrong about dragons being more powerful than ancestor-beasts. He knew I was coming here to help you, and said he wanted me to succeed. I do not know about killing Riversong, but we do have power to do what is good, the three of us, if we love each other in the human sense of the word."

Love is a way to power for me, said Distance. *I am a dragon. You cannot make me into a person. Take me to the great lands, the forests, and farmkeeps. I will find them in your minds eventually. Give this information to me now and share my power longer. I may not eat you until I reach full majesty.*

"She is half-asleep," said Bellchime. "She babbles."

"She is arrogant, telling us that she will eat us one day, but trusting us not to kill her while she sleeps."

"We cannot kill her. We are dragonbound."

"I could kill her," said Periwinkle. "I choose not to. Bellchime, I thought four years with a dragon would make you powerful and dangerous, but I see that you are neither." Periwinkle stopped, aware of alien thoughts coloring her own. "I am sorry. She tries to make me scorn you, be disappointed in you."

"You want to love me and do not," said Bellchime.

Periwinkle considered this possibility, but said, "For love of you I rode for miles through snow and night, not knowing where I was going or what I would do."

Bellchime looked into her eyes, with his mouth half-open in wonder. "She is trying to make me think I am unworthy of you," he said.

Periwinkle laughed. "I trust my own judgment of your worth. You are clever, warm-hearted, and gentle, and I want you to kiss me."

His lips nibbled hers ever so lightly. She put her arms around him and twirled her tongue in his mouth until they were both out of breath. She touched his face, his soft reddish beard, and slid her hand over his shoulder and down his sleeve. His hand felt smooth and warm.

"I promised you more than a kiss, earlier," she said, setting the remains of their meal aside and unlacing her leather jacket and taking it off. She untied her pants, stood before him in bloomers and thin white shirt. Bellchime needed no more encouragement to undress, and while he did, she removed the rest of her clothing.

"This is real," she said, reaching to pull him to her side and looking at his body with curiosity. "I will not suddenly wake up and find myself alone."

"This is real," he said, and the soft straw tickled them through the mammoth-hair blanket while they kissed.

In the steamy warmth their bodies melted together. His hands smoothed and tingled her breasts, better than any dream, exciting and relaxing her at the same time. She reached to touch his erection pressed against her, felt the soft skin that slid over the hardened core, and the wet tip. Shifting beneath him, she opened her legs and felt the shock of his hip-shivers driving him deep, tasted sweat on his lips, and held his slippery back and behind.

The whole cave seemed to be vibrating, or was that the dragon purring?

Her breaths became gasps became screams. Jolts of energy ran up her spine and all through her body, and a new pulsing filled her with fluid. Over and over she kissed him, brushing away tears from his eyes, and telling him, "I love you," with a voice that came from her whole being.

"It feels so wonderful to be able to tell you I love you with you really here," he said, squeezing her tight.

"She is purring," Periwinkle said, after some moments passed. "We made her happy."

"I have been so alone," Bellchime said.

"Tell me more about it," she urged him. "I know I should be tired after being up most of the night, but—"

"I have been up all of the night and most of the day. Finding you took hours. I thought you would be on a mammoth trail, but there you were, right on the ridgecrest."

"That was the only way I knew my directions. I hope the horse did not stumble when he ran away."

"I saw him with the men when we left. Froth was one of them, was he not?"

"Froth and Heroncry followed me."

"Froth is obsessed about me. He was in the inn when I became dragonbound."

"You became dragonbound in an inn? I assumed it happened somewhere in the wilderness."

"Right in the Blue River Inn, in the center of Upriver, and I was even—" he hesitated.

"Sleeping with a barmaid?" Periwinkle guessed, and laughed when he nodded.

"We were asleep in a room on the second floor when something woke me. I got out of bed to use the chamber pot, and saw, by the moonlight, a dragonling looking up at me, projecting feelings of love, of needing to be with me, of offering me a rich new world. I suddenly felt, well, disgusted that I had needed to pay this woman silver to be my companion, and even then she only gave me something that had the shape of love but not the substance. I found myself thinking that no human I had ever known could offer me as much as this wonderful creature staring up at me. I found myself resenting my father for sending me away from the sea so that I could not become dragonbound. I found myself feeling that I was destined to become a great and powerful dragonbound wizard."

"She gave me all kinds of wild ideas, too," said Periwinkle.

"Then Trillium woke up and saw me kneeling on the floor, rubbing the dragonling's head, and screamed."

"Oh, no!"

"Oh, no, indeed! She ran out to the hall naked, shouting, 'Dragonbinding!' The terrified dragonling looked this way and that, made a funny swallowing noise, and wiggled under the bed. The next moment, three armed men rushed into the room. The one holding the lantern was a fishcatcher named Froth, and I was frightened, for I knew that he had a certain amount of wizard's intuition.

" 'What is the meaning of this?' I stammered. 'My woman had a nightmare.'

" 'Trillium does not have nightmares,' Froth said.

" 'Perhaps not in the arms of a strong man like you,' I said, and the other two men laughed. I was naked, he fully dressed, and the size difference between us emphasized. He stooped down to hold the lantern close to the floor, then looked at the windowsill. I knew then that I was saved, because he was looking for wet marks, and my dragonling was dry. It had taken her some time to crawl from the river by whatever improbable route to my second-floor room.

" 'The floor is dry,' he said, shaking his head.

" 'My aim was perfect,' I said, gesturing toward the chamber pot."

"Bellchime!" Periwinkle said with pretended shock, laughing.

"The other men laughed, too. Then Trillium returned, wearing a robe, with Stout, the innkeeper, who wanted to know just what the bloody death was going on. If only the dragonling kept still and quiet, all would be well, I thought, and she did.

" 'You had a nightmare and caused all this ruckus,' I accused Trillium. 'I paid for the whole night, but I do not think I want you now.'

"My story stuck, and in another hour it was dawn, and I left the inn with the dragonling hidden in my pack. I realized by this time that she could sense the emotions of nearby people, and somehow communicate this to me. Before too long, she was using words, much as she does now. I named her Distance because her color reminded me of distant mountains."

"I had the same thought when I first saw you riding her," said Periwinkle.

"I bought a hatchet from an Upriver blacksmith, and used it to build a tree-house in Cricket Swamp, and lived at first on fish and tubers. Later on, I lived in caves, and moved each time the goblins found me. Sometimes I walked the human roads in disguise, and learned a few things; that Froth had become Tarragon's new storyteller, for example, and that Riversong had left Moonport to attack Newport. That was when I first thought of killing Riversong."

"Newport is destroyed," Periwinkle said. "The survivors are

fighting a war with the goblins of Goblin Plain, and losing, some say."

"I was afraid it would come to something like that."

"Go on with your story."

"I already told you about meeting Gar, and making the storm. When that happened, I knew I needed help, but did not know where to turn. One day while Distance was sleeping, I was stretching a deer's hide, wishing that none of this had ever happened—and I thought about you, and really wanted to talk with you. I did not think you could do much about my predicament, but I knew at least you would understand."

Periwinkle smiled and caressed Bellchime's hand.

"I did not dare come to the keep, even in disguise, so I tried a dreamsending that night, and I reached you, and—I was surprised. I knew you were a woman by then, or almost a woman, but I never guessed how much you loved me, or how strong you had become."

Periwinkle laughed, squeezing Bellchime hard. "Of course I love you! Even my mother guessed that, though I tried to hide it from her, even before you disappeared. Can you believe that my parents somehow kept all knowledge about you being dragonbound from me and the other children? When Froth got captured by the goblins, I did not even know he was looking for you."

Bellchime said, "That is what finally made me have to leave Oak Lake. The goblins thought they had a choice between trouble with me and trouble with Tarragon's warriors. They confronted me, and Tomcod somehow strengthened their spirit-beasts, so that Distance could not sense the threat in their approach.

"'We can kill the dragon,' Tomcod said. 'You must leave.'

"Distance was ready to fight, but I had enough confidence to be firm, and we moved here."

Periwinkle said, "I was so angry when Froth finally admitted the truth, but I feel better after talking to him and Heroncry on the ridge. They will look for us, because they must do what they believe is right. They fear for the safety of the keep."

"I think it will take them some time to find us here," said Bellchime.

4

LITTLE DRAGONSTONE MOUNTAIN

15.

Froth and Heroncry spent a cold night wrapped in their furs beneath an overhanging ledge. The morning sun shone on the Silver Mountains, and forests below, but nowhere near their camp. "By the blood my bones are stiff," groaned Froth when he took a few steps down the trail to pass urine. His breath was thick and white, as was that of the three horses huddled together behind him.

Heroncry stirred. "Bloody fire went out," he said.

"A bigger one would not have."

"A bigger one might have gotten us speared in our sleep."

"We have crossed maybe forty miles since leaving the keep and not seen a single goblin yet, except Gar," said Froth.

"We are a long way from home and could easily disappear without a trace. I trust the goblins' honor enough to talk to them, but not enough to let them surprise me asleep."

Froth shivered. "Let us be off," he said. "The sooner we reach sunlight, the better."

The two men munched hard biscuits for breakfast while they rode, Heroncry first, Froth following, leading Black Rose's horse by a rope. The fir trees gave way to a mixture of pine and oak while they followed the mammoth trail down the west side of the ridge. Snow was patchy on some of the meadows here, and when the two reached a sunny place, they stopped to allow the horses to graze.

Froth had the disquieting feeling that they were being watched. Heroncry looked at the brush, as if his hunter's ears had heard something there. Lightly as possible, he stepped toward whatever it was.

A small sound like a giggle came from a different direction, and Froth turned to glimpse something furry disappear behind a tree at the edge of the clearing. Heroncry was already stalking it.

"Your step is heavy as a mountain mammoth's," said a voice from the direction of another tree. Froth ran behind the tree but saw only a hole like a rabbit's. "Heroncry, watch the horses!" he shouted. "I saw a pook!"

"A pook in this country? Are you certain?"

"Either that or the rabbits here know how to speak."

"Rabbit indeed!" huffed the voice, and there was no mistaking the woman who stood next to the tree for anything but a pook. She was little more than knee-high to the two humans, wore no clothing, and was covered head to foot with golden-brown fur. "And what may the likes of you be doing on this land?" she asked.

"Grazing our horses and enjoying the sunshine," said Heroncry.

"A likely story," said the pook. "What is the sword for?"

"Do not waste time talking to her," said Froth in a low voice. "We were just leaving," he told the pook, and taking the rope to Black Rose's horse in hand, he mounted his own horse. "Our apologies for disturbing you," he added.

"Oh, I am not disturbed," she said. "Let your horses graze. Come dance in the meadow with me. I have not danced with humans before." She spun around twice and danced a couple of steps, opened her eyes wide and grinned at them, posing with furry hands on furry hips.

"Think she might know anything about the dragon?" Heroncry asked Froth in a low voice.

"I have never heard of a pook giving anyone a plain answer. All they think about is singing and dancing and eating."

"You left out lovemaking," said the pook. "We pooks concentrate on the important things in life and leave the dragonslaying for fools like you." She laughed and disappeared into the forest.

"You know more about pooks than I," Heroncry said to Froth when she did not reappear. "Will she bring us bad luck?"

"I do not think so," said Froth. "We did not anger her."

They mounted their horses and rode on. By noon, the forest had become mostly oak, bare trees with buds tipping every twig. No clearings or hills opened the view to show them where they were. Each time the trail forked, Heroncry chose the way that ran toward the trees' shadows. When they finally came to a meadow showing Blue Dragonstone Mountain above the trees, the cone of Little Dragonstone was to the right of it.

"Oak Lake should be less than thirty miles from here," said Heroncry.

"So far yet? Are we coming a roundabout way?"

"It is at least seventy miles from the keep, even as the dragon flies. You think it is closer because some of their people are usually camped near the keep."

"No wonder Stonewort had to hire warriors from Upriver when he took the war there," said Froth.

Something snorted, heavy feet trampled the ground, and on the far end of the clearing a shaggy bull mammoth, with tusks as long as a human, stood, eyeing the men and horses. Another mammoth stepped out of the woods beside it, and another. The first decided he felt safe, then began to pull up grass with his trunk. Slowly Froth and Heroncry rode out of the clearing.

"Lucky he did not charge," said Heroncry. "Swords and arrows are little use against those beasts."

"They are blocking our way."

"Nothing we can do about that but wait."

From the woods they watched five more mammoths, including two young ones, amble into the clearing and begin eating.

"Now we can go around them," said Heroncry, leading Froth a winding way behind the brush at the edge of the clearing to the far side, where the freshly trampled trail was muddy and slushy, and wide enough for the men to ride side by side.

"At least we know the weather will keep improving if the mammoths are going back up the mountain," said Froth.

"Where mammoths march, goblins will be close behind," said Heroncry.

"How do they kill such beasts with spears?"

"They throw many spears."

Not too far down the trail they saw tracks of something stalking the mammoths, but they were not goblin-tracks. The horses stomped and whinnied.

"Fangcat," said Heroncry.

"Blood! I can see that as well as you."

"What is the matter?"

Froth took a deep breath and sighed. "That attack of the Great Mother Cat at Gar's hut felt entirely too real."

"This cat will not put you in a trance. May eat you, though."

"The tracks go off the road away from us."

"I hope it has not doubled back."

Despite the long ride, the horses needed little urging to move faster, splashing mud on their legs with every trot, until they came to another fork. The mammoths had trampled up the left way, and they turned right. About a quarter-mile farther, they came to a four-headed totem pole, about five feet high, with a bear carved on top, then a fangtooth cat, a great elk, and a speckled condor.

"These are totems of Oak Lake," Heroncry said in a low voice. "Must be a camp nearby."

The two men rode, leading the third horse, a short way before reaching a flat clearing, with seven goblin tents arranged in a circle. The tents were conical, made like miniature versions of a castle tower's roof, with poles instead of rafters, and leather instead of lead. Each was about ten feet in diameter, and no more than seven feet high. This was a hunting camp, easily moved. The smell of smoked mammoth meat was strong.

"Truce of Stormbringer and Tarragon!" bellowed Heroncry. "We want to speak with you!"

"No one is here," said Froth.

"In the bushes," said Heroncry, and out sprang seven goblin warriors with spears. All were shorter than Froth, stocky and beardless, with pointed ears and large lips; all wore sleeveless fur jackets, short fur breeches, and soft shoes; and all stood with power and pride.

"Dismount and throw down your weapons," said the leader, who wore a bear's tooth necklace over his jacket. He spoke the humans' language with a noticeable accent. "You trespass here. This land is never yours to hunt in."

"We do not hunt," said Heroncry.

"We have had no meat since we left the keep two days ago," complained Froth.

"Why are you here?"

"We seek the dragon and the wizard Bellchime," said Heroncry.

The leader mumbled something in his own language to the shaman, who wore a moonstone on his headband, then said, "You have no more right to hunt dragon here than to hunt mammoth or unicorn."

"I will speak," said the shaman, who was much more fluent in the humans' language. "The dragon is gone. Tomcod of the Speckled Condor Clan overpowered the wizard Bellchime this past summer. We forced him to leave our land because the storyteller Froth from Tarragon's Keep was captured trespassing, looking for him. We want no troubles with humans over this matter."

"I am Froth, and I *saw* the dragon fly around this side of the mountain yesterday afternoon. Do you expect us to believe—"

"Froth!" broke in Heroncry. "Let us assume these warriors speak the truth until proven otherwise."

Froth looked at the goblins' spears and saw the wisdom of this. The leader and the shaman were mumbling in their own language to each other when a third goblin threw down his spear and jumped up and down shrieking and shouting.

"He says the dead deer was killed by dragon, not fangcat," Heroncry told Froth.

The other goblins looked at each other slowly, and one by one quietly dropped their weapons.

"Truce of Tarragon and Stormbringer," said the leader. "I am called Redfox."

"I am called Drum," said the shaman, "and I am Tomcod's spirit son. I was with Tomcod when he and Stormbringer and Redfox and other warriors confronted Bellchime and his dragon. We did this after Tarragon spoke with Trout of the Great Elk Clan about releasing Froth. Tomcod fasted and prayed for four days. He told Bellchime that now he had the power to kill the dragon. The dragon bellowed, but our spirit-beasts kept her out of our minds, mostly, and this time Bellchime made no storm. He looked small and powerless standing in the cave facing all of us."

"Why did you not kill them?" asked Froth.

"Because Tomcod dreamed a vision battle and won, but there was no killing in the dream, only exile. A shaman cannot kill another shaman without dreaming it first. Otherwise, the death curse—"

"Of course," interrupted Froth, thinking of how he had killed Taproot years before. "But this wizard is losing power. Dragons give a wizard power, as spirit-animals give a shaman power, but when a dragon reaches a certain size, it begins to drain the wizard, taking back the wizard's power along with his knowledge. I know that this is happening now, because Bellchime has summoned a helper from our keep."

"Ah, that is why you come now," said Redfox.

"Humans do not go out much in cold weather," cackled one of the other goblins. "Not strong, like goblins."

"Truce means respect, Toadstool," said Redfox. Toadstool glared but kept his mouth shut.

"Trout was a fool," Drum said to Froth. "I say that you are a man of power, that you have had experience with dragons before."

"Trout would not listen to me at all. His attitude toward my kind was like Toadstool's or worse. But I do know about the growth of dragons. Four years ago, it was about as long as my arm; two years ago, its body was as big as a wolf's, and with neck and tail it was nine feet long; now, its body is as big as a horse's, its wingspan—"

"When we first learned of the dragon and Bellchime, it was as you say," said Redfox. "How big will she become?"

"I have seen a dragon with a head at least five feet long, and a body as bulky as two mammoths."

"We have heard stories of a dragon even larger than that," said Redfox. "Far to the south, where thousands of goblins fight a war with thousands of humans, the humans speak of Riversong, whose head alone is eight feet long. Who can believe that?"

"That is the same dragon," said Froth. "I saw Riversong twenty years ago when he destroyed Moonport. He ate the burnt body of my wife in two bites."

The chief and shaman looked at each other with bulging eyes, Toadstool scowled, and the others asked in their own language what Froth had said.

"Your story must be true," said Redfox. "No husband would say that he watched his wife being eaten and did nothing but escape with his own life, if the story were not true. Your story humiliates you, and you are a man of pride."

"Tomcod was wrong!" said Drum. "We must kill the dragon!"

One by one, the goblins picked up their spears, and Heroncry his sword.

"Kill the dragon!" bellowed Heroncry.

"Kill the dragon!" yelled the goblins.

Redfox whistled four times, and other goblins, women and children, came running into camp. One of the goblin women ran into her tent and brought out a drum and began to beat it.

"The women agree with our decision," said Redfox.

He began dancing around the circle, followed by the other goblin warriors, and by Heroncry and Froth trying to imitate their steps as closely as possible. This had to be a first, Froth thought to himself, two humans dancing a war dance with the goblins. Would either Tarragon or Stormbringer believe this?

The drumbeat quickened, became more complex when another goblin woman's drumming added to the first. Froth's legs began to cramp, but a power in the drumming kept him going. He saw Redfox as a bear, Drum as a fangcat, Toadstool as a condor, the four other goblin dancers as elk and bear, Heroncry as a unicorn, and himself as a weasel. Froth began to dance weasel, to feel the power of subtlety, of hiding his true self, of peeking at the world through small holes and dashing out to catch a mouse.

Froth did not remember leaving the dance and sitting down next to one of the goblin women. She gave him a cup of hot drink, which kept his head from spinning. Heroncry and the goblin men were also sitting down, drinking cups of this brew.

"How will we find the dragon?" asked Froth.

"As you lead us in the dance," said Redfox. "We will hunt like weasels."

"Watch the sky at night," the woman who was the first drummer said, with a heavy accent.

"Cricket speaks true," said Drum.

"Are there caves you cannot climb to?" asked Froth. "Caves the dragon would have to fly into?"

"I have seen such caves near the top of the smaller cone," said Toadstool.

"Do goblins often go near this place?" asked Heroncry.

"Hunting is terrible there," said Redfox. "That cone is all rock, no soil, and few trees."

"It sounds like a good place to look," said Froth.

"Attacking that place will not be easy," said Toadstool.

"You make it sound even more likely."

"But we can do it," said Heroncry, and grabbing his bow and an arrow to demonstrate, he aimed high and sent an arrow above the treetops beyond the camp.

"A goblin gets close to what he hunts," snorted Toadstool.

Redfox said, "If we watch the caves night and day, when the dragon leaves, we can climb into the cave and kill her when she returns."

"Where do we hide the ladder?" asked Heroncry.

"It is worse than that," said Froth. "The dragon would hear the thoughts of anyone planning an ambush."

"No," said Drum. "Our spirit-beasts can hide our thoughts from her."

No one said anything for a few moments, then Cricket struck her drum and spoke. "Go watch the cave and find out if they are there. You cannot know how to attack without more information." She struck her drum again.

"We watch the cave in pairs, one to watch, one to return if the dragon is seen," said Redfox.

"Froth and I will go first," said Heroncry. "If the dragon appears this evening, I may be able to shoot her down."

"That seems right," said Redfox. "Toadstool will show you the way. Drum and I replace you at Moonrise."

Froth and Heroncry looked at Toadstool.

"Come," he said sullenly.

The humans started over to their horses and packs.

"On foot," said Toadstool. "Where we go, horses cannot."

"Let us ride as far as we can," said Froth.

"And leave your horses for the wolf and fangcat? On foot, I said."

"Toadstool knows the country," said Heroncry.

"Take just your weapons," said Cricket. "We will have a meal for you when you return."

Toadstool snorted and led the two humans out of camp the way they had entered, back to the muddy mammoth trail, back to the meadow where the mammoths had been, and though the journey on foot was slower, the way back seemed shorter for being familiar.

Here Toadstool led them off the trail and up the lower slope of Little Dragonstone Mountain, warmed now by late afternoon sun. The ground between the pines became rocky with outcrops of dragonstone. The forest thinned above them as though they were climbing toward a ridge, but when they reached the last trees, they saw the slope continuing steadily but more slowly upward, nothing but naked rock, all the way to the bottom of a sheer cliff, with several caves halfway up.

"Blood!" said Heroncry. "There is no cover."

"Perhaps we could attack from above," suggested Froth, "or does that cliff go all the way around the peak?"

"It does not," said Toadstool.

"If I shoot the dragon out of the sky while Periwinkle rides her—" said Heroncry.

"She might be badly hurt or killed," said Froth. "We could try Redfox's plan. After what happened with Gar, I am no one to underestimate the power of spirit-beasts."

"A rope lowered from above could get us in," said Heroncry.

"Did you say 'she'?" asked Toadstool. "A woman? Most likely this wizard seeks a mate, not a helper. He may still have all his power. Oh, fools, have you dreamed his death?"

"Many times," said Froth.

"But dreams do not always come true," said Toadstool. "We do not even know for certain that anyone is up there."

"Is there no closer place to watch from?" asked Heroncry.

"See for yourself," said Toadstool, gesturing at the open wasteland of jumbled rocks between the forest and the cliff. "I return to camp. Redfox and Drum will meet you here late tonight as they said."

Heroncry and Froth did not watch Toadstool leave, but stared at the cliff and argued about how well the dragon could see by sun and stars, whether various rocks might hide them, and whether there might be pits in the dragonstone flow. Sunset touched the gray cliff with yellow, then orange and pink, and the sky deepened to stars.

Slowly and awkwardly, Heroncry and Froth walked over the boulder-strewn flow, glancing constantly at the dark spots on the cliff.

"I think I see a glimmer," mumbled Heroncry, but if so it was too faint for Froth's eyes.

"It is gone now," Heroncry said somewhat later, when the constellation of Wintercress the wizard-king rose behind the top of the cliff.

"If the dragon does go out, what do we do? We cannot climb around to the top of the cliff in this dark."

"Bold frontal attack tomorrow, with as many goblins as we can muster. Periwinkle can either stand aside or fight us."

"I think she will fight us, and that will be hard," said Froth.

"Wish we had some warriors from the keep."

"We could get them."

"No, let us do this with the goblins, improve on Tarragon's truce, and try to save his daughter. We danced with the goblins; let us try to kill the dragon with them. They will take pains not to kill Periwinkle once they know who she is."

Something giggled, and told the men that their voices were louder than a fangcat's roar.

"Bloody death, it is that pook!" said Froth.

"You would not dance life with me, but you danced death with goblins," said her voice from somewhere among the rocks.

"Dragons kill," said Heroncry. "We are trying to save lives."

"She knew where the dragon was all along," said Froth.

"I do know where Periwinkle is," said the pook's voice.

"Yes, but will she tell us?" asked Froth.

"Right here," said the pook.

"Periwinkle?" asked Froth, thinking she might be with the pook.

"At your service, my lords," said the pook.

"Your name is Periwinkle?" asked Heroncry.

"Beautiful name, is it not? I like it so much better than the name I used before."

Heroncry suppressed a laugh.

Froth said, "What did I tell you about pooks wasting your time?"

"Not much else to do while we watch this bloody hole," said Heroncry, but the pook did not say anything more, and did not answer when he called her by name.

"I suppose she is gone," said Froth.

A few uneventful hours later, when the moon began to rise, a sound like a wolf's howl startled the two men, and there stood Drum and Redfox.

"Nothing," said Heroncry.

"Heroncry thought he saw a glimmer of light in one of the caves," said Froth, "but nothing more. The dragon may not hunt tonight."

"Or she may wait for moonlight," said Redfox. "Go back to camp and sleep. Sooner or later we will see her."

"One thing we must tell you," said Heroncry. "The helper Bellchime summoned is Tarragon's daughter."

"Aha!" said Drum.

"Now it all makes sense," said Redfox. "We attack the dragon without harming her, and there is substantial reward."

"Um, yes," said Heroncry.

"The humans wanted us to realize that we had our own reasons to kill the dragon before telling us about Tarragon's daughter," said Drum.

"We did not lie about Bellchime wanting a helper, whatever Toadstool says," said Froth. "This woman, Periwinkle, is a warrior and one of the best. I know, for I was her storyteller."

"Humans are like fangcats," said Redfox. "The women can be as dangerous as the men."

"The same could be said about cave bears," said Drum.

"I meant your clan no insult," said Redfox.

"Or ours, we presume," said Heroncry.

"Anyway, good night," said Froth. "We have a long walk."

The two humans worked their way back over the dimly lit boulders while the two goblins watched the face of the cliff.

16.

Periwinkle startled awake at once when she felt something tapping her shoulder.

"Periwinkle," said a small voice that was not Bellchime's.

"Periwinkle?" asked Bellchime drowsily.

"Someone is in here besides us," she whispered, and Bellchime got up to light a candle with his sparker.

In the shadow of their straw bed stood a golden-furred pook woman, looking somewhat out of breath and very nervous about the dragon snoring in the steamy dimness across the cave.

"Hello," said the pook. "My name is also Periwinkle."

"You seem to already know our names," said Bellchime.

"I know Periwinkle's, but not yours, my lord."

"Bellchime—the wizard. I am no lord."

"You may become one," said the pook. "I look at this beautiful cave, at the fierce blue scaly one sleeping, and I am sad. Please dance with me."

"Does this make sense to you?" Periwinkle asked Bellchime.

"I guess she means that we will have to leave this place soon," said Bellchime.

"Very well," said Periwinkle to the pook, "we will dance with you as best we can, though there is not much room here for people our size to dance."

"Dance sitting on your bed then," said the pook. "The feeling is what matters."

The pook bowed to each human, spun around on her right toes, and leapt onto the straw bed where Bellchime and Periwinkle both sat, naked as the pook was.

"I think I get the feel of it," said Periwinkle, rocking her head and gesturing gracefully with her arms. Bellchime watched both Periwinkles and began a tentative imitation of the human woman's movements. None of them sang songs or played music, but they danced to the dragon's snores, which seemed to become musical.

"The dragon's thoughts!" said Bellchime. "Distance dreams music at us."

"How delightful!" said Periwinkle the Pook, who imitated the larger Periwinkle's arm and torso movements while dancing on and off the straw. She stopped, and the humans stopped, and all three looked at each other.

"You must leave your home tonight," said the pook. "They are watching this cave. They danced a war dance with the goblins and all will attack tomorrow."

"She must mean Heroncry and Froth," said Periwinkle.

"I am amazed that they found us so quickly," said Bellchime, "and even more amazed that the goblins would dance with them."

"We are their common enemy, or Distance is, or so they believe," said Periwinkle. "As I said this morning, if we must become homeless wanderers, staying nowhere long enough to make enemies, we should take the opportunity to learn all we can about the ways of power. Years will pass before Distance can do—what you want her to do. Even this pook has taught us something. Did you feel the power of her dance?"

"More than power," said the pook, holding Periwinkle's gray eyes with her own dark ones. "Life! We dance life!"

"Would you care to come with us?" Periwinkle asked her. "We do not know where we will go, but—"

"No, no, my place is here," the smaller Periwinkle said. "And I see death in you, though you dance life. The two below desire to kill your dragon, and you, I think, also want to kill something— "

"Riversong," said Periwinkle.

"The great god demon of the sea?" asked the pook incredulously.

"—is only a dragon, like this one, but much bigger," said Bellchime.

"If Riversong were killed," said Periwinkle, "humans would keep their cities on the coast, humans and goblins would not fight wars— "

"They do not fight wars now," said the pook.

"Farther south they do," Bellchime said grimly.

"If I advised you, I would say, live here, be now, and dance!" said the pook. "Do not worry about dragons and wars far away. But you must go far away, that is what I come to tell you. Oh, you big people and your foolishness make me so sad, I do not know what to do. I must leave this cave, return to the green woods, and dance, dance until my sadness is gone."

"I wish we could be like you," Periwinkle said, but the pook danced to the mouth of the cave and climbed over the edge with no more words.

17.

Not too much later, Redfox and Drum saw something large flying from the cliff, difficult to make out until it flew beyond the edge of the mountain into moonlight.

"I go, you stay," said Redfox, and hurried back through the night to his camp to rouse the warriors. Three other goblins, Heroncry, and Froth scrambled back with him over the boulders.

"The dragon has not returned," said Drum, and the seven made their difficult way over the rest of the dragonstone flow to the foot of the cliff, having agreed to challenge the dragon to a direct battle when she did return. Otherwise, Heroncry would shoot her out of the sky the next time she emerged from the cave, whether anyone rode her or not.

However, the dragon did not return. The moon faded in the west as the sky brightened, removing the stars. At noon a large group of goblins, including Stormbringer and Tomcod, arrived. A few goblins followed the bottom of the cliff to a passable section, climbed it, then walked the top, back to where the caves were, and lowered themselves on a rope. In the cave they found nothing but a pile of straw, a stool, an empty shelf, and a piece of deerskin covered with human marks-that-talk. This they brought to Froth. What it said was, "Goodbye and bless you, Bellchime and Periwinkle."

⟨5⟩

UPRIVER

18.

Periwinkle looked at the seven symbols Bellchime wrote on a piece of deerskin and told him it was beautiful, but Distance, who understood the meaning of the marks through the humans' thoughts, considered this a most odd message to leave their enemies.

"They choose to be our enemies," said Bellchime. "We need not agree with their choice."

Bellchime and Periwinkle mounted Distance, who assured them that she could carry Bellchime's books in addition to the two humans, because these weighed much less than the deer she tried to lift two days before.

From footing in steamy warmth to flight through dry freezing air was a sudden change, though Periwinkle had expected it. Close on their left passed the cliff, blocking out almost half the sky, until they circled Little Dragonstone Mountain into the light of a gibbous moon already high, and then the ground fell away, farther than ever before, to textures of rocky, snowy, and forested ridges, moving very slowly beneath the dragon's legs. The wind in their faces seemed biting cold.

The moon was moving west when Periwinkle recognized the ridge where she had ridden her mother's horse to meet Bellchime. Farther west they passed over what looked like the road from

Tarragon's Keep to Slot's Keep, which greatly interested Distance. Why not fly over Tarragon's Keep and show them all what Periwinkle had made of herself, tamer of a mighty dragon? Periwinkle realized with mixed amusement and annoyance that Distance was at it again, and to distract her, she looked at the far-off Silver Mountains curving from west to south, ghostly blue in the moonlight. Bellchime reached up and scratched behind the dragon's ears, which seemed to calm her mind.

They turned toward the southwest, flying directly toward the mountains while the sky brightened toward dawn. The first sunlight made the tips of the snowy peaks a brilliant pink, which brightened to orange and yellow while moving down the jagged slopes. In front of the foothills still in shadow curved a river's shining strand. This river enlarged rapidly; the texture of ground became bumps of treetops, the river rough and swollen with spring flood. Periwinkle felt the muscles of Distance's flapping roll beneath her legs while the dragon set down on a broad bank of gravel several times the width of her castle's courtyard.

"That was a long ride," said Periwinkle, dismounting and rubbing her legs. Even in the sunlight it was still cold. "Where are we?"

"The Silver River, I would say, twenty miles from Hammer's Keep," said Bellchime, dismounting. "I do not think anyone, human or goblin, is likely to be nearby, but here we cannot be suddenly surprised."

"This is a huge river," said Periwinkle, "much bigger than at Slot's Keep." She unlashed the packs from the dragon's hips, began eating a chunk of cheese from hers, and offered Bellchime some. "This never tasted so good," she said, and Bellchime conceded that at least that was true, for he had never liked the cheese made at Tarragon's Keep. She also offered a nibble to Distance, who found the flavor interesting. Scratching the dragon's scales behind the ears until she began purring with pleasure, Periwinkle asked her if she might hunt them something.

A deer, perhaps? asked Distance.

"Smaller than that, unless you will eat also," said Periwinkle. "Go up into the mountains across the river, I think," she added, and Bellchime nodded yes.

The dragon jumped into flight and coasted low over the treetops on the far side of the river.

"You manage her better than I have been able to for months," said Bellchime.

"Stop being so hard on yourself. You managed a dragon for four years, and you are neither power-mad, insane, or dead. I can think of no dragonbound wizard more recent than legend who could claim so much. I learned where she likes to be scratched by watching you."

Bellchime hugged her, saying, "You are truly a wonder."

Periwinkle looked into his eyes and said, "Now for the real question: Where are we going to go? We were still talking it around in circles when we had to leave."

"You have a new plan," said Bellchime. "I know that much."

"As we flew, and Distance became interested in my father's keep, I began thinking that we should have our own keep. We might find ourselves a people among those humans from Newport who are caught between Riversong and the goblins."

Bellchime thought seriously before answering. "Once Distance breathes fire, this might be done. She could help defend a site."

"And I know how to lead a keep. How soon will her flame come?"

"Soon, I hope," said Bellchime, "but we will have to find another cave to live in until then."

"We should go to Upriver now, before there is any rumor of a dragon in the Silver Mountains."

"Yes, it would be a good place to gain news of the war, and certainly the only city east of the sea that we can come anyplace nearby with Distance. I hope I can disguise myself well enough. Two summers ago, I shaved my head and passed for a wandering priest."

"That might be fine for walking the back roads, but Upriver is full of real priests."

"That was how I went to Upriver. I made a point of pretending not to be a priest, so of course people thought I was one."

"You paid a barmaid to sleep with you, I suppose?"

"Hmm, not exactly," he said, and Periwinkle laughed.

"You would make a most scandalous priest coming to the city gates with me," she said, "and besides, I want to marry you."

"And I want to marry you, but it might be risky. I would have to use my real name, and Froth has done all he can to make Bellchime an infamous name."

"So what?" asked Periwinkle. "Bellchime the Wizard is not the only Bellchime east of the sea. You can be Bellchime the Merchant. If you can make storms and dreamsend, you should be able to change the look of your face enough to be someone else."

Bellchime turned away from her, walked a few steps, pressed his hands to his face, and turned back, saying he was Bellchime, a trader from Bigfish. His face seemed a bit changed, but Periwinkle had no trouble recognizing him.

"You have looked into my eyes too deeply for this trick to fool you," said Bellchime.

"So has Trillium, probably," said Periwinkle. "Try harder."

"She did not recognize me when I was the priest."

Periwinkle burst out laughing. "You mean you slept with *her* again?"

"She kept saying she always wanted to sleep with a priest, and I kept denying I was a priest. She did not even ask me to pay her."

Periwinkle laughed again. "Let me think. If you are a trader, where are your goods?"

"I was robbed."

"Robbed, you say, and they did not take the beautiful young woman from you? She must be a warrior. If so, why did she not protect you?"

"She was hunting when the robbers attacked me. Periwinkle, no one will believe any of this nonsense!"

"Of course not. They will think we are a young couple getting married against my parents' wishes, and making up stories so no one will stop us. We should gather wood to cook with. Distance will return soon."

"I sensed her kill something, also."

They picked up sticks from the river's edge that had dried awhile in the sun, and had the fire ready to be lit when Distance appeared overhead, carrying the hind leg of a goat in her forelegs. She bellowed, dropped the meat, and flapped to a landing.

"How do we explain to her?" asked Periwinkle.

"It is all right. This is a wild goat," Bellchime said, and thanked Distance for killing it.

It is delicious, she said.

Bellchime struck his sparker to the kindling, which caught fire, dwindled to a red glow, and went out. Periwinkle asked Distance to blow on the wood like a bellows, and Bellchime's next spark flashed the entire pile into flame.

"It will not be long before you breathe fire," Periwinkle told

Distance, scratching the scales under her chin, while Bellchime cut the leg into steaks.

Soon the meal was cooked and eaten, the leftovers fed to Distance, who loved the taste of cooked goat even better than raw. Then the dragon sprawled out on the gravel to doze in the sun, which Bellchime let her do, for he did not want to approach the Upriver gate until late afternoon, when travelers on foot would naturally time their arrival.

While Distance slept, Periwinkle and Bellchime talked, about everything from their own beliefs about the purpose of life, to the keep they wanted to establish, to what might be the true story behind the fabulous events described in the *Epic of Wintercress*, to the contents of Bellchime's well-worn map, which showed the entire coast from Swordwall to Southport and the Isle of Hod.

Southport had been the realm of a dragon named Redmoon for many years, but Periwinkle said that this dragon had either died or disappeared, and some traders, or pirates, from west of the sea, who spoke a foreign language, were settling there now. This much she had heard an overland merchant tell her father.

"Tales get twisted when passed from traveler to traveler," said Bellchime.

"I have heard some wild ones," said Periwinkle, "islands that explode and darken the sky for days, or places where for many miles in every direction it is as barren as this beach, or places where the sun moves north at noon."

"Well," Bellchime hesitated, "those stories are probably all true."

"If they are, then I am glad to be here, where everything is forest and meadow, and the sun stays where it should. How could an island possibly explode, anyway?"

Bellchime had no answer for that, but he had heard of it happening.

When the sun touched the trees on the hill across the river, they tied their packs onto the dragon's back, mounted her shoulders, and flew high above the course of the Silver River, until the gray towers of Hammer's Castle became large enough to make out.

"Do not go close," said Bellchime. "They will shoot arrows through your wings if they see you coming. Stay south of the river until that keep is behind us, but cross the river before the forest ends."

Perhaps I will not go near them this time, said Distance.

"Do what he says, Distance," said Periwinkle firmly.

Over the deep forest south of the river, toward the Silver Mountains they flew, until Hammer's Keep was small and the river a dark thread. Slowly they turned, and when the river became closer again, Periwinkle saw cultivated land far away to the right, angular patterns of pale green and brown that stopped abruptly at the river. Upriver was the only place this far from the coast where humans farmed outside the walls, for here the goblins had all been killed or driven across the rivers many years ago.

The river changed from darkness to bright blue to silver when they passed over it. Suddenly, Distance half-folded her wings, and the texture below became treetops, some green and conical, some brown and feathery, rushing rapidly toward them.

"Distance!" shouted Periwinkle.

You will not fall off, answered Distance in her mind, but Periwinkle's stomach lurched when the dragon spread her wings and powerglided very quickly just above the treetops. Gradually she slowed down and began flapping. The roof of what looked like a distant tower appeared over the farthest treetops, and Distance sank a little lower and flew until the roof appeared again, then landed in a small clearing surrounded by trees. Periwinkle heard the river not far away; Distance walked through the trees toward this sound.

"Good dragon, Distance," said Bellchime. "That was beautiful flying! From the looks of that tower roof we saw, we are less than two miles from Upriver, in broad daylight, and they did not get a glimpse of us."

Periwinkle tactfully restrained her comment, but Distance was purring with delight at Bellchime's praise, and paid Periwinkle's emotions no heed.

"Now what?" Periwinkle asked Bellchime.

"We ride Distance on foot to the river, make sure no one is watching, then she flies us across, flies back herself, and we walk into the city."

What do I do then? asked Distance, stopping her purring.

"Hunt animals or sleep, whichever you wish, but stay on this side of the river and make certain no human sees you. We will return and call you either tomorrow or the next day."

You go to learn about the great lands beyond us, said Distance, purring again.

"Yes," said Periwinkle.

Patches of water showed between the trees, then they stopped and looked over the river at the trees on the opposite bank and the open farmland stretching toward the hills and mountains. No one was in sight.

"Let me get our packs," Periwinkle said and twisted around to untie them from the dragon's back. Bellchime's pack was quite heavy, but she managed to pass it to him.

"Fly as low as you can," said Bellchime, and Distance's wings almost touched the foaming river when she flapped. They dismounted on the other side, watched Distance fly back and walk into the trees, then climbed up the bank.

Periwinkle removed her bow from her pack and strung it, got out her quiver of arrows, and put her pack back on. "We will not be robbed again," she told Bellchime, winking.

They trudged the road, talking, and before long came in sight of the tower they had seen before, the watchtower of Lord Blackwood's Castle, then other towers of the castle, then towers of the Church of the Second Daughter, then towers of the wall of the city.

"I was here once before, but I was young and do not remember much," said Periwinkle.

"Last time I came here, I walked all the way from Copper Mountain, mostly by night. Distance had only been flying for a few months and was about the size of a wolf, too small to ride, but hard to keep hidden. I left her in the forest a few miles back this road. She had just killed her first deer and was content to remain—"

"Tell me no more stories of former lovers!" said Periwinkle angrily, hearing hoofbeats of a horse behind them.

"Not so loud," said Bellchime.

The rider who quickly overtook them was a woman with wavy brown hair, a warrior from Hammer's Keep, to judge from the marks on her shield and scabbard.

"You look like two with stories to tell," she said, eyeing Periwinkle's weapons.

"Stories are to be told in comfort by the fire, my lady," said Bellchime, "not when one is footsore with miles yet to walk."

"Be comforted. You are not far from the city gates, even on foot," she said, pausing a moment as if in thought. "A marriage?" she asked.

"Yes," said Periwinkle. "Please ask no more."

The warrior laughed. "I was married in Upriver myself eight summers ago, to a blacksmith's son. My parents were angered at first, but they recovered. Good luck to you both," she said and rode ahead of them toward the city.

"I recognize her," said Periwinkle in a hushed voice, "and she may have guessed who I am."

"Soon we will pass the gate and be lost in the city," said Bellchime.

As they neared the city gate, the towers of church and castle sank below the top of the wall, which was faced with larger stones than the walls of Tarragon's Keep, and the road was flanked with two oversized statues of seated warriors, a man on the left, a woman on the right, carved from shining hardstone in the archaic style.

"These were the work of Oakroot the Sculptor in the year when Wentletrap's army killed Mugwort the Dragon," said Bellchime when they walked between them.

The bars and great bronze doors of the main gate were closed, and a guard with a spear stood in front of the lesser gate, which was large enough for only one person on horseback to pass at a time. She looked at Bellchime and Periwinkle and stood aside for them.

"I do not need your names," she said quietly. "Torchfire of Hammer's Keep explained your business. By the blood, begging your pardon, some of those keeps in the wild places are as old-fashioned as these statues. Go on in."

"Thank you, my lady," said Periwinkle.

Once inside the gate, Bellchime saw and noted a large number of hastily built huts against the city wall. Two women dressed in mended clothes, one at least Froth's age, one not much older than Periwinkle and very pregnant, were talking about how they and their husbands scheduled their days of helping with the big clearing project, and how they someday hoped to farm their own fields and have real houses in the city, once the city walls were enlarged.

"Good women of Newport," Bellchime addressed them.

"Never name that city to us," snapped the older woman. "It is a dragon's lair. We are both women of Upriver by the grace of Lord Blackwood and his warriors, and we deserve to be called no less."

"I meant no offense," said Bellchime.

"Endive is bitter because Riversong killed her sister and brother, and the goblins killed all three of her sons. My husband and I lost only our land and our wealth."

"What do you know of the war?" asked Periwinkle.

"We lost," said the pregnant woman. "Others may fight on, but we only want to make a new life for ourselves here."

"Pip," said Endive into her ear, "this woman is a warrior from one of those northern keeps where they live with goblins and hunt more than farm. I want nothing to do with such people."

Pip began to apologize for her friend's behavior after Endive slammed the door to her hut.

"I am sorry myself," said Periwinkle. "I am a warrior, but unlike you, I have not lived through a war, and did not know the depths of the pain—"

"I do not want to talk about this anymore, either," said Pip. "Please go."

Walking down Street of the Market, which paralleled the wall of the city, they noticed more refugees' huts beneath this wall, behind the homes and shops on the street.

"Has all of Newport moved here?" asked Periwinkle.

"Hardly," said Bellchime. "There must be many others on Goblin Plain, or Spirit Swamp, or even hidden in the Foggy Mountains."

"Unless the others were all killed. That older woman hated goblins so much, she reviled me for Tarragon's truce."

"That is why I want to kill Riversong," Bellchime said in a very soft voice. "The goblins of Goblin Plain lived in peace with the humans of Newport since Wentletrap's time; they allowed human trade to pass on the river with minimal tolls; and they even all speak our language, though they keep their own way of life. No war is ever more bitter than one fought between two peoples who were formerly friends."

"We should get a room," Periwinkle said, pointing at the sign on the Green Oak Tavern and the yellow sun sinking behind it.

"The Sleep and Spirits is cheaper, and its beds are softer."

"All right," she said, squeezing his hand.

The Sleep and Spirits was a smaller inn not far from the main market and the docks, a place once frequented by sailors; but the innkeeper, whose name was Gable, told Bellchime and Periwinkle that business was bad even for winter, because the destruction of

Newport and the goblin wars had stopped most of the boat traffic, except local runs to Hammer's Keep and Fallow's Keep, and refugees, who seldom had money.

"Goods from the coast come over Cat's Tooth Pass now," he said.

"How much for a room?" asked Periwinkle.

"Four treemarks," said Gable.

"Two treemarks sixpence," said Bellchime.

"Three treemarks and not a split penny less, but I will give you my best room."

"What do you think?" Periwinkle asked Bellchime.

"All right," he said, and they both shook Gable's hand.

"I will have Filaree show you your room. Filaree!"

"Got a customer, Pop?" asked a voice hurrying down a hall toward the common room. "Aw, too bad he is not single; we could make a lot more."

"Curb your tongue, girl," growled Gable. "Our guests are a warrior and her husband, so let us show respect. I will worry about the money. We may do well on drinks tonight, once people from the clearing project get back. Show these people room eleven."

Filaree led them down the hall to their room and left them there. They dropped their packs and fur coats against the wall, sat on the edge of the bed, which was stuffed with feathers, and kissed. Bellchime flopped down, pulling Periwinkle on top of him.

"Let us get married," she said.

"Very well," he said.

She sprung off of him and put her fur back on; he did the same. They closed the door to their room, went back through the hallway to the common room, told the innkeeper they were going to church, and stepped outside.

Twilight was fast darkening; bells of the Church of the Second Daughter rang sunset; and a lamplighter was busy at work lighting the lamps of Street of the Market. People filled the streets, on foot or horse, returning from Lord Blackwood's clearing project, or wherever else they worked that day, to their homes, or to church, or to the taverns. When Periwinkle and Bellchime passed the Market, she noticed that tomorrow was a market day, and the last day of the year. The day after tomorrow was the spring equinox.

"But what do we want to buy or sell?" asked Bellchime.

"I do not know. Information, perhaps?" she replied.

Beyond the Market, Street of the Market curved away from the river and rose uphill. Towers of the church appeared and disappeared above nearer buildings along the street. Bells rang for the evening chant and prayer. Periwinkle and Bellchime entered the great church and sat down on a bench near the back among a mixture of Newport refugees and earlier city residents.

The chants led by the lesser priests in purple were the same chants done in Tarragon's Keep before each evening meal, but chanting them in this great hall of stone and colored glass with more than a thousand other people felt incredibly powerful. Then the high priest, dressed in robes of red velvet with golden trim, walked out and kneeled in front of the church's centerstone, engraved with the symbols for each one of the sixty-four greater names of God, and offered prayers that the new land being cleared become fruitful, that the older and newer inhabitants of Upriver unite to become one great city, that Lord Blackwood and his warriors remain unconquerable, and that these prayers be granted in such a way to bring the highest good to all concerned, in the name of the Mother, the Father, the Three Daughters, and the Three Sons, so be it. Then he rose, and the lesser priests rose, and they stood in silent meditation for what seemed a long time, then ever so softly sang the hymn to Light and Darkness, then the entire congregation stood up and chanted the sixty-four names, the priests withdrew, the bells rang, and it was over.

"We should have sat nearer the front," said Periwinkle when she realized that the two of them could do nothing but flow with the multitude of others leaving the church.

"There will be priests at the door bidding us goodbye," said Bellchime.

At the front doors, they managed to stand aside from the others, and waited, and waited, for all the people to leave.

"May I help you?" asked a voice behind them, and they turned to see a young priest in purple.

"We want to be married," said Periwinkle.

"I do not understand," said the priest. "You are already married; any priest would tell you that." He squinted his eyes and looked at them again, told them to come with him, and led them through a small door in the vestibule down a stairway to a small but opulent room, with tapestries and upholstered chairs.

"Sit down," he said. "I am a priest who knows things, and I do not dispute with the major forces. If you want me to perform the rite that binds you two together, who are already so bound, I will do this and consider it an honor, Bellchime and Periwinkle."

"You know our names," said Bellchime.

"And your dragon's name, Distance. Do you know mine?"

Bellchime was too stunned to say he did not.

"Relax and it will come to you," said the priest.

"Father Cumin," said Bellchime at once.

Father Cumin nodded yes and said, "You are a new thing in the world, two people sharing a more-than-human power and hardly using it, one of you a human warrior watched over by a goblin totem animal. Where this path will take you I cannot say. The future is never certain until it is now, for God works with the present, and all your possible futures are unlikely. Bellchime, answer me, what is a warrior?"

"A warrior is one who protects and defends the others of the keep or city, one trained to use weapons against others that speak, but who will not do this unless absolutely necessary."

Periwinkle smiled at Bellchime's image of her.

"And what is a lord, Bellchime?" asked Father Cumin.

"A lord is a warrior whose presence brings peace to farmland beyond the walls of his keep."

"And what is a king?"

"There are no kings east of the sea."

"What would a king be, if one existed?"

"I would say a king is a lord whose presence brings peace to all his kingdom."

"You may be a king," said Father Cumin, "or you may not. Do I marry you now?"

"Yes," said Periwinkle and Bellchime together.

"Stand facing each other and look into each other's eyes. See the part of you that is human and the part of you that is God. Remember always that you are each both of these things, and remember always that you love each other. Will you do this?"

"I will," they said together.

"Then in the name of the Mother, the Father, the Three Daughters, and the Three Sons, I say that you are husband and wife. You may kiss." They did, and Father Cumin sprinkled drops of holy water over their heads. "So be it," he said.

"I will write your names in the church register tomorrow at sunset. I suggest you leave Upriver before then, lest someone who wishes you harm read the register and look for you. You are a hope few people east of the sea could imagine. Go in peace." He bowed to them, and they walked up the steps and out of the church.

And so it was recorded that on the 367th day of the 202nd year of Humans East of the Sea, Bellchime the Storyteller and Periwinkle the Warrior were married by a priest of the church.

"I, a king?" said Bellchime softly, while they walked Street of the Church back to where it crossed Street of the Market.

"God works with the present, according to Father Cumin," said Periwinkle, "and this is our wedding night. Let us think mostly of that."

"So be it," he said, laughing, and kissed her.

Back to the Sleep and Spirits they walked hand in hand, and asked Gable at the bar to have dinner for two sent to their room. The crowd in the common room looked like they were enjoying themselves drinking and singing, but Periwinkle and Bellchime passed through them and walked straight to room eleven.

A few minutes later, Filaree knocked on the door, saying, "Your dinner is here." Bellchime got up from bed, opened the door, and brought in the meal, a steaming plate of grain and vegetables with bits of pork mixed in.

"Wonderful," said Periwinkle. "I have not had vegetables or grain since I left the keep."

"Which was only three days ago."

"Mugwort the Dragon still sat on the ruins of Turtleport then, it was so long ago," she said, "or no, Windsong the Mariner first glimpsed the Foggy Mountains and knew for certain that there was land east of the sea then, it was so long ago."

Bellchime joined her game, saying, "If you have not had a dinner like this for so long, I have not had one since Wintercress ran from house to house in the form of a wolf, searching for the woman who would one day be his queen."

"Ooh! It is much spicier than what I am used to," Periwinkle said after a few bites, "but I think I like it."

"It reminds me of Midcoast," Bellchime said. "Some of these spices came from west of the sea. We are certainly getting our money's worth of food."

"It makes me feel warm inside," she said, unlacing the top of her jacket and sipping some water from a clay cup. "So do you," she added, squeezing his hand while taking another bite.

Bellchime smiled and ate some more. Soon the plate was almost empty, and they split the last bite, put the plate on the floor, and hugged and kissed each other. Periwinkle pulled off her jacket and shirt together while Bellchime turned down the bed.

"Your pants look too tight all of a sudden," she said, giving the bulge between his legs a playful squeeze, and stood up to untie her own pants and push them down.

"You are beautiful," he said, taking off his shirt.

Periwinkle wrinkled her nose. "I am a warrior, not a barmaid. I am beautiful to you because you love me."

Bellchime said, "Your nose is straight, your eyes are big and gray, your lips are soft, your hair is black and shiny, your breasts are small and shapely, your stomach is thin, your hips are graceful, your arms and legs are strong. You are beautiful like a well-made sword is beautiful."

"You are the one like a well-made sword," she said when he took off his pants.

She wrapped her strong arms and legs around him and kissed him, tumbling onto the featherbed, and felt the contrast between the cool room, the soft mattress, and the heat where their bodies pressed together, the wetness penetrating her, the push-pulling, tingling and shuddering.

When they finally blew out the lamp, they fell into a deep, dreamless sleep, their bodies pressed together under the warm blankets.

19.

They awoke with sunlight streaming through the window and Filaree knocking on the door, with a delicious breakfast of hot apple pastries.

"You will not be staying tonight?" asked Gable when he saw them leave with their packs.

"No," said Periwinkle, "but we will recommend the Sleep and Spirits to any who ask us where to stay in Upriver. Your food and bed were excellent."

Filaree cackled at this remark and they walked to the street.

"We have time to go to the market, do we not?" asked Periwinkle.

"As you wish," said Bellchime.

The market was a huge rectangular building walled with a

colonnade. A large gate to the docks opened through its back wall, which was part of the wall of the city. Despite roaring fires in both hearths, most people wore coats or other heavy clothing. The tables were bustling with activity.

"If this is what Gable calls poor business, I wonder what it looks like when business is good," said Periwinkle.

"I think most of the sellers are former Newport people, trying to get cash for what is left of their belongings," said Bellchime.

One such person was an old man trying to get ten gold starmarks for a sword and shield. "You look like one who would use these well," he said, noticing Periwinkle's bow and quiver. He pulled the sword from its scabbard and handed it to her by the hilt. "This is an excellent sword, worth much more than the ten starmarks I ask for both sword and shield."

"One moment," Periwinkle said and took off her pack and quiver. She raised the sword, feeling its balance, and angled its shining blade to the light.

"The sword and shield belonged to my son who was killed in the war," the man said, adding in a hushed voice, "I know of a house for sale, a real house for sale in Upriver, up on Street of the Silver Mountains, with a view of the river and near the castle, which I can buy for my family and myself for only five pounds of gold, and all we need is ten more starmarks to do it. You will never find another sword like this at that price."

"Let me talk with my husband," said Periwinkle and led Bellchime some paces away from the table. "Bellchime, I want that sword. How can we get ten gold starmarks?"

"Is it that good?" he asked.

"The blade is firesmoothed silversteel, worth more than the entire value of the house this man wants to buy. Lord Blackwood would pay that much for it if he knew about this. Few weapon-makers east of the sea have ever learned how to forge such steel. Why, this sword could cut Riversong's largest tooth in half with one blow."

"I have heard stories of such swords but would not know how to recognize one."

"You watch the way light glints on the blade near the hilt," said Periwinkle. "Steel is made of fine crystals, and the finer the crystals, the better the steel. Slot, who has such a sword and let me examine it, explained this to me. Bellchime, this sword might nick even Slot's sword if swung hard enough, and also the shield is well made. How can we get ten starmarks?"

"We find a witch," said Bellchime. He tapped the shoulder of a girl about seven standing nearby, looking wistfully at jewelry, and said quietly, "I am looking for a witch." She immediately pointed at a redhaired woman dressed in mended wool clothes selling perfumes two rows of tables away. "Children always know who the witches are," he told Periwinkle while they made their way to the perfume stall.

"I have a book you may be interested in," he said to the woman, who looked not much older than him. She smiled and motioned for him to step around her front table and sit beside her.

"In your pack?" she asked.

"Yes," he said, and took it off, fumbled inside it, and brought out a small leatherbound volume of *Mysterious Conjunctions*, which like most books of magic was written in a tight hand on thin parchment, so that the book was small enough to be easily carried, or hidden.

"It is worth about six starmarks to me," she said.

"What of this one?" he asked, showing her his copy of *Uses of the Esoteric Names of God*.

"You have some hard-to-obtain items here. How many more?"

"For now, only these two."

"Fifteen starmarks for both of them."

Bellchime carefully examined each gold starmark she counted out. "They are real," she said, "and of standard weight."

"Thank you, good woman," he said, "business with you has been a pleasure."

"Hurry!" said Periwinkle, who had just returned from the stall of the old man with the sword. "Another warrior wants to buy the sword." Bellchime passed her the gold coins, and she ran back around the row of stalls, saying she had the money. The warrior, a gruff burly man of nearly forty winters, looked at her in surprise.

"If she has the money, I promised it to her," said the old man.

The warrior glared at Periwinkle as if he wanted to test her skill with her new sword against his own in personal battle, but turned and walked away without a word.

"I do not like the way he looked at me," said Periwinkle, counting out starmarks into the old man's hand.

"A promise is a promise, and I am sure he is warrior enough to know that," said the old man, while Bellchime joined them wearing his own pack and carrying Periwinkle's. She fastened the belt of the scabbard around herself over her coat, tied the shield to her pack and put it on, and trudged with Bellchime out of the market and down the blocks of Street of the Market to the northgate. The same guard who was there the day before waved them out, smiling.

"Got yourself new weapons," she said.

As they walked between the seated statues, Periwinkle asked, "Did you mind selling those books for me?"

"No," Bellchime said, smiling hesitantly. "I valued them little. Magic is more in the wizard than in the book."

"Then what worries you?"

"The luck of your new sword. Good as it is, it did not save the life of the last warrior who used it."

Periwinkled laughed, saying, "Luck is more in the warrior than in the sword. Whatever happened before, it is my sword now, and it feels better in my hand than any other I have ever held."

"Then it is probably meant to be yours," said Bellchime. "I think you are right about luck, and there is much to be said about how a weapon feels."

They walked in silence for a few moments, then Periwinkle said, "What were those books about?"

Bellchime smiled. "*Mysterious Conjunctions* is about how everything is connected to everything else. In one section, after thirty pages of tedious prose detailing every theory ever advanced about why dreamsendings work, it gives a convoluted ritual that obscures the essential. *Uses of the Esoteric Names* is a manual for priests, and contains knowledge forbidden to the uninitiated, but most of that is obvious knowledge."

"You know much more magic than you use," said Periwinkle.

"Since I made that storm at Oak Lake, I have tried no sorcery at all, except for the dreamsendings to you. That storm was what changed my dragonbinding from a relationship of love to one of power."

"Thunder and Love are both members of the Holy Family. For us, the gentle Third Daughter must be stronger."

"If you had not come, I do not want to think of what might have happened."

"Of course not. Why think of things like that? I am your wife, I share a dragon with you, I love you, and I love her."

It gladdens me to hear you say that, for I am lonely without sight of you, said Distance's voice in their minds.

"How long have you been listening to us?" asked Periwinkle. "Where are you?"

Shall I come to you?

Bellchime and Periwinkle looked up and down the road, at the bare brown and fallow green plots of farmland, which would be busy with farmers plowing and sowing in another month, depending on the weather. They saw no one. "Come fast," said Periwinkle.

The dragon flew low over the Silver River and landed on the road. They mounted and crossed back over the river without noticing a man who happened to be walking from Hammer's Keep at that moment, who wondered if he was really seeing two humans ride a dragon over the river.

— 6 —

BLOOD AND DEATH

20.

"If we fly north of the farmlands, cross the river, and go directly toward the mountains, we can come close to Cat's Tooth Pass without being seen, where I think we can find a cave," Bellchime said, while he and Periwinkle secured their packs to the dragon's back.

"Do we want to live so near the road?" she asked.

Bellchime shrugged. "Upriver has few hunters. If we stay home by day, we will not be discovered. When the cold weather ends "

"Will she not breathe fire long before then?" Periwinkle asked, watching Distance's breath steaming in the sunny woods while her own and Bellchime's could not be seen.

"I do not know," said Bellchime, mounting her. Periwinkle mounted also, and they flew at treetop level away from the roof of Lord Blackwood's watchtower, then across the river.

Hills fell away and mountains loomed ahead. Beyond the hazy farmland on the right, smoke rose from the clearing project, where people burned stumps and branches after hauling the logs away. Distance was excited by the sight of so much smoke and wanted to see the fire, but Bellchime and Periwinkle dissuaded her from this.

How long must I hide from everyone? she asked.

"For every dragon half Riversong's size that humans kill, they kill dozens your size and larger. Your time will come if you have patience," said Bellchime.

"Do what Bellchime says," said Periwinkle, who could barely hear his words over the rushing wind, but guessed their meaning from the dragon's emotions in her own mind.

You always say that, Distance complained, but continued to fly toward the mountains, away from the distant fire.

"You obey us when we both agree," said Periwinkle. "Is that why you wanted me to kill him when you dragonbound me, so that we could not have this power?"

Distance said nothing, but projected sullenness.

"Do not be angry, Distance," said Periwinkle. "But if you dragons choose us humans to be your teachers, then kill us when you grow up because you want to be free, what then? If you were lonely last night while we were in Upriver, how would you feel if we were dead?"

I do not know. Perhaps I would rage in fury when I realized my loss, and destroy everything human I saw.

"Riversong does that."

The dragon considered this while the Silver Mountains grew to jagged blocks of granite ridged with snow, not far ahead. Bellchime said something that was probably directions, and the mountains swung around to the right and passed slowly.

I will not kill either of you, Distance suddenly said in Periwinkle's mind. *This conflicts with my instincts, which would have me love you and then kill you.*

The dragon said no more but concentrated on finding a cave, and dropped closer to the slopes when Bellchime said something about mortarstone. Dark green and white cones of snow-covered spruce rushed up, and Distance landed between these and a cave at the foot of a high white cliff made of rocks piled like the courses of stone in a wall.

"Did someone build this?" Periwinkle asked.

"This rock that we use to make mortar for our walls sometimes looks like walls itself," said Bellchime. "I do not know why. Shall we look inside?"

It smells damp, said Distance while her riders dismounted.

Bellchime lit a lantern, and they entered a cave unlike any they had seen before. Beyond the low entrance tunnel, it was as large as the great hall of Tarragon's Castle, and from the ceiling hung long cones of pale rock dripping water to blunter cones of rock on the floor. Sometimes these met in the middle to form columns.

"The earth has teeth," Periwinkle whispered.

"To me they seem more like stone icicles," said Bellchime.

"Whatever they are, they drip," she said. "Let us look for a cave more snug and dry."

"Most mortarstone caves are damp. We could make fires."

"We have plenty of daylight left to find other caves. This one is too wet even for bats."

Or dragons, said Distance.

Bellchime laughed, and they left the cave, mounted Distance, and flew to the top of the mortarstone cliff, where a ledge covered with trees and grass sloped some way toward another, much lower cliff. Distance landed in the open, not far from another cave, took a whiff of the air, and told Periwinkle and Bellchime while they dismounted that they would have to fight for this cave.

"Fight what?" asked Periwinkle.

Bear, said Distance.

"Are you sure it is not a fangtooth cat?" she asked.

A mother bear with cubs, said the dragon.

"Distance is no match yet for a full-grown bear," said Bellchime, "least of all in the cramped space of a den."

Watch me, said Distance boastfully, making an ear-splitting bellow into the cave's mouth. Periwinkle drew her sword and followed the dragon, who still had their packs tied to her back.

Distance bellowed again, and this time was answered by a growl from inside, scratches, stomps, and bumps. When the enraged bear came rushing out of the cave mouth, the dragon flapped her wings and rose out of reach. The bear stood on her hind legs and snarled, keeping her face to the circling dragon, not noticing the humans until Periwinkle's sword pierced her heart. The bear screamed, dropped to four legs and collapsed in the middle of her charge toward Periwinkle, while Distance, infuriated, bit the back of her thickly furred neck.

This was my hunt, human! she screamed in Periwinkle's mind, dropping to the ground and pushing her large head with many sharp teeth into Periwinkle's face.

"We killed her together and we are both unhurt," said Periwinkle firmly. "When we work together, we are bigger and stronger than either of us are separately. I could not have killed that bear alone, and you might have been badly wounded."

"She is right, Distance," said Bellchime.

The dragon turned to glare at him, but already her anger was subsiding while another thought occurred to her. *I will kill the cubs*, she said, and squeezed into the opening of the den. With some difficulty, Periwinkle reached under the collapsed bear and withdrew her blood-covered sword, just when something screamed and growled inside the cave.

"We do what they do in the war," she said. "We kill to gain a home."

"The home you were born in was gained that way," said Bellchime.

"—by humans fleeing from Mugwort and killing goblins. I know, but it feels different to do this myself, even though what we kill is only a family of bears." While she spoke she cut the bear's skin with her knife.

Sounds of bones being crunched and swallowed came from the cave.

"She is always hungry," Periwinkle said. "Here, help me turn this."

They worked steadily, removing the bear's skin, cutting meat off the bones, and building a fire, which they lit after dark to smoke the meat. The cliff below them hid the fire's light from any human eyes; the night hid the smoke. Finally they crawled inside the den, which was small but dry. The sleeping dragon left them just enough room to make their own bed.

21.

Here they lived and hunted for the next two months. On some nights while the dragon was hunting, Periwinkle danced in the meadow, remembering the pook of Little Dragonstone Mountain. Pooks also lived in the woods near Cat's Tooth Pass, and one warm spring night, after a time watching the human woman and her mate dance in the starlight, five brown-furred pooks came out of the trees to dance with them, and a sixth, a young one with reddish fur, played on his pookpipes the very song that Periwinkle was hearing in her mind while she danced.

They scattered in fear when they saw the dragon returning, and looked from their hiding places in wonder at the woman and man caressing the fierce scaly head. The dragon seemed to regret scaring the little furry dancers away, but none of them reappeared until more than a week had passed, this time while Distance was asleep in the den and the two humans danced in the moonlight fog. Only the young reddish one with the pookpipes came, and again he played what Periwinkle danced to.

"How did you know what song to play?" she asked him when they stopped dancing.

"From your dance, of course, silly big one."

"Where are the others?" asked Bellchime.

"Dancing to pipe music in another field. They say that you humans who do things but dance the dances of being are too weird to dance with, begging your pardon. Old ones get set in their ways."

"We hunt, we dance, we live in this cave," said Periwinkle. "Do they call that doing things?"

"Humans who keep dragons always die of doing things," said the pook. "You keep a dragon and do very little. No, you are waiting, and while you wait, you dance being. What do you wait for?"

"For our dragon to breathe fire."

"Oho! Blood and death!" said the pook.

"We want to stop—at least some of it," said Bellchime.

"Your dragon's hunger may make it worse," the pook said, and he immediately began playing a wild tune on his pookpipes and danced out of sight.

"I think we made him sad," said Periwinkle, staring into the fog-blurred forest beyond the meadow. "Sometimes I wish we could just stay here, you and I and Distance, for the rest of our lives, and let the world manage as best it can."

"You want to be two feet tall and covered with fur?" asked Bellchime.

"No, but I can admire their good qualities and dance their dances with you. It empties my mind of worry about our future, and seems to have a taming effect on Distance."

"She is still fierce when she hunts, but yes, at other times she seems to have regained the love she lost when I made that terrible storm at Oak Lake." Bellchime turned to look at Periwinkle's face, pale in the moonlight, half-hidden by loose black hair. "You say these dances empty your mind?"

"Yes."

"Mine also, at times, and I like the sensation. What I feared most was Distance emptying my mind, but if I empty it myself, what can she take?"

"Nothing!" she said, taking his hands. "Oh, Bellchime, this is wonderful, and we can do it anywhere, even in the middle of a war! This is what I love most about our life here and now, and we can take it with us!" She danced while speaking these last words, and he joined her.

22.

Distance breathed her first flame two days later, before sunset, when Periwinkle and Bellchime were waking up. Her unintentional flicker smouldered their leafy mattress. While Bellchime urged the dragon outside, Periwinkle doused the fire with the water jug and followed, fanning smoke from her face.

"Do it again," Bellchime was saying, and this time a red flame shot five feet from the dragon's mouth.

No more raw meat for me, she said, eager to hunt something and cook it for herself.

"Wait," said Periwinkle. "It has not rained here for several days, and we do not want you to burn down the forest the way you almost burned our bed."

Beds should be made of piles of gold, not leaves.

"Someday you will have such a bed, but we prefer something softer for ourselves," said Bellchime.

"Before I ever hunted with a bow or sword, I had to practice proper use of them," said Periwinkle.

I am ready to practice now, said Distance.

By midnight she was able to roast a piece of meat on Bellchime's skewer without burning him, though he stood in the line of fire, and could direct a thin jet of flame at the cliff wall from twelve feet away.

I must hunt. Firebreathing hungers me even more than long flights.

"Enjoy yourself, but be careful," said Periwinkle. The dragon leapt into the sky with a joyful bellow.

"Her scales are thickening," said Bellchime when she flew out of sight. "She is growing, also. Soon she will not be able to squeeze into our den."

"Let us dance before we talk about the war."

She led him out on the meadow and began a dance that he felt awkward trying to follow. He had not felt so with her for many dances.

"What song goes with this dance?" he asked her.

She smiled, saying, "You need the pook boy to play for you?" Then she sang:

>Good King Wintercress
>was born a farmer's son,
>in a land without a king,
>where bandits and dragons roamed.

>His mother, Wind the Hunter,
>Goddess of the Moon,
>left him with his father,
>but she taught him things in dreams.

>He said, "If I can swing a scythe,
>I can swing a sword,
>and if I can chant a ballad,
>I can chant a spell."

>When bandits burned his village,
>he escaped in the form of a wolf,
>and fled to the Snowy Mountains,
>where he learned to hunt and kill.

>He gathered a band of warriors
>who fought for what was right.
>They killed the lawless bandits,
>and they built the strong-walled town.

>Wiser than elves is the warrior
>who brings his people peace,
>who gives them long lives and laws
>better than the laws of old.

>Stronger than dragons is he,
>but we live in his sight without fear.

Most gracious is King Wintercress,
who gives us happy blessings.

"I taught you that song," he said. "It comes from *The Oldest
Book of Songs*, and may have been written during Wintercress's
reign."

"Though probably it was written to flatter some later king who
deserved it less," said Periwinkle. "The melody was made by
Dreamleaf the Elf, west of the sea, two hundred thirty years before
the last voyage of Windsong. See? I remember your lessons well."

"Tonight you are my teacher. Show me your dance again."

She did, and this time Bellchime danced with confidence the
soul of a great wizard-king. Then they sat together on the grass
and talked for hours about what the war might be like, and what
they might do to find friends there.

"Call them friends, not followers," said Periwinkle. "One
friend is worth twenty followers to a keepholder, and many more
than that to a lord or a king."

23.

Distance returned before dawn, smug and satisfied, bringing
Bellchime and Periwinkle a meal-sized piece of cooked meat,
which they thanked her for and ate. When she learned that they
would leave for the war the next night, she purred with excitement
and anticipation.

Periwinkle dreamed uneasily that day about walking among
skeletons and rotting human bodies, and about riding Distance
while she swooped down on an army of goblins, burning them
alive with her fire, which Bellchime fanned with a sorcerous
wind. Was this what a warrior truly was, one who killed until all
enemies were dead, then looked for other enemies to kill?
Distance landed on a burned goblin and began to eat him.

Awaking with a start in bed next to Bellchime, Periwinkle
whispered, "Distance, it will not be like that," but the dragon was
asleep.

"What is wrong?" Bellchime asked, sensing Periwinkle's
unease.

"Bad dreams. Distance is too eager. I dreamed we burned an
army of goblins alive—"

For several moments in the dim light of the den they gazed into each other's eyes.

"Do you think the dream is a bad omen?" asked Bellchime.

Periwinkle considered this carefully before saying, "It feels more like a warning for us not to take sides in this war, but to work for a genuine peace. If we keep that ideal, I do not see how the dream could possibly come true."

So they packed the books and cookware, and as many of the furs and hides they had made in the past two months as they thought Distance could carry.

Take them all, the dragon said, stirring from sleep. *I am stronger than before and I would not make you leave behind part of your hoard.*

Distance looked odd with the "hoard" of skins humped over her hips, but had no trouble flying that way. As the ground dropped away Periwinkle imitated the dragon's exuberant bellow. Above the edge of the big cliff they flew, high over the forest.

It was late afternoon when they passed over the road from Upriver to Cat's Tooth Pass, then over the deep canyon of the Mortarstone River and the road from Cat's Tooth Pass to Fallow's Keep, last keep on the Blue River. To the right loomed the Cat's Teeth, twin snowcapped peaks on either side of the pass; to the left the forest sloped down to the distant Blue River, then up again into vague hills.

At sunset the gorge where the Blue River cut through the Silver Mountains yawned beneath them, and Distance settled to the level of the cliffs on either side, hundreds of feet above the river itself, which was broad and steady even here. A smaller river cut a canyon on the left to join it, then the mountains loomed above both cliffs.

The sky darkened to night. Suddenly the cliffs stopped, and beyond this the river flowed through the middle of a starlit plain. Periwinkle looked over her shoulder at the dark cliff split in two by the river, then ahead at the pale grasslands with clumps of dark that might have been trees or rocks.

Distance landed on the grassy riverbank not far from the foot of the cliffs.

"Do you smell any goblins or mammoths nearby?" Bellchime asked her.

No. I smell animals I do not know, but none are nearby.

"Your own scent will probably keep them away from us," said

Periwinkle. "This looks all right to me, though I am not very tired yet."

"Better we wait till daylight to go on, even so," said Bellchime. "Otherwise, we may miss the friends we are looking for."

Periwinkle jumped off the dragon's back and walked over to the river, which looked black and shiny in the starlight.

"I would not want to row a boat up this river through that gorge," she said when Bellchime stood beside her. "Even here the river is swift."

"Much slower than the Indigo River or the Moonstone," he said.

"No one would even think of navigating those."

"Packing goods over Cat's Tooth Pass is even harder. Most of the time, the sailors would wait for a favorable wind before passing this point."

"I do not think Endive's and Pip's boat had that choice."

You might unpack me, said Distance, and the two humans immediately walked back to her and unloaded the packs and all the hides. The dragon stretched her legs and wings and curled up to sleep on the river gravel.

Periwinkle and Bellchime danced another song about Wintercress, undressed and made love on some of the furs, and dressed again to go to sleep, in case they had to break camp in a hurry. The moon rose beyond the end of the mountains across the river.

In her dreams Periwinkle was back in Tarragon's castle. It was winter, and she was trying to listen to Froth explain the goblin wars of her great-grandfather's time in a broad context of coastal economy, the battles between the humans who survived Mugwort's destruction of Turtleport and those who lived in the Valley of the Two Rivers, and the disrespect the humans and goblins of that time had for each other's religions. Froth was as dull as ever, and for some reason she could not hear or understand half of what he said. In frustration she left the story circle and got into an argument with her mother and stormed up to her room. Bellchime was there and said that Distance was waiting on the tower roof.

Periwinkle opened her eyes to a half-moon overhead, the grassland surprisingly bright, and wondered briefly whether Froth might be trying to contact her by dreamsending before she fell asleep again.

She woke again to Bellchime's kisses, the morning sun shining around the edges of his curly brown hair and reddish beard.

"Distance wants to hunt," he said. "I told her we should all stay together until we learn more about this land."

"Yes, I am hungry, too," said Periwinkle, yawning.

They tied all their things to the dragon's back, mounted her shoulders, and flew along the Blue River. Birds flew through the grass; a group of valley mammoths ambled toward a clump of trees.

Then Distance spotted an antelope, which proved more difficult to catch than she expected; it dodged like a rabbit chased by a hawk. Afraid of falling off, Periwinkle asked Distance if she might shoot the antelope, and to her surprise, the hungry dragon gave permission and held an even flight while Periwinkle notched an arrow in her bow and shot. Her second arrow downed the antelope.

"That thing ran almost like a unicorn," said Periwinkle when Distance landed next to its body.

"Let us clear the ground before you cook it," said Bellchime. "The grass is green, but your fire—"

I know that, said the dragon, who already was scratching the ground bare with her claws. She made a pile of grass over and around the carcass, leaving a wide bare swath around this, and breathed a long flame on it. This did not work nearly so well as the sticks and leaves she had used two nights before, and Distance ended up giving each bite a touch of flame before swallowing it. While she ate the meat, her fire became hotter, and each bite was less raw. What she left for Periwinkle and Bellchime was perfectly roasted.

They were just finishing this meal when Distance bellowed louder than ever before and simultaneously said in their minds, *Goblins attack!*

Periwinkle had only enough time to draw her sword when goblins rushed toward them from all directions, shouting war cries and throwing short spears with spearthrowers, two of which Periwinkle struck down with the flat of her sword. Suddenly fire was everywhere, swirling around in a blinding raging wind. Two goblins with faces painted like skulls rushed toward Periwinkle with knives. One burst into flame and screamed, the other Periwinkle cut in half with her sword. Something seized her from behind and lifted her up into the air.

"Where is Bellchime?" she screamed.

On my back, said Distance, and the rage and fear that seemed to be everywhere diminished for a moment. Periwinkle looked down at the swirling firestorm below her dangling feet, at one goblin that ran through the grass in flames, then stumbled and fell, and at the bright red dripping from her sword. She felt numb. Like a heartbeat throbbing in her mind came the thought, *Kill, kill, kill, kill, kill*.

"Distance, Distance, I love you and we are safe now," said Periwinkle, forcing herself to be calm. "No more." Somehow through the bubbling rage she realized that the dragon was wounded. "Fly away from here and land; we will heal you."

After they are all dead.

"An injured warrior who is safe and whose comrades are all safe has no cause to return to battle," said Periwinkle, sighing with relief when Distance accepted her carefully chosen words.

The dragon flew up the river about a mile and lowered herself until Periwinkle's feet touched the top of the grass and dropped her, then stumbled to an awkward three-legged landing, with Bellchime just managing to stay mounted.

The wound was a shallow gash across the dragon's left hind leg, underneath some of the dangling hides. Bellchime and Periwinkle carefully untied these hides and their packs. The blood oozing out of the cut seemed scalding hot.

"We should clean this," Periwinkle said.

I think I can reach it. Stand back, said Distance, twisting her neck around to mouth a thin jet of flame at the wound. She threw her head up into the air and screamed.

"Easy, easy," said Bellchime.

"We need a cloth bandage," said Periwinkle, unlacing her leather shirt and pulling off her worn white undershirt. "Use this," she said to Bellchime, putting her other shirt over bare skin.

He carefully folded the shirt and said to Distance, "Come down to the river first and wash off that blood."

Not cold water, said Distance.

"All right then," said Periwinkle, getting the bronze water jar out of Bellchime's pack and filling it with fresh river water. "Heat this up first."

The trembling dragon warmed the water with her fire-breath until the jar was almost too hot for Periwinkle to hold, then she and Bellchime used this to clean the wound. Distance took several sharp breaths and groaned, but felt better when Bellchime pressed the scales back together and covered it with Periwinkle's shirt.

One of the leather hides Periwinkle cut into shape to bind the bandage to her leg.

"Thank God they missed your wing," said Bellchime.

"Thank God they missed *you*," Periwinkle said to him. "Those bloody backstabbers almost killed us. What happened? Did you make the wind?"

Bellchime nodded. "If you had been close enough to jump on the dragon when she gave alarm, I would not have needed to. Those two spears you struck down with your sword—"

"Why think of that? Next time I will have my shield." Periwinkle looked around at the grass, the river, the distant column of smoke. "We should leave here soon as we can."

Load me up, hides and all, said Distance. *Those furs kept the spear from going deeper*. Periwinkle and Bellchime balanced and tied their belongings to her very carefully, so that nothing would pull on the wound. *The weight helps*, she said. *Where now?*

"We look for humans," said Bellchime. "Carefully. They may also shoot at us without warning."

Periwinkle sighed. "Maybe I do want to be a pook. At least they have enough sense not to hate anybody. I have never killed a—person before, Bellchime. I did not like it. They gave me no choice, and I am a warrior. And you, you only seem to be unarmed. Your wind was deadlier than my sword."

"I only wanted to drive them away from us. That storm I made at Oak Lake hurt several goblins badly, but none were killed. This was my first killing also." He took a deep breath. "We were warned that this might happen by your dream, but what is done, is done."

They deserved to die, said Distance.

"For attacking that way, perhaps they did," said Bellchime, "but that does not make me glad to be the one who killed them."

You humans make a necessary thing so complicated.

Bellchime mounted the dragon and Periwinkle slung her shield over her shoulder and sat behind him. "Dealing with our feelings is necessary, Distance," she said softly, and Distance flapped her wings hard until she lurched into flight.

24.

The land they flew over was incredibly wealthy; herds of valley mammoth, wild auroch, antelope, and quagga roamed the grass;

flocks of ducks, geese, and swans swam the river; small brown birds sang everywhere. The goblin camps were much bigger than even the main camp at Oak Lake; some had as many as forty or fifty tents, arranged in double circles, with three or four cookfire awnings in the middle.

"No humans anywhere," said Periwinkle, leaning forward to Bellchime's ear.

Carefully holding the dragon's neck, he twisted around to say, "Considering how those goblins attacked us, that is no surprise. Pip said back in Upriver that they lost the war."

"She said some still fought, somewhere."

We could ask a goblin, said Distance, as quietly as one of their own thoughts, and when they wondered how, she said, *Several goblins in that camp are looking at me. They know what dragons are, but have not seen one before. I think I can talk to them from here.*

While Distance circled their camp, the goblins ran around like ants, shouting things and gathering weapons. Distance bellowed loudly and belched flame, concentrating a booming mental shout at them, *Attack me and I roast you alive. Where are the humans?*

The goblin warriors stared up at what indeed was a dragon. It spoke in their minds the way the gods spoke to the shaman. What should they say? Dragons were supposed to be the enemies of humans, but two figures rode this dragon the way humans rode the stripeless quagga they called horses.

"We are many," said the chief, whose name in fact was Quagga. "We can kill it if it is not a god."

"Though it speaks like a god, its blood is red like ours," the shaman said. "It flaps its wings like a bird or drakey."

At the same time Periwinkle and Bellchime were imploring Distance not to carry out her threat. The ground fell away rapidly and the spears fell short, some of them among the goblins' tents. Distance circled directly over the group of warriors saying, *Shoot at me now and your spears strike yourselves. Where are the humans?*

"It cannot attack us without coming into range," said Chief Quagga, and Distance saw that this was true, unless she flew upwind of the camp and started a fire.

Periwinkle said, "Fly quickly as you can down to a tent across the camp from where the warriors stand, knock it down and grab one of whoever is inside, and be sure to pin his or her arms."

Oh, that sounds like fun! said the dragon. *Hold on tight.*

Faster than Quagga or his warriors could aim, the dragon powerdived at them, belching flame, then pulled out and rushed across camp, crashed into a tent, banked steeply and flapped her wings to loop back, seized a woman with her forepaws and lifted her into the sky and away from the camp.

Distance flew across the river to a clump of trees. She had to drop their prisoner before landing, because with one hind leg hurt she needed both front legs to land, and even then she had to flap vigorously.

Periwinkle dismounted and drew her sword.

"No need for that. I am unarmed." The woman who stood before them looked terrified and vulnerable.

"You are a human," said Periwinkle with surprise.

"Despite my clothing, yes." She wore a goblin woman's short leather dress and a necklace of bone beads.

I thought you would be especially interested in this one, chuckled Distance.

The woman pulled her brown hair back and turned her head from side to side to show off her round ears, saying, "They kept me because my hair and eyes are brown like theirs, because," she shuddered, "that man I hate needed a wife. When I refused to be his wife, he made me his slave. He beat me and raped me." She burst into tears, screaming, "God, is this how you treat your priestesses? Then I am a priestess no more! From this day I will be a warrior and a witch like this woman, and make my own luck!"

"May I hug you?" Periwinkle asked quietly, and the woman hesitated, then embraced her. "Are there others like you in this camp?"

"One other who claims to love her man, though whether she truly does, I do not know. She actually suggested to me that if I gave the man who kept me what he wanted with love, he would treat me better. Bloody death, I am a woman, not a child! Who is he to say he is my husband, if I do not want him?"

"If she loves him, we will leave her with him," said Periwinkle. "What do you want us to do with you? We intended to take a prisoner to get some information, but it seems we have freed one instead. Can you be our friend? I am Periwinkle, and this is my husband, Bellchime, and our dragon, Distance."

The woman looked at Distance, who was purring and placidly

lying in the sun, though with eyes and ears aimed toward the river, in case the goblin warriors had any ideas of following them. "You do not act like the dragonbound are supposed to act," the woman said, "especially those bound to a firebreather, but you—you have the bloody mother fangcat on your soul!"

Bellchime said, "Where we come from, far to the north and east of the Silver Mountains, humans and goblins are not at war."

"Do they bind dragons there?"

Bellchime shook his head slowly. "We were outlaws because we bound Distance. Perhaps she is relatively tame because we both share the dragonbinding."

I am no more tame than you two, said Distance, *but I choose to love you. Periwinkle taught me the limits of power. She could have killed me that first day but chose not to. Love applied correctly is more powerful than power*.

"She was Bellchime's dragon for several years before she also became mine," said Periwinkle.

"Call me Hope," said the woman. "I am Mother Hope no more. May the rest of my life make less mockery of my name."

"I do not think the Lord of Light and Darkness has entirely abandoned you," said Periwinkle. "Of all the tents Distance could have knocked down, she chose yours, and now you are free."

"What kind of information did you want?" asked Hope.

"Are there other humans left on Goblin Plain?" asked Periwinkle.

"I doubt it. The goblins kill most humans on sight. Last summer I was on one of the boats that did not make it to Upriver. We had few warriors and the current pushed us too near the edge of the river. We could sink their canoes if they came at us that way, but when we came within spear range of the shore, we were done for. The goblins sank the boat, and they killed everyone who swam to shore except me, because they thought my red robe was a messenger's costume. I understood this and tried to plead with them to let the boats go through to Upriver. Their chief told me that Strong Bull knows that the humans they let go to Upriver plan to return with Upriver's mighty warriors."

"Who is Strong Bull?" asked Periwinkle.

"He is the high chief, and he hates humans because we killed his father. That is what the man who kept me said."

"Upriver is swollen with refugees," said Bellchime, "but the ones we talked to seemed to want to stay there."

Periwinkle said, "Lord Blackwood and his warriors have been more than kind to them, but they have no room for more. Bellchime and I want to help any other humans who survive the ruin of Newport to build their own keep."

"Where? How?" asked Hope.

"We do not know yet," said Bellchime.

Periwinkle asked, "Where might we find other humans?"

"I suppose there are some left alive in the swamp, but that is a backstabbing place. Even in the summer it is so wet that you have to build your houses on platforms or everything rots, and then there are leopards and drakeys, and worst of all, swamp sickness. My Overmother died of it, and I was sick for many weeks."

"Then they will almost certainly want to live somewhere else," said Periwinkle. "We can find some place on Goblin Plain where we can build a keep, perhaps those hills, and Distance can help us defend the site until we get the walls finished. If we can find as many as a hundred people, we could enclose a big enough area for farms in two summers."

"I have heard stories of keeps like that, with everything inside the walls," said Hope.

"That is what my great-grandfather Tipspear built, in the time of Lord Wentletrap, and where I lived all my life until the end of last winter."

"But you said you lived in peace with the goblins," said Hope.

"We do, but that has only been the past twenty years. Let us go look at those hills. Care to come along?"

"What else would I do?" said Hope. "But how can three ride your dragon all the way to the Gray Hills?"

One of you sit on my hips and hang onto the packs, said Distance.

"I will do that," said Hope. "It will be better than dangling from her claws thinking I was about to die, and you two may need to be together." She scrambled up onto the dragon's back and Distance made an eerie whine like a cry of pain.

My leg is hurt, she said. *Shift your weight to the left.*

The dragon shuddered, then exhaled with relief. Bellchime and Periwinkle mounted her shoulders, and with a leap that caused her to howl again, she flapped into flight.

≈7≈

SITTING
THE PEACE CIRCLE

25.

Hope tossed and turned, unable to sleep, though it was probably safe to camp here in the Gray Hills, miles south of the Blue River, especially with an easily roused dragon dozing nearby. She sat up in alarm when she realized Bellchime and Periwinkle were not in their bed of furs beneath the oak.

Calm down, said Distance, turning her head toward Hope and half-opening her eyes. *They are only dancing.*

"Dancing?" wondered Hope, but she could see by the starlight that they were dancing. To her church-trained eyes, it was clearly a dance of power, though nothing like the goblins' war dances. Somewhat hesitantly, she walked out of the trees to the flat where they danced.

"Would you like to join us?" asked Periwinkle.

"What kind of dance are you doing, something they do in the north?"

"We were dancing peace, the way the pooks might dance it, to bless this possible site for our keep," said Bellchime. "Do you know 'When the War Ends'?" he asked, and sang very softly,

> When the war ends,
> we will tend our gardens

and use our weapons for the hunt;
may the war end soon.

When the war ends,
we will have no enemies
and open our hearts to all;
may the war end soon.

When the war ends,
we will feast
and the crows will starve;
may the war end soon.

"I use this hand movement," said Periwinkle, "to bring compassion from above and pour it into my heart, and this one to draw life up from the earth."

"Who taught you this?" asked Hope, trying to duplicate Periwinkle's gestures.

"A pook," she said.

"Give yourself more credit," said Bellchime. "Periwinkle the Pook taught us one dance, maybe two. The rest you taught yourself, and I learned from you."

"You are seekers, then," said Hope. "You go beyond what is taught to find what is real."

"Well, yes," said Bellchime. "When I was storyteller at Tarragon's Keep, I encouraged all the children to do that."

"My storyteller at Newport did not, nor did my Overmother when I was in the church. Riversong's devastation and my years of exile have made me a seeker, and yet often I would lie awake while that goblin slept next to me, wondering whether my misfortunes meant the teachings of the church were false, or whether God was punishing me for my doubt."

"I have no answer for that," said Bellchime.

"I want to do another dance," said Periwinkle. "How about a dance of serenity? We all need sleep. You might think of this as a dance of Lake, the Third Daughter, if you want, Hope."

They danced serenity and returned to their beds.

26.

Hope woke up with the bright sun beaming on her, feeling, if not happy, at least not angry and bitter. Already it was warm, and the dragon lay sprawled out like an oversized lizard with overlong legs. Periwinkle and Bellchime lay close to each other under their cover, and Hope wondered for the first time in many years whether she herself wanted that kind of closeness.

Of course you do, said Distance in her mind.

"Can you hear my thoughts?" Hope asked quietly, looking at the dragon.

Only the loud thoughts. The rest is confusing murk. I understand you better when you talk aloud, though I do not need to hear your voice.

"I hate the only one who ever mated with me."

Now you are confused. I am sorry. It was not my concern.

Periwinkle stirred, saying, "Who can dream through all that dragonspeech? But I am glad she likes to talk to you, Hope."

"I think she wants to find me a husband," said Hope, and both women laughed.

"Good morning," said Bellchime, rubbing her eyes. "How is your leg, Distance?"

The dragon pulled her front legs beneath herself, stretched her right rear leg, and stood up, then put some weight on her left rear leg and hissed. *Still sore*, she said, but took a few steps and then a few more.

"Stiff, but healing," asked Bellchime.

Yes.

"Good." He then turned to Periwinkle and said, "Tell me what you think of this dream: You and I and Distance are living in a camp like a goblin camp, but some of the people are goblin and some are human. We are all sitting around a fire, listening to Father Cumin talk with Tomcod, the shaman from Oak Lake. At the edge of camp, two statues of seated warriors like the ones at Upriver's north gate flank a totem pole. Then I am somewhere else listening to my master Rush discuss the best way to tell the story of how this camp came to be. He said the children would understand me better when I talk aloud, but they did not need to hear my voice, then he apologized to me for confusing me."

Hope laughed and said, "That was what your dragon said to me before you woke up. I asked her if she could hear my thoughts."

"Finally one of us had a positive dream about this work," said Periwinkle, spontaneously hugging her husband. "Why not have a community of humans and goblins living together and sharing their wisdom with each other? What a beautiful vision! Much better than the battles and skeletons I dreamed about before, and that more or less came true. But how do we get to this camp from here, where we cannot even cook breakfast without someone rushing in with spears to kill us?"

"You want to live with goblins?" asked Hope incredulously.

"I would rather live with them than burn them alive," said Bellchime.

"I suppose we cannot ask you to forget whatever pain you went through as their captive," said Periwinkle.

"But all the same, could I forget it, please?" said Hope. "Do not be so surprised, my lady! As a priestess I was hearing thoughts as loud as that one years before your dragon was spawned."

"So pardon me for thinking," said Periwinkle irritably. "Are all Newport refugees so touchy? I suppose I cannot blame you for that any more than I can blame Endive or Pip or any of the others we met in Upriver—"

"Endive made it to Upriver?" asked Hope. "She was on the boat before mine. She is one of the lucky ones."

"You know her then," said Periwinkle. "She and her husband have a home of sorts there, and work on Lord Blackwood's clearing project, but she is very bitter. She would not hear the name of Newport mentioned, and slammed her door in my face when she learned I was from 'one of those northern keeps where they live with goblins,' as she put it, which is not quite true, though we have had twenty winters' peace with them." Periwinkle sighed, then smiled at Hope. "All my life I have known peace with goblins, until yesterday, when we burned several goblins alive who attacked us without warning. I may be young, and impatient for the world to be better than it is, but I have experienced both peace and victory. I prefer peace."

"It has gone too far for that," said Hope.

"We could talk for weeks without resolving anything," said Bellchime. "What about breakfast?"

We must all stay together, said Distance. *Load me up and let us go hunting*. They did this, with some groaning from the dragon at take-off, and over the low grassy hills they flew, toward the plain and the river. *How about one of these?* asked Distance when she startled a flock of ducks into flight.

"You must not be hungry," said Periwinkle, "but a duck would be delicious."

Distance chased one of the ducks into range and belched a jet of flame at it. Its quacking became a scream and it died, and she caught it in her mouth as it fell. *By the time we land, it should be well baked*, she said. *Shall we go back to the dry hills?*

"Anywhere far away from goblins or animals they might hunt," said Bellchime.

The duck was not "well baked" by any human standard when Distance landed on a grassy knoll and they examined it. The feathers were all burnt off, and the skin quite crispy if not charred, but the meat was raw. Periwinkle, Bellchime, and Hope sliced it into thin portions and stuck them on Bellchime's skewer, which, with the help of some dry grass, Distance was able to cook in a few minutes.

After their meal, they flew back toward the river and followed it downstream, passing near two more goblin camps by noon. Though Distance kept well out of spear range and did not try to talk to the goblins, she noticed their louder thoughts and was amused that they had never seen a dragon before. When they passed a third, much smaller camp, about a quarter-mile north of the river, Distance turned and flew toward it.

They are much more disturbed by the sight of me, she said. *Something is different about these goblins.*

"Be careful," said Bellchime.

This camp had only nine tents, with one cookfire awning in the center, and the totem pole was not even twice the height of the five people who stood beside it. Perhaps this was a hunting camp, but if so it was the first one they had seen on Goblin Plain.

The dragon flapped with sudden vigor to make the ground fall away. Periwinkle turned to see how Hope was hanging on and almost bounced off herself. Five arrows rose toward them. One touched the dragon's left wing but without enough momentum to break the skin; the others fell short. Distance barked and circled higher, frothing with anger, but not without noticing how surprised and impressed the people below were at her anticipation of their attack.

It is unwise to shoot a dragon who wants to talk, she said to them. *Are you humans or goblins?*

"We are goblins," said the people below, but in their thoughts they doubted this.

"They are as human as we are," said Periwinkle. "They shoot arrows, and I am almost certain that some of those warriors are women. This is so stupid. They do not even know who we are and they shoot at us."

"We are riding a dragon," said Bellchime.

Periwinkle felt tears in her eyes and wondered for an instant what kind of warrior she was, then the energy of one of her dances the night before came into her and she sang,

> When the war ends,
> we will have no enemies,
> and open our hearts to all;
> may the war end soon.

I gave your message to those below. They threw down their weapons and told me to land, said Distance, flapping down to the grass beyond the totem pole and landing with a hiss of pain. The five who faced them, three beardless men and two women, were dressed in goblin-style leathers, and the women wore necklaces much like Hope's.

"Welcome to our camp," said one of the women. "We badly misjudged you, and I am very sorry. Will you sit the peace circle with us?"

"Of course we will," said Periwinkle, taking off her shield and weapons while Bellchime and Hope carefully removed the packs and hides from the dragon's back.

The woman who welcomed them was small and thin, with curly brown hair framing a still-young face that had come beyond suffering to something else. Her smile seemed as much nervous as welcoming, but Periwinkle found her immediately likeable. The other four, who also looked young, deferred to her.

She opened a small pouch she wore at her waist and sprinkled a fine white powder on the ground to outline a circle. "Enter here and be seated," she said when only a small gap was left in the ring. She stepped into the ring after everyone else was seated and completed it. "Are you ill at ease with our customs?" she asked Periwinkle.

"Not ill at ease, but I have many questions."

"So have we," she said, glancing at the dragon sprawled out near the totem pole. "Shall we begin by each telling who we are? I am Coral, daughter of the Condor, and first woman of this camp, wife to Rockdream, our chief, who will return tonight. I was born a human in Newport, but now I live the goblin way and call myself a goblin. It is a good way to live, and the goblins who have always been goblins have not disturbed us since we became goblins last summer. Then we were a camp of three tents. Now we have nine. Shall we go around the circle?"

The first man, short and heavy-set, whose wavy black hair fell to his shoulders, said, "I am Bloodroot, son of the Great Bear, hunter and warrior, husband to Salmon. In Newport I was a sailor."

The woman next to him, who was also stout and muscular, with long brown hair, said, "I am Salmon, daughter of the Mother Wolf, warrior and healer, wife to Bloodroot, and I was also these things in Newport and in exile. Bloodroot and I expect a child this coming autumn, our first, an affirmation of life after all the death we have experienced. We both joined this camp four months ago. There is no swamp sickness here."

"I am Periwinkle, daughter of the Mother Fangcat, who was given to me by a shaman named Gar. I am a warrior from Tarragon's Keep in the dragonstone mountains north of Upriver, where humans and goblins share the land and keep a truce that has lasted twenty years. I am outcast there because I am dragonbound. Bellchime is my husband."

"And I am Bellchime, the storyteller, born in Midcoast and apprenticed there to Rush who was storyteller at Tarragon's Keep. Though I had only eighteen summers when Rush died, Tarragon allowed me to continue storytelling there each winter. I became dragonbound to Distance two summers later, in Upriver. Periwinkle, Tarragon's daughter, who had been one of my students, joined my exile and married me this past spring. With her love and wisdom she has changed our dragonbinding from a thing of awe to a thing of beauty. We—"

"You are both bound, and with love, to this dragon?" asked Salmon.

"Let him finish," said Coral. "Is there more?"

"Only that Periwinkle and I have danced with the pooks."

At this remark the five people of the camp looked thoughtfully at the three strangers. Why was the older woman dressed just like Coral and Salmon?

"I am Hope," she said. "I was priestess of the Church of the First Son in Newport, but now I use my powers in no name but my own. I have lived this past year in Quagga's camp as prisoner and slave-wife to one I will not name. The dragon rescued me from this. We are looking for—Let me say that it is hard for me, who was forced to live as a goblin, to understand why any human would do so willingly. But how much choice do any of us have, and how much is fated to be? For many centuries the Mothers and Fathers of the Church have disputed this, and if they do not know—I am disillusioned and bitter, and your faces, like my friends' faces, are filled with hope and kindness. Why did no one in Quagga's Camp ever mention you? I thought they were still killing every human they saw."

"Quagga's warriors probably would kill any human who went up the river as far as his camp, but we are allowed to live," said Coral. "He was one of two chiefs who were against the agreement we made with Drakey and Strong Bull, so I am not surprised we were not discussed in his camp. Have you more to say?"

"The ice in my heart is melting, and it hurts."

"We can see that, Hope," Coral said gently.

The next man, thin and intense, with an angular face, brooding dark eyes, and stringy hair, said, "I am Feathergrass, and I—I was the one who most believed we had to kill your dragon, though I saw you riding her. Um, much of what I believed has changed this past winter and spring, this past hour. My second wife was killed by goblins, and now I am one. My first wife died in Riversong's fires, and now I sit a peace circle with the dragonbound. I have doubts, worries. And I sit next to another goblin's slave-wife? We want no trouble from Quagga's Camp."

"Tell us who *you* are yourself," said Coral.

"My feelings are part of myself," said Feathergrass. "I guess you want me to say that I am a warrior and a hunter, and that I was something else in Newport several centuries ago or whenever it was. Without stone walls and farms and horses and carts, we must all be hunters and warriors, unless like the other goblins we force our women to keep to the drums and cookfires. We live in tents, honor spirit-beasts, and for this we are alive."

Bloodroot sighed at Feathergrass's words but said nothing.

The last man, of average weight, with reddish-brown hair, light brown eyes, a hooked nose, and lips as full as most goblins, said, "I am Ironweed, and I have been at this camp since the beginning. All five of us shot at you, and I thank my Great Mother Cat that our arrows fell short. In Newport I was a merchant's bookkeeper.

The merchandise was all burned, and the merchant killed, so now I mostly make arrows and shoot them. My wife, Stonewater, is hunting with Rockdream and the others."

Coral looked at Periwinkle and Bellchime, saying, "Hope is a refugee from Newport, that much is clear, but you two could have gone anywhere. Why, of all places east of the sea, would you choose Goblin Plain?"

"It was my idea," said Periwinkle. "We were living in a cave in the lands of the Oak Lake Goblins, when the humans of our own keep persuaded them to drive us away. We are outcasts of human civilization, but potentially useful to those with great enough need. I thought perhaps we could join with some humans from Newport here and establish our own keep, with our dragon's help." Here Feathergrass and Salmon tried to interrupt, but Periwinkle said, "Please let me finish. After only two days on this plain, I see that any such effort would only prolong the war and cause more deaths. Your approach is much, much better. Nothing I heard from any Newport refugees suggested that some had found a good way to live here. The goblins who attacked us yesterday morning gave us no hope. Their faces were painted like skulls, and they charged us throwing spears without the least warning while we were eating an antelope."

"What did you do?" asked Feathergrass.

"We—we killed them," said Periwinkle.

"Was this near the camp you rescued Hope from?" asked Coral.

"No, no, this was before that happened," said Periwinkle.

"This does not make sense to me," said Coral. "Why would they be wearing warpaint? How long had you been at the place where you were attacked?"

"No more than an hour," said Bellchime.

"This is a matter for our entire camp to discuss," said Bloodroot.

"It sounds like some whim of Strong Bull's to me," said Salmon.

"We promised to sit the peace circle," said Coral, "and as our first woman, I say it is time for us to link hands and close our eyes to complete the circle, and I will ask my Grandfather Condor for guidance and wisdom, as you may each ask your own spirit-beasts."

She took the hands of Ironweed and Bloodroot, and when the others joined hands, she said, "Now picture a bluish-white spider's thread connecting us all to each other," but instead of the thin thread of energy she expected, a vast silvery river swirled through them all.

Above this river's surface was a mist, and from this mist flew or galloped totem spirits, her own condor, the bear and wolf of Bloodroot and Salmon, Feathergrass's unicorn and Ironweed's fangtooth cat. These melted into mist, then the fangcat returned— no, this was a different fangcat, much stronger and larger, Periwinkle's version of the Great Mother Cat. Now what were the spirit beasts of the other two? Every person, human or goblin, had a spirit-beast, whether they realized this or not. Here was a young woman walking on the river, the Third Daughter probably, for she was dressed in blue, but what animal was she? Show yourself as an animal. A weasel, perhaps, no, an otter. Hope was daughter of the Mother Otter, then. Coral let the otter dissolve into the mist.

Are you looking for me? said a voice in her mind.

She saw a dragon, the same grayish-blue as the young dragon dozing on the edge of her camp, but much bigger. "No, dragon," she told her with her inner voice. "I am looking for Bellchime's own spirit." The dragon vanished into mist and seven pooks danced around the circular river, followed by an owl, no, the owl was a condor, much bigger than her own. Bellchime's Father Condor? Yes, of course, anyone with that much imagination had to be a condor. The condor imagines and the fangcat makes it happen, much like her own marriage to Rockdream. But these were people of far greater power.

Coral let this condor dissolve into mist and sought her own spirit Condor. "What should I do?" she asked him silently, and already she knew.

She took a deep breath, felt Bloodroot and Ironweed's hands in her own, and slowly opened her eyes. The afternoon sun on the brightly painted leather tents and green grass and everyone else's faces was blinding at first. Everyone was out of trance except Bellchime, who just now opened his eyes.

"This is what I was told to say," said Coral. "Hope, daughter of the Mother Otter, on behalf of our camp I welcome you as one of us, if you choose to be. You are a gifted shamaness and your sorrows will heal here."

Hope was stunned and silent for an endless moment, then found herself saying, "I have come home," and crying unexpected tears.

Coral nodded and smiled lightly, then continued, "And you,

Bellchime and Periwinkle, I have no right to interfere with. You will stay or go, whichever you need to do. You are dangerous friends but even more dangerous enemies. I believe you are innocent of stirring up the battle you described, but I am deeply disturbed at what such a battle might mean. You may bring us danger or you may protect us from danger or both. Your brightness is so bright that I cannot see your darkness. Your dragon seems to mean us well. She was in the circle through you two. Bellchime, you are my brother, another child of the Condor."

"Do you want us to stay or go?" asked Bellchime.

"As a person, I like your energy, both of you, and would welcome you to stay. As a leader of this camp, I am not sure. If you stay, you are welcome. If you leave, we will remember that you sat the peace circle with us. If others in the circle have anything to say about this—"

Salmon immediately waved her hands and said, "We have what may be the two most powerful shaman-warriors east of the sea come to our camp offering us their friendship after we tried to kill them! How can we do anything but welcome them fully?"

Feathergrass said, "But if they stay, the camp that the ones they killed belong to may challenge us, and then we must battle them, for these two cannot be killed or given as slave-hostages. They are bound to a dragon! I ask you, please: Ride your dragon as far from here as you can."

Ironweed said, "If they leave us, they may go to the humans of Spirit Swamp and rouse them to war again."

"I do not think we will do that," said Bellchime, "though that was our plan, before we met you."

"What will you do?" asked Ironweed. "There may be as many as a thousand humans left in the swamp who cannot or will not try our way, and many of them will die of swamp sickness. What will you do for them if not bring them back here? Kill Riversong?"

Bellchime glared at Ironweed and said, "Not if people discuss the possibility years before we are ready!"

Periwinkle gasped. Of all possible responses to the taunt, why did Bellchime have to say that? He must have consciously decided to let these people share his improbable ambition. How would they react?

Feathergrass mumbled with disbelief, "He means it."

"This is a peace circle," said Coral sternly. "Consider the bad fortune that has followed the breaking of a peace circle, for I will have to break the circle if this continues."

"Perhaps Periwinkle and I should be cast out," said Bellchime. Periwinkle said, "Bellchime, no, stop—"

"Casting you out of the circle would break it," said Coral. "What I meant was, we cannot talk the talk of a war dance while sitting the peace circle. Please, all of us, let our minds become calm again, let our spirit-beasts give us wisdom. Link hands, close eyes, and this time let a tiny bright thread connect us all, not a wild broad river."

Everyone did as she said, and this time the channel of energy was only as large as a heavy rope, until she said, "Make it thinner and brighter," then it collapsed to a finer and finer thread of bluish-white light. The fineness of this thread was important, she realized now, a measure of group control, and all the more impressive for the amount of energy this thread carried. She felt the pulses that were the spirit-beasts, but she had already seen them above the river and had no need to examine them now. She did not even need to ask her Father Condor for wisdom, for the insight she had before was a dull mist compared to what she realized now. She blinked her eyes and stretched her shoulders, looking around at the circle of calm faces in the bright afternoon.

"I misunderstood," she said. "By inviting Periwinkle and Bellchime to sit the peace circle with us, we have already welcomed them to stay in our camp as long as they wish. Do you see that this is so?"

"This is so," said Feathergrass without hesitation, and the others nodded yes.

Coral looked at Bellchime and Periwinkle and said, "Stay with Rockdream and me in our tent tonight. I think we will have much to talk about. You are guests of this people."

Everyone nodded agreement to this.

"Then let us stand together and thank the great spirits for bringing us together this day in peace," she said.

This they all did, then Coral stood up and stepped over the circle, and they all followed her out. She then took her pouch of white powder, made a spiral into the center and stood there, saying, "The peace circle is completed," and everyone came running into the circle shuffling their feet until the pattern was obliterated.

"You are a better priestess than I am," Hope said to Coral after Ironweed and Feathergrass returned to their tents.

"Why a group of spirits called the Mother, Father, Three Daughters, and Three Sons would demand celibacy from their priests and priestesses has never made sense to me," said Coral. "The humans called me a witch and looked down on me for the most part, except whenever they wanted my help for whatever a priestess would not do. Here I have both the freedom to be who I am, and respect for doing it well."

"But how did you learn these rituals?" asked Bellchime.

"From a wise old shaman named Drakey, who moves from camp to camp teaching, who saw that I have talent and thought that this camp of ours was an excellent idea."

A woman who was not in the peace circle came out of one of the tents with three children, one of whom was Coral's son, Wedge. Her name was Birdwade. She had a round face, a turned-up nose, and wavy black hair, and looked almost as young as Periwinkle, but was not, for the older girl, seven-year-old Ripple, was hers. Coral introduced Hope as a new tribeswoman to her, and Periwinkle and Bellchime as guests. Birdwade offered them each a loaf of freshly baked flatbread.

"You have bread here and do not farm?" asked Periwinkle.

Hope laughed at this remark and Birdwade said, "We live in this vast field of wild grain, and you wonder that we have bread? It may be harder to harvest than wheat or oats, but it is so much easier to grow! The great spirit grows it for us."

"This bread tastes very nourishing," said Periwinkle. "Too often we have eaten only meat, mushrooms, and wild lettuce."

"Wild lettuce?" asked Birdwade.

"It grows in the forests on the other side of the Silver Mountains," said Bellchime.

"We have some furs and hides of forest animals that would make soft, warm blankets for the winter," said Periwinkle. "Would any of you be interested in trading for some flour?"

"Show us the furs," said Birdwade.

After the trades were negotiated, Coral was standing near the dragon with Periwinkle and Bellchime and a sack of flour, and talking to Bellchime about how at first she had trouble finding his spirit condor. "The dragon's spirit may suppress your own," she warned him.

"Only if you let it," said Periwinkle.

"Periwinkle taught me that," said Bellchime.

Distance sat up with a snort, turned her eyes north, and said, *People come*, meaning the barely perceptible specks in the distant green grass.

"That is the hunting party, I hope," said Coral.

They are tired but happy and carry heavy loads, said Distance.

"How do you know that?" asked Coral.

Their thoughts are loud, said Distance, *and now you are thinking I may be useful*.

"You are impressive," laughed Coral, tentatively patting the dragon's neck.

Behind my ears, she said and lowered her scaly head, purring with pleasure while Coral scratched her there.

"There are not many places she can feel a caress now," said Bellchime. "Her scales are thickening."

"I should meet my husband and tell him how it is with us and the dragon. Bloodroot will go with me," Coral said, leaving the dragon and walking to Bloodroot and Salmon's tent.

27.

She walked with Bloodroot toward the hunting party, seven more humans who called themselves goblins, each with a heavy load of meat, and was worried about why only seven returned when nine set out.

"We killed a young one," said Rockdream, a big stout man who had been a warrior and a guard in Newport, and was now chief. "Swanfeather and Flatfish stayed to guard the rest of the meat."

"You killed a mammoth?" Coral asked, walking beside him.

"Yes, finally, our spirit beasts gave us one," Rockdream said. "The herd crossed the Goblin River some hours before, and this mother and calf were unable to keep up, because the calf had a lame leg. We made a lot of noise to panic the mother. The calf was as tall as a full-grown auroch, and much heavier. Even crippled, it was hard to kill."

"I never imagined how much meat was on one of those things," said Holdfast, the small, tenacious man who became Birdwade's husband after the death of Ripple's father.

"Was it wise to leave only two with the meat?" asked Coral.

"We built a watchfire to keep away the wolves and fangcats, and will go right back for the rest," said Rockdream.

"I came to tell you that we have accepted a new tribeswoman named Hope—"

"Hope?" asked Limpet, a tall, red-haired woman with a bad sunburn. "Is she about Holdfast's age, with brownish skin and a broad nose? I think I knew her from Newport. She was a priestess—"

"Yes, that must be her," said Coral, "but let me tell you about our guests, Periwinkle and Bellchime, and their dragon, Distance."

"Their—dragon?" asked Rockdream and several of the others.

"Yes, they are dragonbound," said Coral. "We saw them in the sky and shot at them, but the dragon knew we were going to shoot and flew out of range. The dragon said she wanted to talk to us, and projected an emotional plea for peace that we could not refuse. We sat the peace circle with them. I know all the stories about dragons and the dragonbound as well as anyone who ever lived in Newport, but these people are different. You will like them. I saw their totem beasts, fangcat and condor, like ours."

Other people gathered around to listen to Coral.

"I understand why you came to meet us," said Rockdream.

"You trust my judgment, do you not?" asked Coral, looking at the assemblage of faces.

"This is a hard matter," said Rockdream, "but if Feathergrass and Ironweed were convinced—"

"Rockdream, besides being your wife, I am first woman of this camp, and just because we are goblins now does not mean that the men are suddenly wiser than the women, whatever the other goblins of this plain may think."

"I agree with Coral," said Stonewater, "and Ironweed is my husband."

"I only meant that those two men, and they only happen to be men, were most prejudiced against dragons of all those left behind. Perhaps you and I should sit our own peace circle tonight, Coral. Anyway, let us go home."

28.

Periwinkle and Bellchime sent Distance to help carry the rest of the mammoth's meat back to camp, then spent long hours that evening talking in Rockdream's and Coral's tent. Bellchime told little Wedge a bedtime story about Wintercress; then after he went to sleep, they talked about their ambitions, even the pros and cons of eventually trying to use Distance to kill Riversong.

"Let the dragon have Newport," said Rockdream. "We can live without it."

"But if Riversong attacks another city—" said Bellchime.

"Would he?" asked Periwinkle. "Does anyone know why he left Moonport?"

"The only reason I can think of is a larger dragon driving him away," said Bellchime.

"Larger than Riversong?" asked Rockdream. "No, whatever his reason was, it cannot be that. I think he wanted Newport because it was the largest city east of the sea."

"You should understand that," said Coral. "You seem to have the same lust for glory."

"We would all be safer if Riversong was dead," argued Bellchime.

At this remark, Coral smiled and shook her head. "There is no such thing as safety. We lived in a city of stone, with nothing inside the inner walls that a dragon could burn, defended by warriors armed with the same crossbows and steel arrows as Wentletrap's army, and Riversong came in the fog and dropped stones on us. It took him months to destroy Newport and make us all homeless, but he did it."

"But that is exactly what I am saying," said Bellchime. "If Riversong was dead—"

"Another dragon would come, sooner or later," said Coral. "Now I live in a city of leather, which, at least if a dragon ever does destroy it, can be quickly rebuilt."

"At least we have survived our first dragon," Rockdream said, and Periwinkle and Bellchime laughed.

"Before I forget," said Coral, "smoke messages came this morning about Drakey calling a council of shamans, men only, on the sacred ground, two days before the new moon. I wonder why he called a council on such short notice, and why before the new moon rather than on it. Something important may be happening."

"I would not know," said Rockdream. "Councils of shamans are not my concern."

"I hope this has nothing to do with our battle," said Bellchime.

"Whoever attacked you that dishonorably deserved to be killed," said Rockdream.

"This war was dishonorable from beginning to end," said Coral. "We trust our spirit-beasts to lift us above the curse of the broken peace circle, and pray that the other goblins will not break their circle with us."

"I do not think they will," said Rockdream. "Drakey speaks well of us in other camps, and he is more respected than Strong Bull. Drakey would condemn the warriors who attacked you, even as we do."

"Strong Bull is powerful," said Coral. "He is one of very few who sat the broken peace circle who are still alive. Your battle may have been near his camp."

Rockdream said, "My best guess is that you were attacked by a hunting party from Strong Bull's Camp. Even though he openly would condemn such an attack, he would secretly reward the warriors who did it if they succeeded. Fortunately for us, his camp is far away from here, in the morning shadows of the Silver Mountains."

8

THE HIGH CHIEF

29.

Two days later at midmorning, while Salmon was talking to Periwinkle and Distance near the totem pole, the dragon sighted something tiny and red hurrying toward the camp.

"Call Coral and Rockdream at once," Salmon told Distance, then explained, "This is a runner bringing a message from another camp. I fear this means trouble—"

"Can you hear anything in the messenger's thoughts about the message?" Periwinkle asked Distance.

The dragon hesitated a moment, then said, *He does not like his message. Strong Bull is dead, killed by sword, fire, and sorcery. A new high chief must be chosen.*

Neither woman said a word. Salmon squeezed Periwinkle's hand as Bellchime, Rockdream, Coral, and many others came up to the totem pole to meet the messenger.

"So Strong Bull himself attacked you," said Bloodroot.

"You can go," said Feathergrass with restrained anger. "You can go to Spirit Swamp and tell the humans there that you killed the high chief. Dragon or no, you will be a hero to them."

"We sat the peace circle with you, and we will face this messenger with you," said Periwinkle, finding in herself the same calmness that she had struggled for after the battle itself, when she had to regain control over Distance.

"So be it," said Rockdream.

In the moments of waiting Bellchime got an idea, then silently shared it with his dragon.

Yes, we can do it, Distance said very quietly with a mental smirk.

Only Periwinkle heard this. She looked at Bellchime and the dragon and knew what they planned to say, and took a slow deep breath, and smiled ever so slightly, as if she needed to make even this much visible affirmation to her dragon and her husband.

The messenger came, a small lean goblin man wearing a bright red vest, panting and sweating.

Rockdream offered him some water and said, "I am Rockdream, chief of this camp. What message do you bring?"

"I am Tusk, messenger from Gorge's Camp, relaying a message from Strong Bull's Camp, now Elkhorn's Camp. Strong Bull was killed in battle three days ago, by sword, fire, and sorcery." He looked briefly at Distance, then at the man and woman in human clothes, and said, "Rockdream, I know that Drakey and Beartooth and Sundance and others sat the peace circle with you because Drakey had a vision, but if you share your camp with the killers of Strong Bull, Elkhorn's camp will surely make war."

"Did the message say anything about the circumstances of this battle?" asked Rockdream. "These people say they were attacked without warning by warriors in warpaint, and killed them to save their own lives."

Tusk said in a low voice, "Rockdream, exile them now, and I will say nothing about seeing them here."

"I say Strong Bull was killed by the curse of the broken peace circle," said Coral. "Strong Bull attacked Periwinkle because he hated women warriors, because he considered it a dishonor that one such killed his father. The warrior Canticle, Newport's great general, and Strong Bull, Goblin Plain's high chief, both broke the peace circle to make war on each other's people. Canticle died in battle, and Strong Bull lived, but Periwinkle brought back Canticle's sword from Upriver, and killed Strong Bull with it in self-defense, thus innocently fulfilling the curse."

Tusk said, "Yes, shamaness, it may be that the curse killed the high chief. Drakey would say so. He refused to sit that circle. But it is not for Drakey to decide, and not for me. Either you must exile the killers, or let them stand to judgment before the new high chief."

"Is there a new high chief?" asked Bellchime.

"That is the rest of my message," Tusk said to Rockdream. "If your camp wishes to submit a candidate for the trial—"

"I claim blood-right," said Bellchime. "I say that I have the power to be high chief of all the goblins on Goblin Plain, from the time I win the trial until my death."

Only Periwinkle and Distance were not astonished by this statement.

Tusk frowned and said, "The trial will be held on the sacred ground, at dawn the day of the new moon, which is the fourth day from now. Send your best runner to Skyrock's Camp with this message."

"That would be Holdfast," said Rockdream. "Our camp must council in private now, but you may rest in the shade of that oak, and share our noon meal when it is ready."

"I understand," said Tusk and walked beyond the circle of tents to the tree Rockdream indicated.

"Now I understand why the shamans' council will be before the new moon," said Coral. "At this council they will set the trial that will choose our new high chief."

"If none of us are among these shamans, how can the trial be fair for our candidate?" asked Periwinkle.

"The shamans make the test based on what we most need in a high chief, without knowing who the candidates will be," said Coral. "The spirit-beasts will make certain the best one wins. Bellchime, please forget my remarks about you lusting for glory. You do have a sense of what is right, and you will make a good high chief."

"First we must accept Bellchime and Periwinkle as people of this camp," said Feathergrass.

"Done," said Rockdream.

"You should have your beard, and both wear clothes styled more like ours," said Coral.

"I will still kiss you, Bellchime, even if your face is rough as oak bark," Periwinkle said, and everyone laughed at this.

"We will have a power circle and dance this evening, and then we will decide who will go with our candidate," said Rockdream.

30.

The power circle began at sunset, with Coral and Hope, who had newly become Coral's apprentice, invoking the totems of the camp and beating on a large drum. This circle was much larger than the peace circle had been, for the entire camp was in it, twenty-two people, including three children. The youngest was Jay, with three winters; the oldest was Hope, with thirty-four. Despite the shortage of children, Salmon was the only woman who trusted their new way of life enough to let herself become pregnant, though Birdwade and Swanfeather were talking about it.

The ritual of the power circle involved sending crossed streams of energy through the center of the circle, while maintaining a flow around the edge. Periwinkle had trouble concentrating and felt something struggling inside her that she dared not let out of control.

The dances were worse, wild and savage, the totem animals enraged beasts in each dancer, her own fangcat like one of Distance's fits of dragon temper. She looked up and saw Distance swooping back and forth in the sky, gleefully belching flame.

Finally they subsided to chanting, then to talk, mostly about who would go with Bellchime to the contest. They honored the custom of the other camps and chose only men: Rockdream, Bloodroot, Holdfast, and two others. Bellchime then said that his spirit condor told him this was time for him to withdraw from the circle with Periwinkle. Coral agreed to this and within moments they were undressing in the relative quiet of their half of Rockdream's tent. Outside, the chanting resumed.

"They will probably go on until the frowning crescent moon rises," said Periwinkle. "Did your spirit condor really send us to bed?"

"My spirit condor has a certain amount of common sense. I have a long walk tomorrow," said Bellchime. "But mostly he meant I need your wisdom—"

"My wisdom?" said Periwinkle. "I am a woman of only fifteen, well, sixteen summers, married to a man who I may never see again alive after tonight, bound to a dragon, and feeling at the moment very young and very scared. Distance has confidence in you, but she is also young, and has a dragon's arrogant fearlessness. You must win this contest. The new high chief decides the life and death of the losers, and if he is not you, and if he has you killed, I think my anger would melt into the dragon's and we would burn, burn, burn—"

"If you love Distance, and if you love yourself, how could you let that happen?"

"If you love us, how can you—" Periwinkle began, then stopped herself and said, "I must let you be what you are. I said we could lead a keep together; I danced dances with you about Wintercress the King." She hugged him, crying quietly and trembling. "Even though I am frightened, I am proud of you."

"I will win," he said. "You and Distance will see to that."

"By making a storm as you did at Oak Lake? That might be almost as bad. Why is it the more we try to do, the more we destroy? Never mind. You were wise to leave that dance; it was wrong for us. We already have enough power to do anything, if only we knew the right way to use it."

Bellchime brightened with inspiration and put his hands on Periwinkle's shoulders. "We already are using it the right way. My spirit condor inspired me to say what I said to Tusk. Both Father Cumin and the first pook, the one who warned us about Froth, saw me as a lord, and what is a high chief but a lord of goblins? But we must do our part to make this destiny real. What I need to do is win, in the best possible way for everyone concerned. If we put all the power of our magic into that desired result, just as we might put power into swirling clouds if we wanted to raise a storm, and if we pray for our spirit-beasts to guide us to say and do the best things at the best time, it should work."

"So you want me and Distance to concentrate on you winning, in the best possible way, whatever that might be. We have been given an incredible opportunity." Periwinkle sighed. "They say the goddesses and gods watch the people they help very carefully."

"I am certain the same is true of spirit-beasts," said Bellchime. "We will continue to do what we do with love."

"Love applied correctly is more powerful than power, according to our dragon," said Periwinkle. "I pray that we prove the truth in that." She pulled him close and kissed him. His face did feel nearly as rough as oak bark, but she did not care. While the others chanted power, she and Lord Bellchime would make love.

31.

Next day, after Bellchime and the five other men left camp, and while Wedge was playing with the other two children, Periwinkle said to Coral, "I know that women are not allowed at the trial, but I will be there."

Coral nodded. "On Distance? I wish I could— "

"You can. Please come with us."

"Can I go, too?" pleaded Wedge.

"The little boy has big ears," said Coral. "Mommy's new friend needs her help right now, and you can help Mommy by playing with Ripple and Jay."

Wedge sighed and said, "You always say that."

Periwinkle said to Coral, "Bellchime suggested I put the dragon's power into an image of him winning the contest, in whatever is the best possible way."

"That sounds stupid," said Wedge. "Make the dragon burn everybody up, then you will win."

"If we use the dragon's power directly, we fight a war, and our victory destroys who we are," said Periwinkle.

Coral said, "Something like that almost happened to Lord Wentletrap after his army killed Mugwort. Do you remember that story, Wedge? He would have killed so many people in Moonport and Midcoast by trying to conquer them, if he had listened to his generals and not to his wise wife, Pip the Elf."

"How would you make Bellchime win?" asked Wedge.

"I would improve the victory spell. Bellchime is the high chief."

"Bellchime is the high chief?" asked Periwinkle.

"Bellchime is the high chief because he is the best possible high chief. Let us put our power into that. Wedge, go play."

This time he left without a word of protest.

"He knows he has to leave when I am doing magic," said Coral.

Near the totem pole, across camp from Coral's tent, Distance stirred awake, feeling the touch of Periwinkle's mind pulling power through her, which someone else—it was Coral—was twisting into the finest possible thread. *Has Bellchime won already? What are you doing?* asked the dragon, then suddenly she understood and laughed, saying, *What a marvelous game this is.* Pieces of the thread broke off and drifted away like silken-haired seeds into the sky.

32.

Bellchime woke at dawn on the day of the trial, in the tent the other five men brought with them. His legs ached. He had not walked so far since his journey with Distance from Oak Lake to Upriver two summers before. His shaven face felt as unnatural as his shaven head had felt then. He rubbed his hands over the stubble and reached for his knife to shave again.

"Are you ready for this?" asked Rockdream, who, like the others, was already shaved and dressed.

"I am the high chief," said Bellchime. "This contest merely confirms me."

Outside, the shamans blew huge horns. Bellchime hurriedly finished shaving, pulled on his clothes, and walked out with the other men.

Beyond the cluster of tents, more than two hundred goblin men were gathering into a circle around Drakey and the other shamans; in front of them Bellchime and the other candidates formed a line. He pulled his shoulders back and looked up at the sky as if stretching his neck. There was Distance, a vague bluish form as high as some of the clouds, soaring in circles like a condor.

Bellchime missed Drakey's signal but sat down when all the goblin men did. The high shaman looked at the row of candidates at his feet, at the other shamans, at the circle, as if making certain all was in order. His eyes met Bellchime's for an instant. Had he dreamed about this one? He could not remember, but it was good that the human camp had a candidate for high chief, and one who might win.

Drakey's voice was loud and clear as a young man's, though his face was wrinkled, his hair and eyebrows white. "We come here to choose our high chief. These are the men who would be high chief. Each is the choice of his own camp. Each claims he has the power to be high chief. This is what we who know things say that the high chief must be. He must be young. He must be strong. He must be wise. These are the reasons. He must be young because our world is changing. A new time begins, and our people face unfamiliar dangers. A young man is flexible enough to find new solutions to new problems. He must be strong, so that we will accept his leadership. He must be wise, so that what he does is correct. Many young men are strong, but not many are wise, and who is the wisest, strongest young man? This is the test we must make. Do you accept this test?"

The candidates answered in this manner:

"I, Blue Trout, accept the test."

"I, Catsclaw, accept the test."

And so on, through Stormcloud, Elkhorn, Beartooth, until it was Quagga's turn, and he said, "If these are the standards, I have already lost, for though I say I am strong and wise, I am not young but have over forty winters."

"Do you accept the test?" said Drakey.

"I, Quagga, do not accept the test."

"Mmm," said Drakey. "Do the rest of you accept the test?"

Bellchime, Redbark, Spincloud, and Bright Owl accepted; no one else declined.

Drakey whispered something to the shamans standing next to him, they whispered back, then Drakey said, "We say that Quagga has already failed the test. If he had accepted the test, despite his age and his fear that he would lose for that reason, he would have shown flexibility, but he did not accept the test. I say that Quagga is too old to be high chief."

"This is not—" Quagga began angrily, then stopped himself. This was not how Strong Bull was chosen, fifteen summers ago? Drakey was right. Quagga stood up and walked to the edge of the circle without a word.

"This is the test for youth, strength, and wisdom," said Drakey. "We the shamans of Goblin Plain are agreed. You will choose from among yourselves one who is young, strong, and wise. You will decide among yourselves how to do this, but you must all agree on the same man. You will surrender your weapons and go into the tent we will call the high chief's tent, and you will not come out until we have a new high chief."

A number of goblin men carried tent-poles into the center of the circle and efficiently set up a tent. The heavy leather cover was beautifully painted with totem animals. Bellchime looked up at the cloudy sky but did not see Distance, though he knew she was up there somewhere. She said nothing to him, but remained in subtle mental contact. He was aware of Periwinkle and Coral both riding her.

The eight goblin men and Bellchime sat in a circle inside the tent, which was already uncomfortably warm. Stormcloud and

Catsclaw looked around at the others with curosity, as Bellchime did; but the others stared at the matting in front of their crossed legs with grim expressions. No one said a word for several tense minutes.

"We will never choose a chief if we do not talk to each other," said Catsclaw.

"Fool," said Beartooth.

"Would one who was wise call another a fool?" asked Redbark.

"Fool," Beartooth said to Redbark. "Same thing, more words."

"Drakey is the fool, to think we can choose a high chief this way," said Redbark. "This has never been done."

"The chief must be able to do what has never been done," said Stormcloud.

"Ah," said Beartooth.

"Who is strong?" said Elkhorn. "That is easy to decide. We can wrestle elbows."

"A child's game," said Redbark.

"You talk like children," said Elkhorn. "Let us learn who is the strongest child."

"Why should I accept your trial, even if it is a good one?" asked Catsclaw. "You would not suggest a trial you yourself could not win, and if you win you might put me to death."

"We could agree that the new high chief must not kill any of the losers," said Spincloud.

"If I win, I could never agree not to kill the man who burned my triboomen!" shouted Elkhorn.

"You lose," said Beartooth. "For you to be high chief, we must all agree, and would Bellchime agree now?"

Everyone looked at Bellchime, but now that he had the attention, he said simply, "We must all sit the peace circle."

"Yiyiyi!" shrieked Beartooth, clapping his hands and stamping his feet. "Do what has not been done, yes, yes! We must all sit the peace circle."

"Beartooth is right," said Spincloud.

"Fool," said Beartooth. "Bellchime is right. A chief must not lie to himself."

"We argue nothing," said Catsclaw. "We must all sit the peace circle."

There was general assent to this, except for Elkhorn.

"You lose, I say again," said Beartooth. "You are not high chief."

"If not I must still approve the one who is high chief," said Elkhorn.

"You refuse to accept the trial we all agree on," said Catsclaw.

"A peace circle is no trial," said Elkhorn. "No one can win or lose a peace circle."

"Strong Bull lost a peace circle," said Catsclaw.

Bellchime listened to more debate, knowing that he had already won, he was already high chief, unless he made some foolish remark now. Finally Elkhorn agreed to sit the peace circle.

The men clasped hands and began to pass a thread of energy around the circle, a very fine thread, for these men were all powerful. Twelve pulses of energy chased each other. Bellchime slowed his breathing and his pulse, relaxed his mind a little, and four of the pulses merged into one. He was soaring high above the river, in two women and a dragon, feeling the wind and the gray clouds, and sitting in the sweltering tent, connected hand by hand to a ring of white energy finer than the smallest spider's thread, feeling three other minds behind his closed eyes.

If you want strength, I am strong. If you want wisdom, I am wise. If you want love, I am kind.

What was this? A totem beast with a condor's head, the body of a great cat, and wings like a dragon. A griffin from the last desert? The four pulses merged?

Keep the energy fine, twist it finer, do not get lost in visions of spirit-beasts. This is the way of the peace circle.

Bellchime opened his eyes and looked at the eight goblin faces, seeing a calmness on each one that he had never seen on any goblin's face before.

"Now we can decide who is high chief," he said.

"Ah," said Beartooth. "Who is wise? Who suggested we sit the peace circle? Who is strong? Who pulled the circle so thin and so tight that we all feel like friends now? Who is young? Who has left behind the ways of the people he was born with and does things no one has done before?"

"I do not like to agree," said Elkhorn, "for Strong Bull and several others who died were my friends. But he was wrong to break the peace circle, and if this circle is whole, Bellchime is also— " he grimaced at the words, "my friend," but relaxed as he saw the truth in this.

"But is this real or are we enspelled?" asked Redbark.

"Would not a shaman with power to enspell all eight of us have the strength and wisdom to be high chief?" asked Spincloud.

"Be strong as you would have our chief be, fools," said Beartooth. "Let us say that Bellchime is high chief of all the camps of Goblin Plain, *now.*"

The other seven, and Bellchime himself, agreed that he was high chief, and they all walked out of the stuffy tent into a breeze and the dazzling midday sun shining between clouds.

"I am high chief of all the camps on Goblin Plain," said Bellchime in a loud voice.

Each of the other men said, "I say it is so!"

Disbelief and rage swept around some of the goblins in the outer circle. Some turned toward the five human men who had come with Bellchime.

"Stop!" shouted Bellchime, and a whirling wind blew dust in the goblins' faces. "I have sat the peace circle with your own chosen candidates, who say that I am high chief, as the high shaman ordered. If I must prove myself to you all, sit the peace circle with me. You are my people and I do not want to have to hurt or kill any of you."

Four separate lightning bolts, about a quarter mile from the circle in each of the four directions, simultaneously struck the ground, and their thunder shuddered the plain. That took imagination and control, Bellchime thought, and he felt for a moment the pleased excitement of three other minds watching the frightened goblins through his eyes. Even Drakey was breathing faster.

"Fools!" shouted Beartooth. "Sit the peace circle with your high chief now!"

"I did not want to do anything like that," Bellchime muttered, while the candidates and shamans walked to the outer circle. Bellchime deliberately did not sit with Rockdream and the other humans, but between Beartooth and Drakey.

Emotions washed around the circle like waves of the sea when they first clasped hands, with over two hundred spirit-beasts running in random directions, some fighting each other. The griffin was there, much larger than the others. With some effort, Bellchime shrank the griffin down to a small bead of light, and as the griffin shrank he became calmer. The other spirits were also collapsing to points of light, and beginning to move around the circle in a stream about the thickness of his own arms. Some of the larger light beads nudged the others toward the middle of the stream. Bellchime was breathing deeply and slowly. The energy circle spun off three lightning bolts, and as it did it collapsed to the thickness of a heavy rope, a thinner rope, a string, a network of threads twisting closer together into one fine thread, because the space between threads was no space at all. Beads of light passed along it as effortlessly as sun-reflections on a spider's web.

Bellchime opened his eyes and looked at what was now his people, over two hundred of them, from camps all over Goblin Plain, and saw that three blackened bodies lay outside the circle, and did not understand what had killed them. More surprising than this, even though one of the bodies was Quagga, a chief, nobody seemed disturbed by the deaths. Bellchime looked briefly at Drakey, wishing strongly that the old shaman would explain.

After what seemed like endless stillness, Drakey said, "Not in my lifetime or my grandfather's lifetime has there been a peace circle strong enough to kill directly those who would break it."

Bellchime waited an equally long time before he said, "I will send messengers to Spirit Swamp and to Upriver. If there are any in either of these places who would live with us on Goblin Plain, let them come and sit the peace circle with us. There will be no more broken peace circles while I am high chief!"

At this remark many of the goblins jumped up and down clapping or shouting, "Yiyiyi!"

When this demonstration ended, Bellchime said, "I will live with my wife in the tent you made for me, at Rockdream's Camp. I will call council at the midsummer round moon."

Drakey then said, "Let us clasp hands once more and thank the great spirits for the strength and wisdom of Bellchime, high chief of Goblin Plain."

After this, the goblins all hurried back to the camp and began taking down the tents.

Drakey said quietly to Bellchime, "Let us sit in front of your new tent and talk." They sat beside each other, watching the bustle of activity, and Drakey said, "When I saw you among the candidates, I thought I had dreamed of you. You will make a good high chief."

Bellchime said, "The night after Strong Bull's death, I dreamed about goblins and humans living together in a camp, sharing wisdom with each other. My wife thought it would take generations to make this happen, but we found Rockdream's Camp."

Drakey looked at Bellchime with piercing brown eyes surrounded by a labyrinth of wrinkles. "Elsewhere, goblins and humans took generations just to end their wars with each other, but Goblin Plain made peace with Chief Wentletrap even before Newport was built. In that time we spoke another language, different from humans and different from other goblins. Some goblins still do this. We learned that all humans speak the same language, and many goblins from far away know this language also. We made it our own language, and now only a few elders like me know any other. Then three springs ago there was war. Too many humans, too many goblins, all wanted control. They sat a new peace circle, but neither side wanted peace, and the peace circle was broken. Battles became massacres. Hundreds died, maybe thousands. Hearts hardened. When Rockdream and Coral came to me, dressed in the red of messengers, I thought their idea of humans becoming goblins was a good one. I had also dreamed something like this. This is what the Newport people should have done from the beginning. It has led us to you, high chief."

Drakey raised his chin and pursed his lips, then continued, "It is good that you won the contest as you did. I know what you could have done, and I know what flies above us even now. It is good that you killed who you had to kill through the peace circle."

"I did not know that would happen," said Bellchime.

"Ah," said Drakey, "that is even better."

"What will happen to the dead ones?"

"I will see to it, then I will go to Quagga's Camp, I think. You do not need me now. They need me to comfort them and help them choose a new chief."

The old man rose to his feet and walked toward the goblins who were disassembling Quagga's tent. Not too far from that, Rockdream and the other human men were arranging the parts of their own tent for portage. Beartooth was talking to Bellchime about which goblins might make the best messengers to send to Spirit Swamp and Upriver, with Bellchime saying he wanted to send humans and goblins together to these places, when Rockdream and Bloodroot finished with the tent and came to Bellchime.

"We almost got killed," said Bloodroot.

"Some of our people needed to see power," said Bellchime.

"You did exactly what you needed to do," said Beartooth.

"You did," said Rockdream.

"You have two tents to carry and you are few. Do you need help?" asked Beartooth.

"Yes," said Bellchime.

"I will talk to the men who carried it here."

In the background, somewhere, Distance killed an animal and Bellchime sensed it. The camp was gone; most of the groups of goblins were fording the river or already across it. Beartooth and three other goblins were taking the new tent apart. This help was good. The tent was too large and heavy for Distance to carry all at once. Most goblin tents could be carried by three people; this one would take at least five. Two pack horses could manage it, but Goblin Plain people never used animals that way; killing an animal for food was taking its body, but making it do work was taking its spirit.

The six humans and four goblins carried the two tents across the ford. Though the water was colder than it had been yesterday evening, in the muggy afternoon sun it was a welcome sensation. They had not walked far along the east bank beyond the joining of the two rivers when Distance appeared overhead.

I can help carry some of that, she said.

"Ah," said Beartooth. "The dragon does talk inside your head like a god. But who is riding her?"

"Periwinkle and Coral," said Bellchime.

The dragon flapped her ribbed, leathery wings and landed not far in front of the ten men, her scales gleaming in the sunlight like stormclouds reflected in deep clear water. Two young human women dressed in goblin-style leather dresses dismounted. One wore a sword at her waist and a shield over her back; she took off the shield.

"What are *you* doing here?" Rockdream asked Coral.

"The high chief's wife asked me to come," she said with a smile.

One of the goblins mumbled, "These human women are pretty when you see them dressed in proper clothes."

"Aye," said the goblin next to him. "With hair like that, who cares if they have round ears and thin lips?"

"Hush, fools!" hissed Beartooth. "These are chief's wives and women of strong magic."

"We did it," Periwinkle said quietly to Bellchime and Rockdream.

"We will talk about it more tonight under the stars," said Bellchime. "Coral, your skill made the difference."

"I never thought I would sit a peace circle half a mile up in the sky," she replied, then said to Rockdream, "Our son is with Birdwade and Salmon is in charge of the camp."

"I am proud of you," said Rockdream. "If I seem unhappy, it is only that I wish I could share the spirit world with you three and the dragon."

"Oh, but you can," said Coral. "I will explain how later."

The two men looked puzzled.

Periwinkle whispered in Bellchime's ear, "By working that much magic with us, Coral has become dragonbound to Distance."

Bellchime's throat went dry, his heart beat fast. He did not want to share this with anyone else but Periwinkle. Coral suddenly looked small and frightened, like a child who had done something wrong. As for Distance—a dragon's emotions cannot be read from facial expression, and Bellchime felt cut off from the dragon's thoughts. Then something broke inside him, and with watering eyes he put one arm around Periwinkle, one arm around Coral, and Coral pulled Rockdream into a four-person hug.

"Nothing the humans do makes sense," said the first goblin.

"You just want to hug those women yourself," said the second.

⟞9⟝

SPIRIT SWAMP

33.

Wedge kept interrupting Bellchime's story about Wentletrap and Pip to ask when Mom and Dad would come back. "I want to ride Distance, too," he complained.

"Are you sure you do not want to go swimming?" Bellchime asked. "We can stay in the shallow."

The afternoon was warm, with slight breezes that bent the tall grasses and boughs of a lone willow tree; they were both sitting on a coarse sand beach at the bend of the Blue River, watching Periwinkle swim.

"Too cold," said Wedge.

Periwinkle bobbed her head up, treading water. "If you want to swim, I can watch Wedge," she called.

"All right," said Bellchime, taking off his soft shoes and breeches and setting them beside her dress. At five winters, Wedge was as young as anyone Bellchime had taught, and though he sometimes liked Bellchime's stories, today there was no pleasing him.

The water was cold, and Bellchime had to wade some distance before it was deep enough to swim in. When Periwinkle stood up to wade ashore, her skin was textured like a plucked bird.

"It feels fine once you get used to it," she said and splashed him.

He took a breath and dove into the water; she watched him till his head bobbed up, then walked ashore to dry in the sun and play with Wedge.

Bellchime swam out to the current and tried swimming upstream, thinking about Ironweed and Stonewater, who with Gray Lizard from Beartooth's Camp had to row a leather canoe upstream all the way to Upriver harbor, to be Goblin Plain's embassy to Lord Blackwood. It would take at least two more weeks for them to get there; the smoke messages yesterday said they had finally reached Elkhorn's Camp; the riverpass lay ahead.

Bellchime turned around and swam with the current until he was again close to Periwinkle and Wedge. She had put her soft deerskin dress back on and was trying to learn a hand-clapping game from the boy, who did not know quite how to do it right, but was certain that her suggestions were wrong. They were chanting,

> Flat bread, flat bread,
> slap it flat,
> flip it over and
> fry it in the fat.
> Turn the down side up
> and the up side down,
> and pile it on the others
> when it turns brown.

They clapped each other's hands and their own in time with the first three lines, then trembled their hands to imitate frying, then clapped hands from above and below, reversed this, then did nothing else till the very last word, when they piled all four hands together at once.

They did this over and over, while Bellchime swam up the river again, and returned, but this time he was not alone.

"Bellchime!" shouted Periwinkle. "River lizard! Behind you!"

The best way to deal with a river lizard is to swim away slowly, using a breast stroke and gentle frog-kicks, because fast splashing movements suggesting prey attract its attention. Unfortunately, Bellchime knew next to nothing about river lizards, beyond their predatory habits, and kicked furiously to try to outswim it. Smoothly it turned and swam straight toward him.

"Stop swimming! Punch his snout!" screamed Wedge, but his voice was too shrill and slurred for Bellchime to understand.

Periwinkle untied her belt, stripped off her dress, ran out into the river with her knife between her teeth, and dove in. Bellchime felt something cold and smooth bump him from one side and slide under his belly, and panicked. Periwinkle, swimming underwater, saw the bubbly blur of Bellchime and the lizard, swam toward the lizard, and slashed with her knife. Leaving a thin trail of blood, it swam quickly toward the middle of the river. Bellchime was already in the shadows when he saw for the first time that Periwinkle was not with Wedge, and turned to see her swim up behind him.

"One cut and it turned tail!" she said, holding up her knife.

"I told you, all you do is punch its snout," Wedge said, with exasperation.

Bellchime, trying his best not to look exhausted and terrified, waded ashore and asked Wedge what else he knew about river lizards.

"Well," he said, "they can eat people, especially children, but not if you hit them hard enough on the snout. They are kind of slimy, like fish and frogs and worms, and taste awful for dinner. I hate them."

Periwinkle laughed. "Do not worry. That one got away before I could kill it, so no one will have to eat it."

"Now what do we do? When will Mom and Dad come back?"

Periwinkle pulled her dress back over her head, tied the belt, and laced up the front, while Bellchime put on his breeches and vest.

"I love this dress," she said. "I copied the one Salmon gave me, but adjusted the fit and strengthened the stitching. This is a real warrior's dress."

"I lived for four years in the wilderness making my own clothes, yet your leatherwork is far better than mine."

"Your dreams and vision are far better than mine, which is much more important," said Periwinkle. "Besides, you did not have my mother's endless criticism to improve your work and drive you to tears."

"Are we going now?" asked Wedge impatiently.

They walked together through the high grass to camp, where Birdwade was kneading flatbread dough, and Salmon and Limpet were preparing a stew. Bloodroot had gone out with three other warriors to the Goblin River to collect willow twigs for arrow shafts. Others were sitting in front of their tents, making weapons or jewelry or clothing, or sometimes doing nothing at all but talking to each other or admiring the beauty of a late spring day. Wedge found a stick and began drawing patterns in the dirt.

"I love living here," Periwinkle said. "This life is even better than the cave, for now we have friends, and do not need to hide."

"I will not be satisfied until we make peace with the humans in Spirit Swamp," Bellchime said. "I fear that when they learn about Strong Bull's death, they will resume the war."

"Is that why you hesitate to send ambassadors?"

"Yes, and also, we do not know where most of the human settlements are."

"We could go there and look for them," Periwinkle suggested.

"I am a creepy crawly river lizard!" Wedge said suddenly, crawling on his stomach and pretending to bite Bellchime's leg.

"Ha! I caught the river lizard," said Bellchime, grabbing the boy. "Shall we cook it and feed it to Wedge?"

"No! Let me go!" he said.

"Shall we punch its snout to make it go away?" asked Periwinkle.

"No!" said Wedge, thrashing his arms and legs.

Bellchime said, "If I let you go, can Periwinkle and I talk about high-chief stuff?"

"What if the Spirit Swamp humans want to fight us?" asked Wedge. "Can Distance beat them?"

Periwinkle said, "The best way to win a war is to stop it before anybody starts fighting. We can talk about things with the other people, and sit peace circles with them—"

"I never get to sit peace circles either," Wedge complained. "Mom says I am not old enough."

"Do you really want to do it?" asked Periwinkle. "Make sure in your heart."

"Are you serious?" asked Bellchime.

"I think it would be good for him, if he really wants to do it."

"Oh, I do, I do," said Wedge.

"We can do it inside the tent," said Periwinkle, and they went inside and sat in a triangle facing each other, hands clasped. "We have to keep holding hands, even if your nose itches or anything," she told Wedge. "Then we close our eyes, and imagine a stream going in a circle through all three of us, and I will tell you when we can open our eyes and talk again."

Periwinkle saw a quiet, misty pool of water, gradually becoming something like a slowly spinning smoke ring, which lasted for about a minute, and that was all. It felt complete, simple, and happy. They all opened their eyes.

"Thank you, thank you," said Wedge, hugging Periwinkle, then Bellchime. "I think I want to—Can I sleep on your bed for awhile?" He was rubbing his eyes.

"Go outside and pass water first," said Periwinkle.

34.

When Coral and Rockdream returned to camp late that afternoon, Wedge was still sleeping, Birdwade was frying loaves of flatbread, the stew was bubbling, and Bloodroot was stripping the bark from his new arrow-shafts while talking to Salmon.

Distance flapped to a landing next to the totem pole.

"How was your ride?" Bellchime asked Rockdream.

"I liked it," he said, dismounting. "I almost shot an antelope."

"You missed it by a mile," Coral said, laughing, and put her arm around the big man.

I killed a quagga colt, said Distance, nuzzling Periwinkle with her scaly snout.

"—and neither of us fell off," said Coral. "I got to meet Silverfish at Skyrock's Camp—we went there—and she gave me a turquoise." She reached into her pouch and brought out a stone.

"What a beautiful color," Periwinkle said.

"How was Wedge?" Coral asked, and they talked about the little peace circle, the flatbread game, the river lizards.

Bellchime said, "After Wedge fell asleep, Periwinkle and I discussed Spirit Swamp."

"I think we can find the settlements with Distance's help," said Periwinkle, "and if we are open, honest, and direct, as we were when we approached your camp, I think we can contact them."

"You know how uneasy I feel about that," said Coral. "What if Distance gets wounded again? Or what if we land and dismount to negotiate a truce in good faith, and they capture or kill one of us? What would you do, Distance?"

She looked directly into the young dragon's green eyes and saw the pupils contract to pinpoints.

I would try to kill them, she said.

Coral looked at Periwinkle and Bellchime.

"Strong Bull surprised us," said Periwinkle. "I never want that to happen again. We will be more cautious."

"How about if you and I went together?" Coral asked. "We can start with the two settlements I know. At least one of them is still inhabited. Probably they both are."

"We were hoping you would suggest something like that," said Bellchime.

35.

Two days later, Coral and Periwinkle were flying Distance over the tangled trees and green bogs of Spirit Swamp, looking for the settlements Coral knew, beginning with the one she used to live in, near Loop Lake, which looked like one of the Turtle River's bends but was cut off from the river itself.

"This lake is the great empire of river lizards," said Coral. From above they could see many, lazily swimming near the surface like overgrown salamanders, only to quickly disappear in the murky water if Distance passed too low.

"Where the lake curves back on itself, there are four cypress trees much bigger than the others—"

Distance flapped her wings to rise higher, wondering why she did not sense any humans below, where Coral thought they would be.

"Are you certain anyone is still there?" asked Periwinkle.

"Several people moved to our camp from this place just two months ago. There were forty humans here then, more than lived here when I did. Rockdream and I helped build many of the huts. They cannot be seen from the air."

No one is here, said Distance.

"Should we take a closer look? asked Periwinkle.

"Give them our message first," said Coral.

River lizards and drakeys do not care if we come in peace, said Distance. She bellowed, and several drakeys, the largest of which was half as long as Distance, with a relatively smaller head and longer neck, flew up out of the trees, scattered in different directions, and dove back among the branches. *You believe me now*, Distance said, and flew down toward the largest cypress.

Here she landed, folded her wings back, and walked between the trees for a view of the village. Beneath the canopy of boughs were the familiar stilt-houses of Coral's former home, but on the muddy ground—

"Oh, no," said Coral. "Oh, no."

What they saw were human bodies, parts of bodies, bones, being eaten and fought over by crawling river lizards. Feeling the revulsion of the two women on her back, Distance turned to leave.

"Wait," said Periwinkle. "We should find out what happened to them."

"Swamp sickness," said Coral, "and they died only a few days ago. River lizards will not touch a corpse older than that. We may catch the sickness ourselves if we go too near the dead." Coral's voice was trembling; she was sobbing. "Distance, get us out of here!" she screamed.

The dragon galloped out of the trees, flapped her wings, and jumped into flight. Periwinkle and Coral were almost thrown off, but soon Distance was high above Loop Lake, soaring slow circles.

"Every summer here, people rot from the inside out," Coral said, choking off her sobs. "Wedge caught it, but he lived. I gave him goldroot, willow bark, sleepflower. He was sick for weeks. In desperation I called upon the Power That Will Help, and when Rockdream learned that, he was furious. I half-think that if Wedge had died, he would have told the others—"

"I know what people *say* the Power That Will Help is, but what is it in truth?" asked Periwinkle.

"You summon—any power that will help, without knowing what the power will be, or what price you will have to pay. The power that helped me was a bird spirit, who I now know is my totem condor. He helped me heal Wedge; he inspired me to return to Goblin Plain—as a goblin! I was very lucky. I might have summoned something terrible."

Where do we go now? Distance asked reasonably.

Coral looked at the direction she thought was right, and before she could think of a way to describe it, the dragon was flying that way. "Stay high. The trail from Loop Lake twists for ten miles. I am not quite sure of the true direction, but the other place is near two bogs and a stand of dead trees."

A short time later, they saw two places that might fit that description, and approached the one that was nearer. Distance swooped down low over the first bog, and Coral thought that it did not look right, until she realized that a distinctive dead tree had fallen.

"This is the place," she said. "Just half a mile beyond the second bog, in that direction."

"Be careful," said Periwinkle.

The dragon flapped her ribbed wings and rose above the dead trees between the two bogs, and higher. *I sense people*, she said with a mental whisper.

"Now," said Coral.

Distance bellowed, then said in her loudest mental voice, *The dragon Distance brings ambassadors from Lord Bellchime of Goblin Plain. May we land in peace?*

Through the dragon's mind, the women sensed the surprise, shock, fear, and panic of the people hidden below.

"Tell them I am Coral! Tell them we are friends of Birdwade and Holdfast!"

The dragon did so, which caused the humans below to argue. Some fled the village, and their fear made them seem like sparks flying from a blacksmith's sharpening wheel. Finally there was agreement, and one man's voice spoke clearly.

"Let Coral walk into our village alone, and we will talk," he said. "I am Driftwood."

Distance did not know whether Coral would be safe, but she did know that Driftwood's intentions were honest, and that none of the people were contemplating attack.

"That is all any ambassador can expect," said Periwinkle. "Will you go?"

Coral sighed. "If Driftwood is willing to talk to me, I should be willing to talk to him."

The dragon flapped to a landing near the roots of a willow, where the ground was firm.

"Is he someone you dislike?" asked Periwinkle.

"He is a bitter, cynical man, who believes in the church's ceremonies and little else, but he must be doing something right, for his village is still alive." Coral slipped off the dragon's back and patted her snout. "I will tell you when to join me."

36.

Coral sensed Distance circling in the sky when she entered the village, a close-packed array of stilt-houses not much larger than the tents of a goblin camp. Most were covered with shingles or thatch, but a few were covered with leather. Coral wondered whether these should be called houses or a new kind of tent?

Driftwood, former Newport merchant, now master of a nameless village, was a middle-aged man, with a balding forehead, and gray streaks in his full red beard. He looked noticeably older, thinner, and tougher than Coral remembered him from two years before. He stood on the ground facing the path, with four warriors or would-be warriors, and a priest. Driftwood and the priest wore cloth, the others leather. All were men, except one warrior.

"I am glad to see you alive," said Coral.

Driftwood spoke brusquely: "Who is Lord Bellchime? What are you doing riding—" He pointed up.

"Strong Bull is dead," said Coral. "Lord Bellchime is the new high chief. I am his ambassador to Spirit Swamp."

"Stop giving me witch's riddles and tell a plain story."

"Your pardon, Master Driftwood," said Coral. "I am telling this as simply as I can. When the high chief dies, there is a contest held to choose a new high chief, and Lord Bellchime was our camp's candidate. My husband, Rockdream, is chief of a camp of goblins who were once humans like yourselves. I am no longer a human witch, but a goblin shamaness."

"You look human to me, except for your clothes," said the woman, whom Coral recognized as a former farmer.

"Let her speak," said one of the men, jerking his head to indicate the dragon high above the treetops. Coral did not know him, but he had the manner of a real warrior.

Coral said, "Good master, your way of life here is not so different from goblins. You hunt and fish; you cannot farm; your horses are of little use; your homes are much like tents. You could become goblins yourselves without changing much, and the hunting is much better on Goblin Plain. I offer you that possibility if you want it."

"We refuse it," said Driftwood.

"The swamp sickness has killed every human at Loop Lake," said Coral.

As used to horror as these humans were, they looked stunned and shocked.

"This cannot be true," said the woman.

"It is," said Coral.

The priest bowed his head, saying, "Whenever we die, we will keep our honor. We will die human."

"Would it not be better to live as friends?" asked Coral. "Goblins are also a people with honor."

"They do not worship the Lord or the Holy Family," said the priest, whose name was Father Brine.

A true worshipper of the Holy Family would have a family of his own, Coral thought to herself, wondering irreverently what this young man would look like in goblin vest and breeches, with his hair grown; but she said, "The spirit shows itself in different forms to different peoples. It is all one."

Father Brine frowned. He was certainly no older than Coral herself.

"Of course you will get blasphemy from a witch," said one of the other men, whom Coral had seen a few times in the Newport Market.

"No," said Father Brine. "This woman's soul is clean, even though she is a witch, even though she is dragonbound."

Driftwood said, "Oh, Coral, in all your unholy practices, I thought you had at least enough sense not to—"

"It is a great honor for Rockdream and me to share this dragon with our high chief and his wife," said Coral. "Lord Bellchime offers your village, at the least, peace and trade, and I offer you a welcome feast if you ever come to Rockdream's Camp."

Driftwood puckered his lips and stroked his beard. "I wish we could offer you the same," he said, "but we have no food to spare, certainly not such as your—" he did not say the word, but looked up, "—may require. I doubt that we have anything to trade, either."

"We have grain and you have wood," said Coral.

Driftwood laughed. "We could certainly use grain, or any other food for that matter, but wood is impractical. There is plenty of that much closer to your camp, and no one to stop you from taking all you want. You clearly know little of the principles of trade. We might, for example, trade swamp pig with the Sharp Bend people for turtle, but not for deer, because we have that right here. Even then, we would have to want very much to make the trade, because it is difficult and dangerous to go anywhere else from here."

"Can I call down my partner?" asked Coral. "She was a

keepholder's daughter before she became the high chief's wife, and understands much better—"

"Call her down," Driftwood said brusquely. "Why did you not tell me she was his wife? I hope she will not consider me rude."

"I took it as caution," said Coral, and called the dragon.

We land in peace, said Distance's mental voice.

Driftwood tried to hide his involuntary shudder by giving a high-pitched whoop that was evidently the signal to the villagers to come out. More faces appeared, from behind trees, and inside houses, to watch their leader stand face-to-face with a dragon twice the length of the largest drakey, and a young warrior wearing a goblin dress, armed with bow and sword, her long black hair tied back with a leather cord.

She dismounted and said, "I am Lady Periwinkle of Goblin Plain, and this is the dragon Distance," and made a bow that was little more than the slightest nod. "Distance will hunt for you if you like, so that we may share a proper feast. She will find and kill the leopard that lives near your village."

"How—how did you know about that?" asked Driftwood.

The sad ones who lost a daughter think loud thoughts, said Distance. *May I hunt?*

"Yes, of course!" said Driftwood. The dragon turned and walked to the nearest relatively open place and jumped into flight.

"I understand we are to discuss a trade agreement," said Periwinkle. "We have everything we need to live, except perhaps metals, which I suspect are also in short supply here. So let us talk about luxury goods."

"You want any cloth?" asked Driftwood.

"If we wanted that, we could make it for ourselves," said Coral.

"Wait," said Periwinkle. "Could you make up the cloth into clothing, of goblin style? We will want the strongest cloth, but finely embroidered with designs we will give you."

"We can do that," said a woman with graying brown hair sitting on the platform of one of the houses.

"You want something sturdy but expensive, and to your design," said Driftwood.

"Yes," said Periwinkle.

"But why?" asked Coral.

"Spirit gifts for the council."

"Oho!" said Coral, suddenly appreciating Periwinkle's plan: to give cloth dresses and vests, embroidered with personal totem-animal or life-story designs, to the other chiefs and their wives, to notable shamans and warriors, at the midsummer council. They would be impressed with their high chief's generosity, and cloth clothing, which on summer days was certainly more comfortable, would likely become accepted. It gave these human villagers something valuable to trade for goblin grain, and making these clothes might even help them appreciate the goblin way of life.

Why had she ever doubted Periwinkle's ability? Here she was, perfectly managing a shrewd man almost three times her own age, making him accept her leadership in his own village, and leading him to a place where he could not possibly dislike or mistrust her.

Now they were discussing the grain, and Periwinkle was saying that though it was possible for Distance to carry what they needed in three or four trips, there were other human villages that they hoped to contact.

"We cannot do all our trading on dragonback," she said. "We will need to establish a trade route."

This was a sore point with many of the villagers because they considered their secrecy an asset for survival.

"Just who is going to attack you?" asked Periwinkle. "Are you saying you want a defense agreement with Goblin Plain? That may be possible, but good trade routes, by river or road, are even more important to making defense workable."

"No—that is—we —" Driftwood stammered, then looked at the priest, then at the others, then said, "Our enemies are Riversong, wild beasts like that leopard, swamp sickness. We are making peace with Goblin Plain."

"Peace," Periwinkle said, quietly but firmly, looking at the villagers' faces. "That means that even the darkest-skinned, fattest-lipped, pointiest-eared goblin warrior from Strong Bull's Camp may, in fact, be your friend. Now, how are we going to get your grain to you?"

"Isolation also protects us from swamp sickness," said one of the warriors.

"It did not protect the Loop Lake village," said Driftwood grimly. "I think that isolation has served us well, but now we have a better choice."

"Once a merchant, always a merchant," muttered one of the hunters.

"I heard that!" said Driftwood sharply. "Today it is a merchant's wisdom that this village needs. Or do you wish so much to hide from a possible death that may find you anyway, that you refuse food from the outside world when you are hungry?"

Distance could not have chosen a more dramatic moment to announce her return, and there she was, large blue ribbed wings spread against a paler sky between treetops, holding the leopard's limp body with her front legs.

I ate one of the legs, she said, dropping it on the ground while she flapped to a landing. *You may have the rest for your feast.*

37.

Periwinkle and Coral returned to Rockdream's Camp late that night. Bellchime was overjoyed at the news of the trade, a joy tempered by the deep sadness of many of the tribespeople when they heard about Loop Lake the next morning.

"They should have come here," said Limpet, crying hot tears.

"We will do a ceremony today, to ease both their spirits and our own," said Rockdream.

This ceremony was planned for the hour before sundown, when the totem pole's shadow came near the old oak tree. People were already gathering around the council circle when Coral returned to camp, after being away and alone for several hours. She spent a moment talking to Salmon and Hope about what each would do in the ceremony, then called everyone to come and be seated.

Hope moved around the inside of the circle, fanning smoke from a bowl of incense with condor feathers, while Salmon offered a prayer to the four directions.

"I give the voice to the east," she said, "where the sun rises behind the Silver Mountains, where new life begins. I give a voice to the south, to the noon sun over the Gray Hills, to summer, to the fullness of life. I give a voice to the west—" and over these words, her voice cracked, and she had to clear her throat, "to the swamp, the Foggy Mountains, and the sea, where the sun sets, where life—changes. I give a voice to the north, to the Emerald Hills, to the winter winds whose rain and snow begins new life, where the cycle begins and ends."

Hope fanned the last two people, then set down her bowl near the small fire in the center of the circle, walked back to her place, and said, "I would like to offer a prayer to the Holy Family, which

I will do in the goblin way, for we of this camp are both human and goblin, and we know that all spirits watch over all people."

"Yes, so be it, yes," said voices around the circle.

She said,

> I give a voice to the Mother,
> who is nameless, who is our whole world,
> who gives birth to all life.

> I give a voice to the Father,
> whose name is Sky, whose light is the golden sun
> that quickens life in the Mother.

> I give a voice to the First Daughter,
> whose name is Wind, the Hunter,
> whose light is the silver moon.

> I give a voice to the Second Daughter,
> whose name is Fire, the Warrior,
> whose light is the red star.

> I give a voice to the Third Daughter,
> whose name is Lake, the Lover,
> whose light is the bright twilight star.

> I give a voice to the First Son,
> whose name is Thunder, the King,
> whose light is the twelve-year star.

> I give a voice to the Second Son,
> whose name is Cloud, the Messenger,
> whose light is the dimmer twilight star.

> I give a voice to the Third Son,
> whose name is Mountain, the Shaman,
> whose light is the slow-moving star.

Coral said, "We are here together in this circle to honor the spirits of the people who died at Loop Lake Village, where many of us lived before we came to this camp. I give a voice to my Grandfather Condor, who helped me make this new song about them and about us." She took a deep breath and sang a simple melody, with no accompaniment but the distant sounds of the river.

> Cry for our friends who have died,
> who know we remember them,
> victims of war, homeless and hungry,
> whose hopes and lives were cut short.
>
> Cry till our tears are a river,
> floating them on their journey,
> till their spirits find new voices
> in the land beyond the night.
>
> Cry till our grief becomes love
> for friends both dead and living,
> renewing our joy in being alive
> and sharing this truth with each other.

Bloodroot said, "We cannot easily tell stories about the dead to comfort ourselves because we do not know who is dead, and who may have left Loop Lake before the sickness came. The only friends who I know for certain are dead are those whose bodies someone has seen, and the only ones who I know for certain are alive are those in this circle. I pray that more friends will come here and join this camp."

"Yes."

"So be it."

Feathergrass said, "I give a voice to Father Unicorn, and Fire, the Second Daughter, the Warrior, who have given me life while others die. Use this moment of sorrow to cleanse me, to end my bitterness, like Coral sang in her song. I am living in peace after three years of war, but there is yet no peace in my heart. You can see that I am crying, but my tears are no longer hot. I am not sure what I am saying or feeling, but maybe I will learn."

Swanfeather said, "I give a voice to the Mother, who is nameless, and to my own and my husband's totem spirits. Two days after Bellchime was chosen high chief was the end of my moon. I have taken no freedomwort since then, nor will I, until Flatfish and I have a child."

Rockdream said, "I give thanks to all the spirits who guided us here, to a time and place where children can again be born, to a time and place where grief can become love."

"Yes, yes," said voices around the circle.

38.

In the following days and weeks, Coral, Periwinkle, and Distance managed to find three more Spirit Swamp villages with whom they made similar peace and trade agreements. The village called Sharp Bend, on a nameless backwater stream, had clay that made an especially fine pottery, and these people agreed to trade jars for grain. Hunters from all four villages, who knew the backwater trails, worked to connect them to make a pack-horse route.

Meanwhile, on some of the days when Distance was not gone to Spirit Swamp, Rockdream and Bellchime would take her hunting for antelope or quagga and then trade the meat for baskets of last year's grain. Some of the goblin chiefs thought it was funny that anyone would want to trade antelope meat for grain; others, like Beartooth, guessed immediately what it was for and approved. All humans were a potential source of metal knives and cookpots, and if these people did not have such things now, they might have them later. Also, it was a sign that the war was over.

The moon became full and waned, the Summer Solstice came with its celebrations, and on the new moon, four days later, canoes from Rockdream's Camp, loaded with grain, met pack horses from the four villages, loaded with pottery and clothing, and exchanged loads.

►10►

MIDSUMMER MOONDANCE

39.

Four days before the midsummer full moon, smoke messages came from Skyrock's Camp, saying that a messenger from Spirit Swamp was coming. Late that afternoon a young hunter named Sharpstone, from Driftwood's Village, walked into Rockdream's Camp, asking to see Coral the Shamaness.

"Over here," she called, and the man found her sitting in front of her tent, mixing a reddish powder into a small bowl filled with what smelled like melted mammoth fat.

Sharpstone was not dressed in messenger's red, but in brown cloth shirt and trousers, with leather boots. His hair was short curly blond, and though unshaven he had very little hair on his face. "What are you making?" he asked.

"Paint for my lyre," she said, and pointed to a framework of fine-grained oak that was probably the first lyre in the world carved with goblin totem designs. "I have to use this while it is still warm," she said, then saw the urgency of Sharpstone's face, and said, "but I can put it on the edge of the cookfire to keep it warm." She did so, said a few words to Hope, then came back and sat down facing him. "What can I do for you?"

Sharpstone was trembling when he said, "The sickness came to our village four days ago. Five have caught the fever, and one was nearly dead when I left. They say that your son had swamp sickness and lived, because of your treatment. Can you possibly help us? Father Brine and Master Driftwood both beg of you to come."

"Sharpstone, is that your name? It took me months to heal Wedge. I used herbs and teas that most humans consider poisonous and called upon spirits that most humans do not trust. If Wedge had died, and if the others found out what I did, I do not know what they would have done to me."

"The Loop Lake people are dead because they refused to accept your knowledge," Sharpstone said with despair in his light brown eyes.

"Your wife has the sickness," said Coral.

"Please, please help us."

"The most I can do is come for a few days, to teach your own healers and witches what I know, and try to encourage the sick. I hope—" she shook her head slowly and reached to wipe the tears streaming down her face. "I hope the sickness did not come to your village because of the trade."

"Some say that it did," said Sharpstone.

"It comes from damp air and foul water," said Feathergrass, who had overhead some of the conversation. "You people should all come here. Look, I once hated goblins as much as you. They killed my wife, and it was not a fair battle. But we have peace now, and the goblin way of life works. Yours does not."

"This is not your concern," Coral said, then turned to Sharpstone. "All right. I must come to your village and do what I can. But you must allow me to do whatever I see fit, and you must not blame me when I fail."

"Thank you," Sharpstone mumbled, making a deep bow.

Coral sighed. "When Distance returns from her hunt, we can go, but for now, I am going back to my painting." She walked to the cookfire, retrieved the clay cup, picked up the lyre, dipped her little finger into the warm red, and began rubbing it into the fangtooth cat. She realized she was painting her sadness about Newport, her worry about her healing skills, and her need for Rockdream's approval, but she was engrossed in her work and could not set it down. After a time, when she was finished, she was startled to see Periwinkle's concerned face.

"What is wrong, sister?" the younger woman asked.

"Am I still crying? I think my spirit needs washing. When did you return? I did not notice Distance."

You were lost in your work, said the dragon's voice.

Coral looked around at the circle of tents and saw Rockdream and Wedge, back from the river, talking to Sharpstone, with Bellchime, Bloodroot, and Salmon.

Rockdream came over to her, saying, "I think what you offer these people is beautiful. Please forgive me for everything I said and did while Wedge was sick. I want to go with you to Driftwood's Village, to help you and support you."

Coral stood up and hugged him, crying intensely. "How many of my thoughts do you know?" she asked.

Rockdream stroked her back and hair. "Before I became dragonbound, I did not understand any of these things, but now—"

When Coral smiled, she felt the strength of her spirit condor inside. "We should eat and pack what we will need," she said.

40.

The next morning Bellchime and Periwinkle moved most of their possessions to Rockdream's tent, took down their own tent, and loaded it in a canoe. Two other canoes they filled with the clothing and pottery from Spirit Swamp. Bloodroot, Salmon, Feathergrass, and Holdfast went with them to the council, two to a canoe.

Their journey to the sacred ground took most of two days, and part of a third. Near their destination they were passed several times by canoes filled with goblins, which with less cargo and more rowers, were faster.

At least four hundred goblin men and women came to the sacred ground, bringing seventy-six tents, which they set up in a large double circle. Many wives and many young women came for the ceremonies and dancing, and some would sit and speak in the council circle itself, because the chiefs knew that their new high chief wanted to hear both men's and women's wisdom. To have women who were not powerful shamanesses speak in council was a new thing, but Bellchime was chosen high chief because he would do new things, good things. He had power and wisdom, and he was ending the war.

Beartooth saw Bellchime, Periwinkle, and the others while they were raising their tent. With him were Gray Lizard, Ironweed, and Stonewater, returned from Upriver in time for the council.

With some difficulty they had gotten to see Lord Blackwood and spoke with him twice. After checking into things, he believed their story, but did not make any commitment.

"He was very careful not to offend us," said Gray Lizard. "He chose every word he said to us as carefully as a spirit gift. He treated us well, in the manner of humans. But we know he plans no invasion. His people are making their own plain, by cutting down the trees."

"We saw no signs that he was enlarging his fleet, either," said Stonewater. "In fact, many of the boats looked like they needed repair. We sat a peace circle with two camps of goblins who live in the forest across the river. They were so pleased with Ironweed and me and what we are doing on Goblin Plain that they promised to send messengers immediately if Upriver ever seems to be readying for war."

Gray Lizard said, "I say the most important thing the three of us did was become close friends. It proves that Drakey's vision is possible."

"Bellchime proved that to me when he became high chief," said Beartooth.

"Where are Rockdream and Coral?" asked Stonewater, and Periwinkle told them about the peace and trade with Spirit Swamp, and the new outbreak of swamp sickness.

"They planned to be here in time for the council tomorrow," she said.

41.

The light of the full moon silvered the ground where goblins danced wild circles to intricate drumming, their arms and legs painted with black and white rings and zigzags. Whenever the drummers changed rhythm, the dancers would do a different dance. Many of these dances were new to Bellchime and Periwinkle, but most of the steps were easy for them to learn.

Suddenly, the drummers changed to a very simple, steady pattern, and everyone clasped hands to form two concentric circles, which did sidesteps in opposite directions, gradually moving faster. From outside the circles came shrill cries of "Yiyiyi!" and one by one, young women ducked under the circles' clasped hands and ran to the center, where they did a wild gyrating dance. They were naked, and their arms and legs were painted with patterns up to their shoulders and hips. When they were all in the center, they made their own circle, facing out, then all turned together to face in, then turned out again.

One by one, young men left their places in the outer two circles to dance with the women in the center. Some seemed to pair off immediately into dancing couples, while others looked for a woman who would look back with a smile. Some were not accepted and returned to the outer circles. The last woman finally saw the man she would accept in the outermost circle, and moved around in time with him, smiling and moving her shoulders to make her breasts bounce. He finally saw her and rushed into the center to dance with her.

"Hoo! Hoo!" someone called, and the drummers speeded up the pace. The circles moved faster and faster, while the couples in the center moved their bodies in frantic shiftings and shakings. The circles became more and more unstable, and finally broke, spinning off everywhere people who were trying not to stumble. At that moment all the couples in the center ran away, in every direction, as fast as they could, while the drummers each played a different rhythm, all of which added up to a throbbing chaos.

Perwinkle grabbed Bellchime's arm, and they both were running, also, past the double ring of tents into the wild moonlit grass, where the drums faded into the distance, where she pulled off her dress and danced naked, moving her breasts and belly like the women in the center of the circle, where Bellchime stripped off his vest and breeches and grabbed her and they tumbled to the ground together, where they made fast and furious love.

"I like being a goblin," Periwinkle said, panting.

42.

They were still naked in each other's arms when they noticed the moon was low in a sky beginning to brighten towards dawn. Drums were still beating at the camp, and they now felt the presence of Distance asleep there.

"How do you feel?" Periwinkle asked. "We should have gotten more sleep, I suppose."

"No, not at all," said Bellchime. "I could feel both our spirit-beasts very strongly, the whole time we were making love. I feel strong and awake, and in my heart I feel like a goblin."

"I feel wonderful," she said. "We should find our clothes and go to the river to wash off this paint."

The sky was a rich blue like Coral's turquoise when they reached the river, where they heard laughter and splashing. They saw two couples sitting down in the shallow water, scrubbing each other's paint off. Bellchime and Periwinkle dropped their clothes and joined them.

Both women laughed, saying, "You were not in the dance," which was obvious because Periwinkle's paint went only slightly above her knees, not all the way to her hips. "Why is your paint so smudged? What were you doing?" They both laughed, as did the men who were washing them.

Bellchime did not know how to respond, but Periwinkle said, "Why should you have all the fun?" and started splashing water on Bellchime's legs, saying, "I know this is cold, but if you sit down, I can scrub you clean much quicker," and the paints swirled off into the water like mud.

"Your father should have let you dance," said the first woman more seriously. "Your body is beautiful, and you are certainly old enough. Which camp are you from?"

Periwinkle laughed. "We are already married. We are from Rockdream's Camp."

"You mean Human Camp?" asked the second woman. "Are you humans? You look just like we do."

Periwinkle stopped scrubbing Bellchime's arm to pull back her hair to show her ear, and Bellchime said, "We are goblins in the spirit."

"Truly you are," said the second man. "You were yowling like fangcats all night." He laughed, and so did the others.

"You should talk," said the first man. "You were trumpeting like mammoths."

"You were all screeching like drakeys," said Bellchime, joining their game and their laughter.

Periwinkle said, "You are clean. Now do me," and sat down in the water. The two goblin couples finished washing, and waded out of the water to get dressed. "Where did you get clothing?" she asked the women.

"You must be human," the first woman said with a giggle. "We each hide our dresses in the bush before we dance, and that is where we run when we leave the circle."

"See you at the camp," said the second woman.

43.

Periwinkle and Bellchime entered their tent not long before sunrise, to find everyone dressing and brushing their hair, and the men were passing around a jug of heated water to shave with. Rockdream and Coral, already dressed in Spirit Swamp clothes beautifully embroidered with fangcat and condor designs, immediately hugged them.

Coral was bubbling over with light. "I think everyone I treated is going to recover, and much sooner than Wedge did. I used the dragon's power in my trances to guide the potency of my drugs, and the results were amazing. Father Condor knew just how much of each herb each person needed, and—"

At that moment the drums suddenly stopped.

"You must get ready," Coral said, handing Periwinkle an embroidered fangcat dress, and Bellchime a condor vest.

"I have to shave," Bellchime said.

"Let me do it," said Periwinkle, with her bodice half-laced. "You always cut yourself when you hurry." She poured some warm water from the jug into her cupped hand, smoothed it onto his stubbled face, and carefully, lovingly, shaved him with her knife. She was just finishing when the horns began to blow.

Soon they joined the large circle of goblins standing in the golden light of sunrise. The shamans continued to blow their auroch horns for some time after it looked like everyone who was coming had arrived. The other goblins would gather grain and kill an auroch bull for the feast that evening; only at times of important ceremonies did goblins take food from the sacred ground.

The horns stopped, Drakey gestured, and everyone else sat down. He welcomed everyone to the council, explained the order of business, and offered prayers and invocations.

Bellchime stood up with his legs slightly apart, his weight evenly balanced, and looked slowly at the entire circle. It numbered almost three hundred people, and at least two out of five were women. He spoke as he had heard other goblin leaders speak, in short firm sentences, with emphatic pauses, about his peace and trade with the Spirit Swamp villages, about his embassy to Upriver and the peace circle with the goblins across the Silver Mountains.

Then other chiefs stood up, one by one, and spoke about their concerns. Two chiefs from neighboring camps on the Bear River had a quarrel about a mammoth herd attacked by hunters from both camps. Only one mammoth was killed, and both chiefs claimed their camps did not get a fair share. Bellchime stood up with his arms crossed, and when they saw him and fell silent, he said, "I thought goblins were not mean-spirited. This sounds like humans in the Upriver Market, haggling over the value of a trade."

This caused much applause and stamping of feet. A weak high chief might have wasted time trying to please these two; an overbearing one, like Strong Bull, would have forced them both to do whatever he himself thought was right; but Bellchime was forcing them to face themselves.

Others stood up to speak, shamans and warriors, about dreams and omens, about successful hunts. One warrior from Redbark's Camp, on the edge of the forest, boasted of tracking and killing a unicorn alone, so great was his stealth, and he proudly held up the horn. Other warriors offered prayers, to spirits of loved ones killed in the war, or to spirits of worthy enemies they had killed, that these spirits would not send new enemies against them.

One of the first women to speak was one of the young women who had teased Bellchime and Periwinkle at the river, without knowing who they were. She tried to make her nervous voice sound strong while saying, "I am Lightstep, and last night Lean Wolf became my husband. I say I am glad Bellchime from Human Camp is high chief, and I welcome all his news of peace. Some may say this is not my concern, but would I not grieve if my husband was killed? Would I not suffer if his heart was hardened by war? Both these things happened to my father. In the name of my own spirit otter, I offer a prayer of thanks for this peace." This was a powerful endorsement, because Lightstep lived at Elkhorn's Camp, and her father was one of the men who died with Strong Bull.

When the council ended, everyone returned to their tents to bring out, display, and exchange the spirit gifts. Bellchime's clothing and pottery were much admired, not only for the fineness of the work, but also as symbols of Bellchime's peace. Before long, many of the important goblins were wearing these clothes.

The hunters returned with an auroch bull, prepared a roast fire, and Distance, finally stirred from her slumber, helped kindle the fire. "You may have a small share of this meat," Periwinkle said to her, "but if you want your usual meal, you will have to catch something else. Go across one of the rivers to do it."

The smell hungers me, she said, and yawning, she stretched her legs and wings and jumped into flight.

44.

The next morning, when people were readying to return to their camps, Distance said that if she had to go back to Spirit Swamp with Coral, she wanted Periwinkle with her also.

You know me best, and understand me when I do not understand myself, she said. *When Coral is healing with me, I need balance*.

Coral had visited two of the villages with Rockdream before the council and wanted to go to the other two now; so she and Periwinkle changed back into leather dresses and packed sleeping furs and medicines. Periwinkle put on her sword, quiver, and bow.

They flew directly west from the sacred ground, over rolling grassland with scattered trees and patches of forest, over a herd of valley mammoths, over flat open marshland with huge flocks of egrets, over the cypresses, rush pines, and willows of the swamp. Nothing looked familiar, though they thought they should be near Loop Lake by now. Distance flew higher to gain perspective, but when she saw what might have been Loop Lake far to the south, she did not turn but instead continued west for about a mile.

I hear people, she said, and Coral and Periwinkle both became aware of pain like many small cuts, of numbness of people wanting to forget they are alive, of anger and grief, strength and determination, and underlying all else, fear.

"You can block this," Coral said to the dragon. "You can listen to it without becoming part of it."

But how? she asked, circling over the dense grove of winter oak and cypress that had to be the source of these emotions.

"You do not feel your own claws and teeth when you bite an animal's neck," Periwinkle said.

Distance's muscles tensed, as though she was about to pounce on something, and the humans' emotions became muted.

That was easy, she said.

"We found a fifth village!" said Periwinkle.

Distance bellowed twice, and said, *The dragon Distance brings ambassadors from Lord Bellchime of Goblin Plain. We have made peace and trade agreements and helped heal swamp sickness in four other Spirit Swamp villages. May we land in peace?*

The responses of the humans below were hard for the dragon to hear clearly, so turbulent were their emotions. Someone seemed to be trying to block the dragon's speech, but a number of others with firm disciplined minds, probably the leaders, agreed that the dragon could land.

"Distance, do you sense any threat?" asked Periwinkle.

Their emotions are murky, but they are willing to talk.

"I think we can chance it," said Coral. "If we do not, we are lowering ourselves to their level of fear."

Periwinkle considered this, but sensed through their mutual link with the dragon how ashamed Coral felt about her own camp's initial reaction to Distance, and decided on caution. "Distance," she said, "wherever they want you to land, land farther away, and take off as soon as I dismount. I will meet them alone. You and Coral stay linked with me, as closely as possible."

Minutes later, Periwinkle was walking toward a thick grove of winter oaks, large, twisted trees with spearpoint-shaped leaves that did not fall off in winter. Beneath these trees, she found a trail leading up a slight slope, but she did not hear the expected sounds of a village.

"Who are you and what do you want?" asked a man's voice, and Periwinkle saw ahead of her a warrior of perhaps thirty summers, dressed in coarse green cloth, holding a sword.

"I am Lady Periwinkle of Goblin Plain, and I want peace. Is it your custom to meet ambassadors with drawn weapons?"

"Whatever else you are, you are a dragonbound witch, and by the laws of our village I could put you to death at once."

"If that is how you feel, why did you tell us to land?"

"If I meant treachery, I would have brought my crossbow, and used it before now," he said. "What did you do, have your dragon burn out every camp on Goblin Plain, and now you come here looking for humans to be your slaves?"

"Nothing at all like that," said Periwinkle. "We are a camp of humans who live the goblin way. My husband was chosen high chief in a fair contest set up by goblin shamans from many camps, and he has sat the peace circle with all the important chiefs and warriors."

"Do you expect me to believe such a preposterous story?"

"Why else would I have a goblin totem painted on my dress? Why do you sneer at everything I say? Can we not speak to each other with honor, as two warriors should?"

"All right, I am Arch of Newport. Show me your mettle with the sword, and if you are a true warrior, I will treat you as one."

"That is a custom that belongs west of the sea, not here."

"Do you accept my challenge or not?"

Periwinkle felt her mother fangcat about to spring, drew her sword, and said, "First blood?"

"First blood," he said, and lunged at Periwinkle. Her sword met his with a clang.

They both parried with the speed of wrestling fangcats. Periwinkle's sword rang like a bell when it nicked the other's edge. The blades locked together. The warriors sprang apart and circled each other. Periwinkle knocked aside a stab that would have cut her throat. Their swords hummed against each other, then suddenly she stopped resisting his pressure, withdrew, and lunged. He recovered his balance just in time to block a cut aimed at his stomach. He was stronger than she was, but not as fast.

"You take your first blood from the throat?" she asked, circling him.

"I take it wherever it flows."

She made a feint from below, withdrew as he moved to block it, and came down hard and suddenly on his sword from above, knocking it out of his hands. She stepped on it with one foot, pointed her own sword at his heart, and said, "Your life is mine."

"I do not think so," said a voice behind her. She snatched up Arch's sword with her left hand and turned to face four men and a woman, all dressed like Arch, all aiming crossbows at her. She felt her mouth go dry and tried to swallow, but did not put down either sword.

"I could have killed him, but did not. He was trying to kill me," she said, feeling the presence of Distance and Coral bring a measure of calmness to her. "I repeat, can we not speak to each other with honor?"

"You are twice our enemy," said the man in the center. "You are a dragon's witch, and you have sided with the goblins."

"I am not dragonbound to Riversong, nor have I fought battles for Strong Bull. You cannot judge me by what they have done."

"How did Strong Bull die?" asked the man.

"I killed him in battle."

"You can kill anyone with a dragon," said Arch.

"She disarmed you in battle, which no one has done since you were a boy," said the woman, whose wavy blonde hair was just beginning to turn gray. "You promised her you would talk to her honorably if she proved herself to you."

"Bronzeberry!" snapped the man in the center.

"This is a woman of honor, Conch, dragonbound witch or no," Bronzeberry said, lowering her weapon. "Arch is right; you can kill anybody with a dragon. Has she once threatened to kill us, even though we are implicitly threatening to kill her? We have tested her enough, I say."

Conch hesitated, then lowered his crossbow, and the others did also. "Well, it is the law of our village that any who find it must be brought to Lord Drill," he said.

"I thought I would be talking with your leader long before this," said Periwinkle.

"Wait!" said the youngest warrior, who still looked like a boy. "I overrule that law! Let her go!"

"You go against your lord's will," said Conch.

"You think he has any will left? In a few days *I* will probably be your lord. Listen to me. Drill may be a frightened fool, but he will not want my head, even if he recovers, which we both know he will not. Do you know how dangerous this woman is? Every word we say, every sight she sees, is known also to her dragon, according to the church."

"What in the world are you afraid of my dragon knowing?" asked Periwinkle. "Where you are? Who you are? That your village is dying of swamp sickness? Distance heard your suffering and we came here to help you. My partner, Coral, is a skilled healer—who sometimes can cure this horrid disease. I cannot understand why six real warriors, under the command of a lord, would treat me with more fear and less reason than a motley group of armed ex-farmers and who-knows-what-else under the command of a fishcatcher. I will see Lord Drill if you want, or I will leave you here and never return if you want. The decision is yours."

"We will take you to Lord Drill," said Conch.

Periwinkle gave Arch back his sword, and they all walked through the forest to the village, where at least thirty houses stood among the trees, which, though no larger than huts, were real half-timber houses complete with curtained windows and little brick chimneys. But though it looked beautiful, the pervading smell was terrible.

They stopped in front of a house slightly larger than the others. Conch and the young man went inside, voices murmured for several minutes, then Conch came back out. "Go in," he said to Periwinkle.

She pulled the curtain away from the doorway and stepped into a dim room that smelled ten times worse than the outside. A man of probably less than forty summers lay in a bed, propped up with pillows. The young warrior kneeled beside him, and a very old woman in red priestess's robes sat on a chair.

The man's voice was harsh and weak. "I am Lord Drill of Newport, you know my son Marten, and this is Mother Mallow."

"I am Lady Periwinkle of Goblin Plain."

"So you say," said Drill. "I mean you no dishonor, but in these times anyone can be an enemy, and I must be suspicious."

"It is a lord's work to judge strangers," said Periwinkle.

Mother Mallow said nothing, but glared at Periwinkle with fierce, deep-set eyes and a wrinkled scowling face, as if she was the worst description of Auroch the Witch come to life.

"You have a good sword," Drill said abruptly. "I had one much like it once, made by Band the Weaponmaker for my father, Lord Herring, when he was a young man. I was the one of his five children who survived Riversong's last attack, but I am no warrior and I gave my sword to Canticle, who was leading the war on Goblin Plain. I know they lost. Some of the survivors came to this place. It was my law that any who come to this village must stay."

"But why?" Periwinkle asked.

"If no one outside this village knows about it, we are safe. Most were glad to live with their lord and his warriors, where it was dry and safe. No more. The sickness and your dragon have both found us."

Drill coughed and wheezed, and Mother Mallow gave him a sip of something steaming.

"We might be able to help you and some of your people," said Periwinkle. "Coral thinks that everyone she treated at Driftwood's Village and Two Willows will recover."

"Coral is the woman riding the dragon," said Marten.

"You told me that," said Drill. "I am only bedridden, not senile." He tensed the muscles in his face, and tried to make his body more comfortable.

"I have looked long enough," said Mother Mallow.

"What do you see?" asked Lord Drill.

The old priestess spoke in monotones as if from a trance. "This woman has a goblin spirit-beast. She has killed people with sword and fire and lightning. She has danced with pooks. She wears a crown on her head."

Periwinkle said, "The people I killed attacked without warning. I had no choice. The rest is true, except the crown, but this says nothing about what kind of person I am."

"With the forces you are using, it hardly matters," Mallow snapped.

"You are a priestess! How can you say that?"

"I became a priestess when I was no older than you, and I have been a priestess for fifty years. The best intentions can lead to thousands of deaths. You use the great powers without the discipline of the church, and your abilities come, not from the Holy Family, but from a dragon and a spirit-beast. Bah!" Mother Mallow made a mystic gesture and turned to Lord Drill, saying, "The crown is on her head, and she already has your sword. Bow down to her or kill her, my lord, it is your choice."

"Bow down to me or kill me?" asked Periwinkle, almost laughing. "My lord, and good mother, I would never ask anyone to bow down to me, nor would my husband, even if we are ever called king and queen of anything. I am first and always a warrior of Windsong's Land, east of the sea, where warriors have honor."

Drill looked at his son and said, "If you were lord of Newport now, what would you do?"

"I would bid this woman begone, and warn her never to return. I told you why before."

Drill sighed a sigh that turned into a wheeze. "Can you prophesy?"

The old woman pursed her lips a few times, then said, "I cannot guide you beyond what I have said."

"Well, Marten, you will be lord of Newport soon—"

"My lord, please let us try to save your life and health," said Periwinkle.

Mallow said, "I am a priestess who knows things, and I know more than any witch. Your life cannot be saved."

"What would Wentletrap say if he knew his great-grandson let himself be condemned to death by a frightened priestess?" asked Periwinkle.

Lord Drill closed his eyes and said, "It shall be as you wish, Lord Marten."

Marten said, "I hereby exile you from all land belonging to the Lord of Newport, from this day until your death—" but Periwinkle had already walked out of the house in disgust. Conch and Bronzeberry led her out of the village.

"My lady—" said Bronzeberry.

Periwinkle turned to look at her.

"I wish you well," Bronzeberry said.

"Thank you," she said and turned to leave.

"Take me with you."

Conch said, "Bronzeberry, you cannot—"

"If she can leave, I can leave. This is not your concern."

"Come," said Periwinkle, smiling, and Conch turned away from the two women walking through the oak grove, toward Distance and Coral, who were waiting.

►11◄

HARD WORDS
TO CONSIDER

45.

A few days past the second full moon of summer, Heroncry and Froth were riding the road through Upriver's farmlands toward the city gate, glad to be done with farmer's work at last. Their unsuccessful attack on the dragon's den had led to a peace circle between High Chief Stormbringer of Oak Lake and Tarragon of the keep, which in turn led to trade agreements and farmland established outside the keep walls, which was what kept everybody busy.

It was hot, and Froth was slouched in his saddle, talking about buying the favors of a barmaid. "The Blue River Inn has the best ones," he said. "These women do the most wonderful things for you."

Heroncry was at odds with his wife and both his mistresses, and not interested. "How can I think of women when my sweat smells like horse droppings?"

"So let the ladies bathe you first."

"Blue River Inn? Is that not where Bellchime was when— "

"Yes," Froth said, chuckling. "He liked the women there as well as I, before he took a fancy to our lord's young daughter."

"I would not joke about it," said Heroncry. "I worry about what may have happened to her."

"Bah! You worry about anyone who is young and pretty. If her father and mother do not care, why should we?"

"You think they do not care because they let Periwinkle make her choice? Not at all! They accepted her decision with love, though it grieved them."

"It is all words," said Froth. "The truth is that we lost their daughter and doubled their farmland and got paid well for our trouble, and now that I am finally free of service for a while, I am looking forward to enjoying the best lovemaking money can buy."

"Sometimes your bitter-mindedness disgusts me."

"I call it being practical and realistic."

Heroncry hesitated before saying, "Froth, your biggest blind spot is love. You do not like to admit that it is a big part of why people do what they do, much less that it is a big part of yourself. You ought to get yourself a new wife and forget the one Riversong killed."

"I could never forget her!" Froth said, shocked at Heroncry's outburst.

"I did not mean forget her exactly, but it was twenty years ago, and life does go on. You know, before we went on that quest chasing Periwinkle, I thought you were a bloody fool, ranting and raving about dragons and dragonbound wizards, but you do have power and wisdom. Was it the baby son you lost? You are young enough to father others, and now we have more land to support more people at the keep."

Heroncry shrugged and stopped talking, realizing that Froth was ignoring him. After a couple of turns of the road, Froth said, "You give me hard words to consider, when tonight all I want is a good time."

"We could both have lighter hearts," said Heroncry.

Ahead of them, beyond the paired statues of seated warriors, the main gates of the city were open, and three armed guards, a woman and two men, stood in the road.

"We are Heroncry and Froth of Lord Tarragon's Keep," said Heroncry.

"Lord Tarragon?" asked one of the men.

"He is entitled to be called a lord, sir," said Heroncry. "Have you not heard that Upriver no longer has the only unwalled farmlands east of the mountains? Have you not heard of the peace of Tarragon and Stormbringer?"

"Peace, not truce?" asked the woman.

"Yes. May we pass?" asked Heroncry.

"We have orders from Lord Blackwood that any warriors from Tarragon's—I beg your pardon—*Lord* Tarragon's Keep, and most especially any man named Froth, is to be brought into his presence at once," said the man who had spoken before.

"I will take them," said the woman. "Follow me." She walked through the gate, and around to a small fenced enclosure with three horses inside, led one of the horses out, and mounted him.

"May we ask what this is all about?" asked Froth.

"You may, but I do not know. I am only a guard. You may call me Iris if you like."

"More refugees here than last year," said Heroncry, looking at the shacks crowded beneath the city wall.

"I am a refugee myself, or was," said Iris. "Now I have a horse and a suite in a real house. So will all the others within three years."

Iris led the two men up Street of the Church to Street of the Castle, which led straight uphill to the fortress. Four great stone towers faced the city, and behind these, four taller towers, though all of these except the famous watchtower sank below the outer wall as they rode closer. The stones were large, and very tightly fit together, and whitewashed with lime.

The lesser gate was open and guarded by one woman. Iris announced herself and the men by name.

"To see Lord Blackwood?" asked the guard. "I think he is in the audience room. Leave your horses here; I will have a servant take them to the stables. Shall I have another guard sent to Northgate?"

"Yes, that would be best," said Iris.

The servant led the horses away, and Iris, Froth, and Heroncry crossed the courtyard to the inner gate.

"The people Lord Blackwood wished to see from Tarragon's Keep are here, Froth and the warrior Heroncry," Iris said to the guardsman at the inner gate.

"He is in the audience room, speaking to the master builders about the new city wall."

"Send a message," said Iris. "He asked for these people more than a month ago, and I am not sure how important they are to him now."

"I will do that," he said, dispatching a message boy. "You

would think some warrior from Tarragon's Keep would have come here long before now."

"None who declared themselves such," said Iris.

"We have all been much too busy to travel," said Heroncry, sharing an expression of mock-weariness with Froth.

Iris said, "They are calling Tarragon a lord, and they say they have peace with the goblins and farms outside their walls."

"I would not spread that news around here," the guardsman said to Heroncry and Froth, "or you will be flooded with rabble from Newport."

"And what do you think I am?" demanded Iris.

"I said rabble, not warriors or guards, my lady."

The messenger returned, panting for breath. "Lord Blackwood will see them at once, sir and lady."

"This way," said Iris, leading the two men across the inner courtyard to one of the tower doors, and up a flight of dimly lit stairs to the door of a room where stood yet another guard.

"I will tell Lord Blackwood you are here," she told Iris.

The guard returned with Lord Blackwood himself, a tall, older man with short gray hair, dressed in a brightly colored silk shirt and trousers, but bearing himself like a warrior in rough leather.

"Froth and Heroncry of Tarragon's Keep?" he asked.

"We call it Lord Tarragon's Keep, now, my lord," said Heroncry.

"Hmmph," said Lord Blackwood. "Take them up to my private conference room. It seems I am now surrounded by other lords."

Iris led the men upstairs to a small room with velvet chairs. Lord Blackwood entered a few minutes later and ordered Iris to leave. She bowed and closed the door behind her.

"Be seated," said Lord Blackwood. "Had I known it would be a month before any warrior from Lord Tarragon's Castle would show up at the city gates, I would have sent a messenger."

"May we ask—" began Froth.

"What this is all about? An ex-storyteller named Bellchime, of course. He has somehow become Lord of Goblin Plain, and earlier this summer he sent me an embassy of three, a human couple and a goblin man, to tell me that his people would welcome any human settlers to Goblin Plain who would be willing to do something called 'sit the peace circle'."

"We ourselves have sat a peace circle, at Oak Lake," said Heroncry.

"This is unbelievable," said Froth.

"How so?" asked Heroncry. "Bellchime lived with the Oak Lake goblins long enough to learn their ways."

"He was barely tolerated, and far from being their lord."

"On Goblin Plain, he is lord," said Lord Blackwood. "My first question was, what happened to Strong Bull, the old lord goblin? The messengers said he was killed by the new lord's wife, with an enchanted sword or some such nonsense."

"Sounds like Periwinkle," said Heroncry.

"And you thought she was way out on the Isle of Hod," said Froth. "We heard from a Coveport merchant that there is a young blue dragon there, but I was certain it must be a different dragon."

"I have heard all the trader's tales from Swordwall to Southport and beyond: the Isle of Hod, Newport, Moonport, and Goblin Plain have dragons. Some say the Moonport dragon is old Redmoon from Southport, but all agree that she is a sizable rust-colored female. I learned about Bellchime's dragon from his own messengers. The human woman even had the insolence to remind me that a lord may make the law for his own realm. What I must know is, what kind of person is this Bellchime? Should a lord who keeps a dragon be permitted to be a lord? I cannot easily go to war against a lord who has conquered, by whatever means, a people who themselves have just won a most bloody war against—well—what have now become some of my own people."

"If Bellchime has brought peace to Goblin Plain, you should thank him," said Heroncry. "Send him a bloody ambassador and be done with it. Send him a bunch of settlers, too, if any will go."

"You think so?" asked Froth.

"Sounds to me like Periwinkle picked herself a better man than any of us knew," replied Heroncry. "I used to find myself sitting and listening to some of Bellchime's stories. He was a bright young man, and at times he would challenge the children with the wildest ideas and ask them what they thought. Periwinkle loved him as a child, and continued to love him after he disappeared. She grew up to be an excellent warrior, with both heart and spunk. If any people I have ever heard about could manage a dragon, those two could."

"It has never been done," said Lord Blackwood.

"Which does not prove it cannot be done," said Heroncry. "Perhaps they have learned something from the goblins. You never hear of goblins getting dragonbound."

"You are wrong about that," said Lord Blackwood. "Far to the south where the goblins have an empire, with cities, farms and all, they have a whole dragonbound priesthood, and sacrifice their own people every day to the dragons."

"You believe that sailor's tale?" scoffed Heroncry.

"I have heard it often enough to be convinced there is something to it," said Lord Blackwood, "enough times to worry about something similar happening on Goblin Plain."

"Blood!" said Froth. "In my worst fears I never imagined—"

"Oh, Froth!" Heroncry said with exasperation. "No self-respecting goblin would do anything of the sort and you know it. Let us forget what sailors tell credulous homefolk about far-off lands and deal with what we know. Goblins around here never get dragonbound. Why not?"

After a moment of thought, Froth said, "Spirit-beasts."

"What do totem poles and mythical ancestors have to do with it?" Lord Blackwood asked impatiently.

"Spirit-beasts are a power of the mind," Froth explained. "I was attacked by a shaman's spirit fangcat when I tried to probe his mind. I was rolling on the floor in agony wrestling with it and blacked out. Could a drangonling bind a person protected by something like that? I doubt it."

"Sounds as unlikely as the misfortunes some of the Newport people attribute to a broken peace circle," said Lord Blackwood.

"A peace circle is an agreement of spirit-beasts to have peace, and I can well believe that a curse would fall on anyone who broke such an agreement," said Froth.

"How can I judge what is real sorcery and what is superstition when it all sounds like nonsense to me?" demanded Lord Blackwood. "I have a dragonbound lord next door and a people with no heart to fight. But you favor me keeping a truce with Bellchime, dragon or no?" he asked Heroncry.

"Yes, of course."

"I cannot say yes or no," said Froth. "I do not know enough about this man to judge him. For almost five years I have tried to kill him, or make others kill him, and now I think I may have been wrong."

"Certainly Lord Tarragon would oppose a war with Bellchime," said Heroncry.

"What concern would it be of his?" asked Lord Blackwood.

"Why, Bellchime's wife, Periwinkle, is his daughter," replied Heroncry.

Lord Blackwood looked momentarily stunned. "Bloody death, of course! I knew I heard that name before somewhere, the moment I found out he married her in the church. The priest refused to tell me anything about them, but I learned from the record that Periwinkle was a warrior. I saw her the last time Tarragon came here. She was just a little girl—"

"She is sixteen now, my lord," said Heroncry.

"So she fell in love with this dragonbound storyteller wizard, and now she has married him and they have their own realm," said Lord Blackwood. "Dare we wish they live happily ever after?"

"Bah!" said Froth. "This is no old legend."

"Sounds like one to me," said Heroncry.

"I must return to my master-builders," said Lord Blackwood. "I wish I could be certain we are not putting all this effort into building up the city, only to have it smashed and burned by some bloody backstabbing dragon! But no one can guarantee that. I will send Lord Bellchime an embassy and hope for the best."

The Lord of Upriver stood up, gave Heroncry and Froth the slightest nod, and walked out the door.

"We ride back to Tarragon tomorrow with this news," said Heroncry.

"You ride back," said Froth while they walked down the tower stairs. "I am staying in Upriver for awhile."

"Suit yourself. I will take the reward."

"What good is a reward if you never take the time to spend it properly?"

"Improperly, you mean."

"Indeed," laughed Froth.

46.

Not too early one morning, about a week later, Lord Tarragon and Lady Black Rose walked into the common room of the Blue River Inn, and asked the innkeeper, Stout, whether he had a guest named Froth.

"May I ask who wants to see him, my lord? He asked not to be disturbed, and he is a good patron."

"Why, Lord Tarragon of Indigo and Lady Black Rose," said Tarragon.

"Oh, my lord, you honor us. Allow me to serve you myself," Stout said, walking into the kitchen. "These rolls are fresh from the oven, sweetened with the best honey and spiced with cinnamon from overseas, which is hard to obtain these days."

"They smell delicious," said Black Rose, picking one up and nodding her head as she bit into it. "Why, these are better than the rolls we had at the castle last night."

"You are kind, my lady," said Stout.

"They are good," said Tarragon.

"I will call for Froth," said Stout and hurried down the hall to room seven. He put his ear to the door, and not hearing any sounds, he knocked a certain pattern.

"What is it?" asked a woman's voice.

"Trillium?" asked the innkeeper. "I thought Feather was with Froth last night."

"You want me?" asked Feather's voice. "I am here, too."

"I want Froth, or rather, the lord Tarragon does."

"Wake up, dear," said Trillium. "Serious business."

"What is it?" grunted Froth.

"Lord Tarragon wants to see you," said Trillium.

"That you at the door, Stout?" asked Froth.

"Indeed."

"Give me some moments to get up, but tell him I am coming," said Froth. "I wonder what he wants," he muttered as he got out of bed and dressed.

"Hey, it was fun," said Feather as she pulled on a loose robe.

"We should do this again," said Trillium. "You can afford it, Froth."

"Perhaps someday," he said with a forced smile as he walked out the door.

"Stop being so bloody sad all the time," Feather called after him.

Froth came into the common room and saw Tarragon and Black Rose sitting at a table set for three, drinking brew and talking about Goblin Plain.

"You are not planning to go there yet, are you?" asked Froth. "Lord Blackwood's embassy only left two days ago."

"Bloody right I am going there now. My daughter is there, and doing something important with her husband and that dragon."

"I do not think I want to ask what this has to do with me," said Froth.

"We want you to come with us, of course," said Black Rose. "Your experience with dragons may be valuable."

Froth sighed. "I suppose I can hardly refuse."

"Finish your breakfast and we will charter a boat," said Tarragon.

An hour later at the harbor, the portmaster refused them. "I will not charter any of my boats to Goblin Plain or anywhere beyond Fallow's Keep until I have word from Lord Blackwood's embassy. I know they say there is peace on Goblin Plain now, but who can believe anything you hear from that place? You want to take a boat to Goblin Plain, you must buy it, and provide your own crew."

"Can we sell it back to you if we return it?" asked Tarragon.

"I would say so, yes, but have you the cash to buy it?"

"You demand cash from the Lord of Indigo?"

"Is that what you call your keep now? I demanded cash from the Lord of Upriver two days ago when he sent off his embassy, and he did not question my right to do so. Look, there is a small boat will get you to Fallow's Keep and through the gorge. For twenty-five starmarks, it is yours."

"Blood!" said Froth. "Any shipwright in Midcoast would sell a boat like that for fifteen starmarks new."

"You a fishcatcher?" the portmaster asked Froth.

"Years ago," said Froth. "I am Lord Tarragon's wizard and storyteller now."

The portmaster frowned at this. "In the early days of Upriver, a man who called himself a wizard would get stoned to death."

"In the early days of Upriver, a warrior like me would draw his sword and take your bloody boat if he had a need for it," said Tarragon.

"A wizard is not that different from a fishcatcher," said Froth. "Both occupations require a sensitivity to the unseen."

"I will offer twelve starmarks cash for that boat," said Tarragon.

"My lord, you must understand the labor situation in Upriver," the portmaster pleaded. "With all the clearing and building work being done, even with all the new people, I have to pay extra for laborers. It would cost me at least thirty-five starmarks to build a boat to replace that one."

"That might be," admitted Tarragon, "but would you replace it? Your harbor is full of boats with nowhere to go."

"All right, twenty starmarks."

"I can either give you eighteen starmarks cash or ten starmarks cash, ten promised. My fortune is farther away from here than Lord Blackwood's."

The portmaster struck his left palm with his right fist a couple of times, then said, "Eighteen cash."

Tarragon counted out ten gold coins, then looked at Black Rose, and she reached into her pouch and counted out eight coins, and the portmaster gave Tarragon the papers.

"I hope some of the servants you brought along have sailing experience," said Froth.

"Old Sedge used to be a fishcatcher like you, and Muffin piloted a cargo boat on the Bigfish," said Tarragon. "They are buying provisions and should be here soon."

Not much later, Muffin, Sedge, and two other servants, all wearing heavy packs, walked through the smaller gate between the market and the docks.

"Sorry we took so long," said Muffin, hunching her shoulders. "Did you charter a boat?"

"He bought one," said Black Rose. "You and Sedge and Froth are the crew."

"We will probably all have to do some hard rowing on the way back," said Muffin.

"Black Rose and I will do our part," said Tarragon.

They boarded the boat, a one-masted rivercraft named *Pook-of-the-Silver*, and stowed their packs.

"Looks like a fine boat to me," Sedge said, examining the rigging and sails. "What did it cost him?" he asked Froth in a low voice.

"Eighteen starmarks."

"Humph," said Sedge. "It may be worth that much, but I cannot say before we sail it."

"The portmaster wanted twenty-five for it," said Froth.

Muffin laughed. "Well, I would ask twenty-five for it, too, if I was selling it. A fool might pay me so much."

"I see ten oars and seven people," said Tarragon. "Do we need more crew?"

"The river is down," said Muffin. "It will be hard work coming back against the current unless the wind blows from the south or west, but we can do it. Take the first, third, and fifth oars on each side and stow the others."

"Are you to be our captain?"

"I did not mean to be presumptuous, my lord," said Muffin.

"She has the experience with rivercraft," said Sedge, and Froth reluctantly agreed.

"This drum," Muffin said, striking the smaller drum, "is for your side and this," she struck the larger, "is yours. Mostly you will all row at once, but when we turn—you understand. Once we reach the channel, Froth and Sedge and I will raise sails. The wind is from the west. You ready to cast off, Froth?"

"Aye, aye."

Muffin beat the drums and they rowed out to the middle of the river and set the sails, and the *Pook-of-the-Silver* took off down the Blue River as if it were flying. Before long, they left the city walls behind, then the farmlands, and the forest darkened both banks.

As the hours passed, the river sank deeper and deeper into the landscape. The Silver Mountains, at first a snow-crested skyline above the west bank, sank below a line of oaks and maples topping a cliff. By the time they sighted the walls and towers of Fallow's Keep, the cliffs on both shores were almost two hundred feet high.

Beyond Fallow's Keep, the wind died, and the *Pook-of-the-Silver* drifted with the current. Rowing might have tripled its speed, but the relentless summer sun that afternoon would have discouraged any captain and crew from rowing.

Evening came, and a flock of white cranes flew overhead; then night, and the seven humans slept in shifts while nightjumper salmon splashed upstream and stars crossed the sky.

At dawn a strong wind began blowing from the south, slowing the boat even more until they began to row. Like a slow heartbeat the drums continued for most of the morning till the wind slackened, then they stopped rowing and drifted through the heat of the day, more rapidly than the day before because the river was now narrower and stronger. When the cliffs became a third as high as the river's width, mountain peaks, gray and jagged, loomed above them. They passed the side-valley of the Pass River, and continued through current which, though far from being white-water, was swifter than seven people would want to row against for very long.

"Or ten people either," said Muffin. "But the wind is strong from the south again, and if the sails were set, we could go upstream easily enough."

Quite suddenly the cliffs stopped, the current slowed, and the *Pook-of-the-Silver* was drifting down the Blue River through Goblin Plain, the sun already low over the high green and golden grass. They did not go much farther before encountering a boarding party of goblins, on unsinkable rafts made from bundled reeds.

"Throw down your weapons if you come in peace; if you do not come in peace you are dead," said the goblins' leader.

Tarragon and Black Rose set down their swords and bows.

"You are human. You must sit the peace circle with the high chief or leave Goblin Plain at once."

"The high chief is who we came to see," said Tarragon. "I am Lord Tarragon of Indigo, and father of his wife."

The goblin leader nodded slightly, turned his head to confer with two other warriors, then said, "The high chief sits the peace circle with the Upriver embassy. I am Chief Elkhorn. You will stay at my camp and we will send the smoke message at once."

Tarragon and his retinue rowed the *Pook-of-the-Silver* to the edge of the river, anchored it, went ashore on the goblins' reed rafts, and walked the trail through the high grass to Elkhorn's Camp. Already the women were making the fire smoky with green reeds, and covering and uncovering it with a wet deerhide to make a series of timed puffs.

"I do not know if this will relay to the high chief before dark," said Elkhorn. "He will probably come tomorrow."

Far in the distance, another series of puffs of smoke from the next camp relayed the message.

"What did that message actually say?" asked Froth.

"Stranger, peace circle, Elkhorn's Camp, now," said Elkhorn. "A smoke message has four parts, who, what, where, and when. Bellchime will know what we mean."

Elkhorn's wife, Shellfly, offered the humans some mammoth stew from a heavy bronze cauldron of Newport make, and they sat with a number of goblins around the cookfire awning, listening to stories such as how Mother Fangcat taught goblins to hunt mammoth, and how Grandfather Weasel stole fire from the dragons and gave it to the goblins.

"I am a son of Grandfather Weasel," said Froth.

"Where did you learn this?" asked Split Hoof, the shaman.

"From a shaman named Drum, near Blue Dragonstone Mountain," said Froth, and he explained where this was.

Elkhorn abruptly said, "Bellchime did get the message."

"I see the dragon also," said Split Hoof, pointing to a dark shape flapping rapidly toward them against the stars. "She will speak in your minds like a god," he told the humans.

Froth could not keep his eyes off the dragon, deep lustrous gray in the firelight, a man and woman riding her back. The dragon swooped low over the fire and bellowed.

"Distance, land," said the woman.

This man is my death, boomed the dragon's voice in everyone's mind. Froth got up and ran wildly through the grass toward the river, and two huge talons grabbed him from behind and above.

"Distance, stop!" screamed the woman. "Put him down!"

The dragon picked Froth about two feet off the ground, dropped him, and then landed. Froth lay unconscious on the trail.

"What did you mean by that?" the man angrily asked Distance as he dismounted and stooped to examine the fallen man.

He is my death, the dragon said with fear.

While humans and goblins gathered around the scene, Tarragon and Black Rose asked the man and woman, "Who are you?"

"I am Chief Rockdream."

"I am Coral. You look much like Periwinkle," she said to Black Rose. "Are you her mother?"

"Who is this man?" Rockdream asked Tarragon.

The wizard Froth, said Distance.

"We came here to sit the peace circle," said Tarragon.

"We have heard about Froth," said Coral, and she asked Distance, "Does he still want to kill you?"

His only thought was fear.

Froth opened his eyes and looked at the dragon, who was at least as large as a great elk and much longer, because of her tail. The young man and woman standing in front of her were clearly not Bellchime and Periwinkle.

"Dragon, I do not even know you," said Froth.

You drove me from my den. You hunted me for four years. Do you want a weapon? Do you want to kill me?

"No, no, I do not want to kill you," said Froth, trying to calm both himself and the dragon. She seemed well under the control of the young wizard and witch, whoever they were, and probably would not attack unless he directly provoked her.

I want to kill you, said Distance.

Froth opened and closed his mouth but could not speak.

"Why do you want to kill him?" Coral asked quietly.

Would you not want to kill your death?

"How is he your death? He is terrified of you."

I do not know how to explain. What is now and what is far from now are not the same for me as for you. Far away from now he is my death.

"You mean you foresee the future?" asked Coral.

It will change if he dies now. It will be better.

"What—what will I do?" stammered Froth. "Tell—tell me and I will do something different."

I do not know. This hurts me. Coral and Rockdream do not understand. They will be sad and unable to dance if I kill you.

To his surprise, Froth found his eyes crying in the deep pool of dragon emotions, and he said, "I understand. I understand how people can love a dragon. I would give you the gold and jewels you deserve if I had them. I do not want you to die. I see—"

Stop, said Distance, taking a few steps backward and shutting off her emotions suddenly and completely.

Rockdream looked at Coral, at the dragon, at Froth, at Tarragon, Black Rose, and Elkhorn. "We came here tonight because Periwinkle guessed her parents might have sent an embassy. Bellchime and she sat a peace circle today with the Upriver people, who mentioned that Lord Blackwood had spoken with people from her father's keep. We welcome you to Goblin Plain. Come down the river to Human Camp."

I want to fly back to Periwinkle, said Distance.

"All right," said Coral. "Excuse us, please," she said to Elkhorn, Split Hoof, and the goblin warriors.

Elkhorn frowned, but said he understood. After Coral and Rockdream mounted the dragon's shoulders, she flapped her wings several times and jumped into flight.

Froth staggered to his feet and dusted himself off. "What do you make of that?" he asked Tarragon.

"You are the one who presumes to know about dragons."

"Could I stay here?" Froth asked Elkhorn. "I will leave Goblin Plain with the first boat to Upriver and never return."

"If you refuse to go with Tarragon and make peace with Bellchime, I must take the dragon's word and kill you as an enemy," said Elkhorn.

"Bloody death, Tarragon, what can I do now?" asked Froth. "I knew I should have stayed in Upriver."

"You made yourself the dragon's enemy," said Black Rose.

"That is not why she wants to kill me," said Froth.

"Enough talk," said Elkhorn. "Back to your boat, all you humans. If any other goblins stop you, tell them Chief Elkhorn and Rockdream said you must go to Human Camp."

Soon after that, Sedge pulled the anchor and Muffin steered the *Pook-of-the-Silver* into the middle of the slow starlit river.

~12~

FIRE AND TEETH

47.

Periwinkle woke with a shudder to the tent's inside darkness and the warm smell of Bellchime beside her.

"Periwinkle?" he asked.

"Distance is coming back tonight," she said. "There was trouble. She is frightened but unhurt."

"Distance, can you talk to us from where you are?" asked Bellchime, but the dragon gave no response.

"I think I am the one she wants," said Periwinkle, fumbling with her skirts in the dark.

"I knew we should have gone ourselves," said Bellchime. "If Froth is one of the people who came—"

"You are lord of one of the largest realms east of the sea, and sending my parents' embassy a messenger was the proper thing to do; it was more than we did for the Upriver people. Coral can manage Distance as well as either of us."

"Perhaps not as well as we both together."

Bellchime dressed and they stepped outside.

"I am still not used to all the new tents," said Periwinkle. Human Camp had tripled in size since the Midsummer Council. It now had twenty-eight tents, and there was talk about more people coming from Spirit Swamp before summer's end.

"Before long we will have to have another human camp," said Bellchime.

"Where?"

"I think in the Gray Hills where we camped with Hope that night. If we dig a well where the ferns grow at the foot of the hill, the camp would not need to haul water from the river. Distance says the hunting is good there. Bloodroot and Salmon could lead the camp."

"Would they want to, with a newborn baby? Salmon is due in a few months."

"You just do not want our friends to move away," said Bellchime, "and we must consider that."

"This camp can sit a council when we need to decide these things," said Periwinkle.

A newer, much larger, but still unfinished totem pole, made from a Spirit Swamp cypress tree, lay at the foot of the original pole, where Feathergrass was standing guard.

"Who is there?" he demanded.

"Periwinkle and Bellchime."

"Distance must be coming back tonight."

"Yes," said Periwinkle, sitting down with Bellchime at the foot of the old totem pole.

"I welcome your company," said Feathergrass. "With nothing to do but listen for intruders who do not come, my mind has been racing like spawning nightjumpers. But I am forgetting who you are."

Bellchime said, "I may be high chief, but I am also, I hope, your friend, and we have nothing to do but wait. What troubles you?"

"Nothing troubles me exactly," Feathergrass said with a sigh.

"What troubles you inexactly then?" asked Periwinkle. "Or should I say who?"

"Has she talked with you about me?"

"She seems confused," said Periwinkle. "Maybe if you give her more time—"

"Are you talking about Hope?" asked Bellchime.

"Who else?" said Periwinkle.

"Sometimes waiting is hard," said Feathergrass. "The other night she kissed me—"

"Distance comes," said Bellchime.

"I see her," said Periwinkle.

From the east, over the dark river winding through starlit grassland, the dragon flew toward them, Coral and Rockdream riding her shoulders. She flapped her wings forward and landed quietly.

Only Periwinkle, said Distance in their minds.

"What could you possibly have to say to me that the others should not hear?"

"She was very upset about Froth," Coral said after dismounting. "She kept saying that he was her death and she wanted to kill him."

"Distance, why?" asked Periwinkle.

Come ride me, she said.

"It sounded like a foretelling of the future to me," said Coral.

Coral, please! said Distance.

"Feathergrass, swear secrecy," said Periwinkle.

"I swear, but I wonder what this is all about."

"So do we," said Bellchime, "but it is not your concern."

"One way to find out," Periwinkle said. She kissed Bellchime, mounted the dragon, and Distance leaped into flight. The ground fell away, and the midnight air felt cold on Periwinkle's bare arms and legs.

"So what is this all about?" she asked when they were some distance from camp.

I do not know, but I hope you will understand.

"I will understand more if you pull your own fear out of my mind. I almost feel like hiding in a cave or a deep grove of trees."

So do I, said Distance, flying over the Blue River and south toward the Gray Hills. At the edge of an oak grove in a valley she landed, and walked beneath a canopy of leaves that hid nearly all the stars, where cicadas trilled and glowflies flashed.

Periwinkle laughed. "Do you feel safe enough to talk now? No one anywhere on the world could possibly hear us over all this racket!"

I wish I knew what I was talking about, said Distance.

"What can make a firebreathing dragon run and hide?" asked Periwinkle. "Only a powerful army, a mighty wizard, or a stronger dragon, as far as I know. Which is it?"

Fire and teeth.

"What does Froth have to do with it?"

I do not know.

"We cannot kill a person just to prevent a foretelling coming true. History is filled with examples—"

I must kill him but I cannot, Distance said with despair.

"I think we need him alive to find out what he knows about all this," said Periwinkle. "It is much easier to change a foretold future when you let enough of it come true to understand the pattern. If you panic at the first vision of disaster, all too often you help it come true."

I need you to dance for me, said Distance. *Dance something filled with life and hope.*

Periwinkle dismounted and looked at the dark shape of Distance's head. "I can hardly see my feet, let alone the ground," she said, "but I will do my best." She began a light-stepping pookish dance to joy, chasing glowflies and catching them in her cupped hands, and singing,

> What is born in a hole,
> dances in the woods,
> laughs at the stars?
> Pook, pook!
>
> What lives in a hole,
> sings in the woods,
> plays flute to the stars?
> Pook, pook!
>
> What sleeps in a hole,
> makes love in the woods,
> sings to the stars?
> Pook, pook!

When she stopped dancing, she looked around, half-expecting to see little furry pooks dancing with her.

They never come when I am awake, said Distance.

"Can you take me home to bed, and can we face tomorrow tomorrow?"

I feel much better, said the dragon as Periwinkle mounted. They flew home to find Feathergrass alone at the totem pole. "You may go," said Periwinkle. "Distance will be here the rest of the night."

"Thank you, my lady!" he said with enthusiasm she did not expect. "Tell your husband you told me so."

"All right," said Periwinkle, wondering what was going on. She walked back to her tent, undressed, and crawled into bed beside Bellchime. "Distance took over the guard from Feathergrass."

Bellchime groaned, then startled awake and said, "What? Oh, but you did not know."

"Did not know what?"

"Hope came to visit him while he was on duty, not knowing I was also there. She gave me some story about being unable to sleep, but I know a lovers' meeting when I see one. You cannot listen for intruders and make love at the same time."

"I think that is wonderful news. I hope he went straight to her tent. They have so much to offer each other."

Bellchime sighed. "Attacks always come when the guards are distracted."

"We have much to offer each other, too," Periwinkle said, lightly nibbling Bellchime's lips and running her free hand down his chest and stomach.

"Were you doing pook dances?" asked Bellchime, sliding his own free hand from her shoulder to her breast.

"Yes—" she said and kissed him again, opening her legs and maneuvering his erection inside. She rolled on top of him, swirled her hips and brushed her long hair across his face, gasping for breath at the wild tingling, the moment of merging, the river of fluids.

"I want more," said Bellchime.

She rolled under him, saying, "We should get woken up in the middle of the night more often. This is wonderful!"

The sky outside their tent was already lightening toward dawn by the time they fell asleep again.

48.

It was afternoon when Periwinkle woke up drenched with sweat and hurriedly opened the door and all the flaps to the tent before pulling on her cloth dress. Bellchime was at the cookfire in the center of camp, talking to the four Upriver ambassadors about the advantages of living in tents.

"Just wait till winter; you will wish you had a castle around you," said one of the men.

"Excuse me," Bellchime said when he saw Periwinkle.

"Tents are much nicer to live in when your husband remembers to open the flaps on a hot day," she said.

"I am sorry; it was cold when I got up," said Bellchime. "Have you eaten? Have some stew; we should go soon."

"Hot food has no appeal to me right now. I will have a leftover roll instead. What I really want to do is swim in the river."

"The sooner we meet Froth, the better," said Bellchime.

"Let me get my roll, and I will eat it on the way."

Bellchime left the ambassadors talking to a number of humans of the camp and two goblins from Gorge's Camp, and then mounted Distance.

"I notice Hope's tent is still shut against the cold of night," said Periwinkle, munching her roll and mounting the dragon.

I feel right about this, said Distance, and she jumped into flying, flapped to a good height, and soared upriver toward the Silver Mountains.

The Blue River did look bright blue that day, with gray beaches or green patches of reeds, and leather canoes or reed rafts of goblins fishing here and there. To either side, the grasslands with patches of oak trees slowly changed to rolling hills. They passed Gorge's Camp, and Beartooth's Camp, and saw a wooden riverboat coming down the river.

Distance slightly folded her wings to swoop toward the boat, saying, *Come to shore. We are here to sit the peace circle.*

"Drop anchor," said Muffin. "Lower the skiff."

In two trips the crew of seven went ashore and pulled the skiff up on the beach.

"Mother! Father!" said Periwinkle, dismounting and running toward Black Rose and Tarragon.

"You come unarmed?" asked Tarragon.

"This is a peace mission, I know who you are, and I did bring my dragon," said Periwinkle.

"Hmm, yes," said Tarragon, looking thoughtfully at Distance. Bellchime walked up to the group and nodded slightly. Froth looked very uncomfortable. "Shall we begin?" said Bellchime. "Form a circle," he said, taking Periwinkle's and Sedge's hands. "Be seated. We all know each other. I am Lord of Goblin Plain, where it is now law that any humans who come to Goblin Plain must sit the peace circle with me. I must warn you that if you have warlike intentions toward me or my realm, this circle may kill you. I have seen it happen."

"I believe you, my lord," said Froth. "But what of your dragon?"

"If you make peace with us through the circle, you make peace with Distance," said Bellchime. "Both Periwinkle and I are dragonbound to her."

"Distance," whispered Froth, as if considering the name.

"Close your eyes and try to imagine a circle of energy connecting us together. What we will be trying to do is make that stream a fine, intensely blue spider's thread."

When Bellchime closed his eyes, the loop of energy he saw as a fairly fine cord, but it was not a closed circle and no pulses of energy moved along it.

He opened his eyes to make certain everyone's hands were still clasped, and said, "We do not have a circle. Let the flow of power be a broad river if necessary, but close the circle."

He shut his eyes again and saw the energy like the great loop of a river that almost closes on itself. There were no spirit-beasts to be seen. He finally found his own father condor flying high above the river, lost. "What do I do, Father?" he asked silently, then knew that Froth was the leak in the circle.

"Froth," he said gently, "what are you doing to the circle?"

"I do not know," said Froth. "I sat two peace circles at Blue Dragonstone Mountain and Oak Lake and nothing like this happened."

"Bring your mind into the circle, totally into the circle," said Bellchime. This time when he closed his eyes he saw Periwinkle's mother fangcat, and Tarragon's bear. With some difficulty they floated around the bend of the river, crossed the neck of land, and floated around the bend again.

I think I can help, said Distance. The majestic dragon self that she always was in trance came around the river loop and began digging a channel across the narrow neck of land. Some of the spirit-beasts, especially the bears and fangcats, helped dig. There were in the end the spirit-beasts of everyone in the circle, plus Rockdream's fangcat and Coral's condor. The condors, including his own, seemed to be high above the river bend, watching for something.

A trickle of water passed across the neck of land, then a broad stream, and the circle was completed. The rest of the river disappeared, and the circle collapsed to a fine spider's thread of blue energy with twelve pulses of light, one for each person in the circle, plus Distance, Rockdream, and Coral.

A thirteenth pulse appeared in the void outside the circle. The circle began to turn brown.

Open your eyes quickly, said Distance, and everybody did except Froth.

"Oh, Limpet, I have a splitting headache," he said, falling backward from the circle.

"Limpet? Who is Limpet?" asked Periwinkle, kneeling over Froth and wiping his forehead with her hand.

"I dreamed a dragon destroyed Moonport," said Froth.

"It really happened," said Periwinkle. "Riversong destroyed Moonport twenty-one summers ago."

Froth opened his eyes and propped himself up to a sitting position. "Are you Limpet? You look different and your voice is changed, but—why are my hands so old and flabby?"

"Was Limpet your wife?" asked Periwinkle.

"I think that was her name," said Tarragon.

"Oh—oh, wait, your name is Periwinkle," Froth said shakily, "and you are Bellchime and Tarragon and Black—Black Rose, right? And Muffin and Sedge and—excuse me." He staggered to his feet, took a few steps outside the circle, leaned forward, and vomited.

"I am all right," he said when he was done.

"Water," said Muffin, offering him a cup. "Just rinse your mouth out and spit it out."

Froth said, "After twenty-one years I am free, whatever there is left of me. Be good to Periwinkle, Bellchime. I love her so much. I love—I can love anybody. But go—go away from this place. He will be curious. Distance, you did this for me. Maybe you are more powerful than he, but you are still much too small."

"Who do you mean by 'he,' Froth?" asked Periwinkle.

Distance hissed. *Froth was dragonbound to Riversong, but did not know it till now*, she explained. *I broke the binding, but did not know it till now. He will be curious.*

Bellchime said, with a sense of helplessness, "I am high chief of Goblin Plain, and if Riversong comes here, thousands will die. I have no time to call a council."

"Does Riversong know where we are?" asked Black Rose.

"He may not," said Froth, "or he may know as much as I do about where I am."

"Which is fairly vague," remarked Sedge.

"I want my sword and shield," said Periwinkle.

"We must fly to Newport," said Bellchime, suddenly seeing the only possible way out of his dilemma.

Yes, that may be good, said Distance.

"You are going to fight Riversong?" said Froth almost in tears. "Distance, I do not want to cause your death."

"We are not going to fight him, I hope," said Bellchime, "but we must find out whether he is reacting to our unintended challenge."

"Bellchime, there is another dragon besides Riversong on the coast, a large female living in Moonport," said Froth.

"Lord Blackwood's ambassadors mentioned this to me," said Bellchime, "but thank you very much. This is the kind of news I need to know."

"You are near Beartooth's Camp," Periwinkle said to her parents. "His warriors are as good as any to make a stand with, if it comes to that."

Distance flapped her wings and jumped into flight.

"To Beartooth's Camp!" said Tarragon immediately, and the seven humans ferried themselves back to the *Pook-of-the-Silver* and pulled the anchor before Distance was quite out of sight.

49.

"Blood!" Rockdream said, while Periwinkle and Bellchime changed into their human-style leather pants, jackets, and boots, after gulping portions of stew. "We should have let Distance kill him!"

"How can you say that?" asked Periwinkle. "The man was dragonbound for twenty years, without knowing it, to the dragon who killed his family. How can you not be glad we set him free?"

"At what price?" asked Rockdream.

"That is what we must learn," said Bellchime.

"Rockdream, this is something they must do," said Coral.

"Riversong killed me once, I think," Periwinkle said, strapping on her sword and picking up the shield.

"Forget the shield," said Rockdream. "Your only hope against Riversong's flame, claws, and teeth, is Distance's flying skill, and you will need your hands free to hold on."

"Distance will be able to hear Riversong's thoughts," said Coral, "but he can also hear hers, and yours."

"That we know," said Periwinkle.

"One thing more," said Rockdream. "What do I tell the Upriver embassy about this?"

"Nothing. This is not their concern, unless Riversong comes to attack your camp, which he will not do unless we are killed—which you would immediately know," said Bellchime. "If I die, there may be no time for a trial to choose a new high chief, and Beartooth should become high chief."

"I will be torn in two if you are killed," said Rockdream.

"Do not say that," said Periwinkle. "Why make something that only *may* happen harder for yourself to face? We know you love us."

"I will be strong," said Coral.

50.

Newport was several hours' flight from Rockdream's Camp. At first Distance followed the river, but when the landscape flattened from grassy plain to marsh to forested swamp, and the Blue River flowed into the Turtle River, the water twisted on itself like a snake, making complicated loops that flowed east as often as west. Distance followed the setting sun toward the sea.

It was deep night when they finally passed over the western edge of Spirit Swamp and saw the ruins of the Turtle River Keeps, destroyed by Mugwort long before and never rebuilt, and miles beyond these, the fogbank at the edge of the sea, with the ruins of Turtleport and Newport on either side of the delta.

Something about a ruined castle feels good to me, Distance said, flying down to the broken towers and grass-covered rubble of the nearest keep.

"I guess Riversong did not immediately leave Newport to look for us," Bellchime said after Distance landed.

"Perhaps he knew we would come to look for him," said Periwinkle. "If Distance can foretell, he certainly can."

"Quiet," said Bellchime. "I hear laughter."

Pooks, said Distance.

"Here, of all places? I feel a strong urge to dance with them but we do not know what we are doing here," said Periwinkle.

Dance what you danced last night, suggested Distance.

"You sense no danger?" asked Bellchime.

"I do," said Periwinkle. "A pook dance is a display of power. Dare we do that so near to Riversong's lair? What if these pooks are dragonbound?"

"She thinks we are dragonbound," said a little voice behind some rubble.

"I do not think we can trust them. They have a little dragon," said another voice.

"Why is that?" asked the first.

"Why, big dragons eat big people, right? That Riversong eats big people, and so does Redmoon. So I suppose little dragons must eat little people."

"We can get together an army of little people to kill the little dragon, and build little castles to keep the little dragon out."

"And cast powerful spells right next to her lair, ha! ha!"

"Oh, we know you are harmless, so come dance with us," said one pook man, finally showing himself in front of a broken tower. "Riversong knows, too, so do not worry." All the pooks laughed at this.

Periwinkle and Bellchime turned their heads to face each other in the starlight, dismounted, and began to dance "When the War Ends" as a dance of trust between strangers. Several pook men with dark fur and a lighter pook woman began to dance with them, then stopped.

"We used to dance dances like that, but now it makes us sad," said the pook woman. "You better get out of here."

You are magnificent, said Distance while Periwinkle and Bellchime jumped onto her shoulders. They both looked up, and there was Riversong, largest living dragon east of the sea, flying quickly toward the ruined keep.

Pay my pets no heed, said Distance. *They fear you, as yours feared me*.

Riversong bellowed, and several stones fell from one of the broken towers. He belched flame, and the ruins were lit as if by lightning flashes. *You trespass, little one*, he said with a mental voice so strong it made heads ache.

I wanted to see how strong you are, said Distance.

Riversong flapped his wings and landed next to the tower where the pooks had danced. His head alone was half the length of Distance's body; his body dwarfed the tower.

"He cannot mate you; he is too big," whispered Periwinkle, trusting Distance's judgment and quieting her own thoughts.

Riversong gave a mental laugh to that remark which left their minds quivering. *In a few more years, if you live so long,* he said.

And why should I not? asked Distance.

These humans will kill you. You should eat them and find new pets. Riversong took a step toward Distance.

Distance also took a step forward and said calmly, *I do not mean to challenge you.*

I only make peace with those who win battles with me, said Riversong.

I only do battle with my enemies, said Distance, stepping to one side just when Riversong lunged with his neck to bite her. In one smooth quick motion, Periwinkle drew her sword and by starlight slashed Riversong's right eye, and in almost the same instant, Distance leaped into flight.

The roar and blast of flame that followed would have burned Distance out of the sky if Riversong's pain and blindness on one side had not made him dizzy. Distance flapped furiously to gain height, then suddenly half-folded her wings to powerdrive away from another blast of flame from Riversong flying below and behind her, a maneuver that almost unseated Bellchime and Periwinkle.

"Merge with her as completely as you can," said Bellchime. "We must know what she is doing as soon as she does."

Periwinkle was only able to hear his words through Distance's mind, in the wild rush of wind while Distance cruised just a few feet above the Turtle River. Suddenly she beat her wings again, banked, and flew around the only intact tower of the second keep's castle, which was surrounded by a moat dug from the river.

Just when Riversong sent a blast of flame so hot and sudden to the tower that flame curved around both sides of the tower to meet behind it, Distance flew straight away from the tower toward the ocean, which was covered with a thick layer of fog. Then she turned suddenly and flew toward the mountains north of the river, avoiding a powerdive by Riversong that took him far toward the ocean before he was able to pull out of it and renew his pursuit. Without so much as a thought, Distance turned and flew toward the mountains south of the river and cruised over the foothills at treetop height.

For miles and miles Distance flew low, tracing the valleys of the Foggy Mountains, which unfortunately were not covered with fog that night, but after awhile it was obvious that if Riversong was still pursuing them, he was far behind, and Distance rose to a level where she could soar.

"His pain must have become stronger than his rage," said Periwinkle. "I blinded him good. He will never use that eye again."

"We were extremely lucky," said Bellchime. "That was a swordstroke to write songs about, but he will never put his other eye within arm's reach of you."

"He underestimated us. If he had scorched first and bitten later—"

Where should we go? asked Distance.

"For now, home, if you can fly that far," said Periwinkle, and Bellchime agreed.

With a victory like that to savor, I can fly all night.

Distance flew more than what was left of the night, for dawn found them crossing over the Turtle River in Spirit Swamp, and it was full daylight by the time they landed, exhausted, at Rockdream's Camp.

Coral and Rockdream ran to hug Periwinkle and Bellchime the moment they dismounted, and Coral scratched Distance's ears. The dragon's legs collapsed under her and she fell promptly to sleep.

"Have some fresh meat ready for her when she wakes up, and call a council of war at Beartooth's Camp tomorrow," said Bellchime.

"What is happening?" asked Coral, very concerned.

In answer Periwinkle drew her sword, which was stained dark with blood at the tip. "I cut Riversong's eye," she said. "We are almost as tired as Distance. At least for now, everything is all right and I am going to bed."

"Me also," said Bellchime, and they staggered back to their tent and fell asleep.

━13━

FACES IN THE SKY

51.

Despite the short notice, most of the goblin chiefs and notable shamans were able to reach Beartooth's Camp at the appointed time of the council. Nearly all came by boat. Rockdream and Coral arrived early, after leaving little Wedge with Hope, who suddenly was eager to care for him. Periwinkle, Bellchime, and Distance were almost the last to arrive, and finally, just before sundown, Redbark, whose camp was at a spring near the Emerald Hills, arrived with another chief from the headwaters of the Goblin River, and the council began.

About sixty goblins of importance, mostly men but with a few first women and other shamanesses, sat with eight humans in a circle around a central fire, near one of the large oak trees around the edge of Beartooth's Camp. Drakey offered a pinch of sacred powder to each of the four directions and invoked the protective spirits of Goblin Plain.

Bellchime said, "I call this council to speak of an enemy who may attack us," and he told the story of the peace circle with the humans of Lord Tarragon's Keep and the battle with Riversong, emphasizing the luck and narrowness of their escape.

What the council was impressed with was Periwinkle's sword-stroke, Distance's skillful flying, and the treachery of the pooks.

"Stand, Lady Periwinkle," said Tarragon.

She gave a quick glance at Bellchime and Coral, at Beartooth, Drakey, and Elkhorn, and decided it would be best to make the most of the attention. She stood proudly and drew her sword.

"Look on my daughter, first woman of Goblin Plain and mightiest warrior east of the sea," said Tarragon. "This is the sword that blinded Riversong's eye!"

And the sword that killed Strong Bull, she thought to herself, hoping Elkhorn would not remember that. Suddenly she felt very small and exposed.

"Father, you embarrass me!" she said. "Had my sword gone clear through Riversong's eye to his brain, I would deserve this display and more. But my victory, if being chased from one ruined keep to another by my defeated foe can be called a victory, means little while he still lives, and was in fact a mistake if it causes him to seek revenge here."

"A mighty deed is never a mistake," said Beartooth.

This was a difference between human and goblin warriors, thought Bellchime. Humans would blame them for attracting Riversong's attention, but Elkhorn was saying, "We defeated the humans of Newport. We can defeat the dragon of Newport. We have many strong warriors and shamans."

Rockdream took no offense at this remark. He was no longer a warrior from Newport, but a chief of Goblin Plain.

Drakey said to Periwinkle, "You won the battle because you had no plan at any moment. Riversong acted, and you or Distance responded correctly because she heard his thoughts. You had no plan, so it did not matter that he heard your thoughts."

"Yes," said Periwinkle, "but I am troubled that we still have no plan."

"Perhaps that is best," said Drakey.

"Is it?" asked Bellchime. "What if Distance bellowed right now and told us that Riversong was coming? Periwinkle and I could jump on her back and do battle in the air, but what of everyone else?"

"We would battle on the ground," said Beartooth.

"I have—a suggestion," Froth said hesitantly. "Riversong is wounded and all dragons sleep much. If you sent dreams— "

"I could do that, I believe," said Bellchime. "Coral, Distance, what do you think?"

We would learn something about his mind and he would not know where we are, said Distance.

"Has anyone ever dreamsent to a dragon in full majesty before?" asked Coral.

"I only know of one such story, almost a legend," said Bellchime, "a wizard named Bog in the Four Lakes Kingdom, over the sea and long ago. He became dragonbound to the dragon whose dreams he invaded."

That could not happen to you, said Distance.

"Yes, as Distance said—"

"I think it would be best if all four of us did the sending," interrupted Coral.

Yes, said Distance.

"Call a recess and do the sending now," Drakey suggested to Bellchime. "We will discuss what you learn, tomorrow morning."

"Yes. We must know more," agreed Beartooth.

"Has anyone anything important to say before we do this?" asked Bellchime. No one did, and the council was adjourned.

52.

The four humans and Distance sat in a line in front of the council fire.

"This should be easy," said Bellchime. "No doubt Riversong is thinking of us already."

"Are we ready?" asked Coral.

They stared into the depths of the fire with closed eyes, something slipped into place, and the fire grew. Immense jaws snapped shut on a woman's body. A harsh, booming inner voice shouted, *You think you are my enemy, but I fear no one*, and Riversong cast the binding spell on a young, slightly pudgy fishcatcher watching angrily from the shelter of a broken stone building. Periwinkle's heartache was so strong that it ripped Riversong's dream apart into a swirling mist of faces.

In a keep on the Midcoast River was a cottage where lived a young, brown-haired witch named Moth, who was angry and wanted to make storms. "It is you who must die, but not yet, not yet," she said to the dragonling Riversong when he promised to love her, then kill her. Now they were in a thatch-roofed shack hidden deep in the woods of the Emerald Hills, where the little furry people danced. "Bind them! Make them serve us!" said Moth.

Again Periwinkle's emotions disrupted the dream. Riversong wondered who was the black-haired woman dancing with the pooks. She drew her sword and he felt afraid, felt the pain in his right eye.

"I did not want to cut your eye, but I am trained to kill," she said. "You attacked us."

In response Riversong scorched Periwinkle's body and bit it in half. Another Periwinkle appeared and said, "You burned me to death once. The person I was wants you dead, but the person I am does not care. Can we talk?"

Riversong felt confused. Why would any human not want to kill him, especially if he killed her earlier? But that made no sense. Death was permanent. *When did I kill you?* he asked.

"In Moonport," Periwinkle said.

"Look south, there is Moonport," said Moth, a few years older than before. "Together we will rule, dragon and queen."

She smelled so delicious that Riversong could not resist burning her to death and eating her while her mind was on something else. When he reached full majesty, he would conquer Moonport without her.

Moth, where are you? he wailed, suddenly missing the dark complexities of her mind.

"She is gone," said Periwinkle gently.

I killed you and you came back, he said, feeling a low dull throb in his eye.

"I did not!" Periwinkle said with intense pain. "Limpet is dead and I am someone completely different now."

I will search the world and find her. I will love her, then kill her again.

"You must stay in Newport or I will kill you," said Periwinkle.

Why should I obey you? I fear no one.

"You fear every human east of the sea," said Periwinkle. "Any one of us may kill you and you know it, no matter how many of us you kill. Why else would you do it?"

Humans taste good, said Riversong.

"Stay in Newport or I will kill you."

Again Riversong killed Periwinkle with a blast of flame and bent his head down to snap up her body, and again another Periwinkle appeared, saying, "Now it is your turn to die," while she rammed her sword through Riversong's eye to his brain.

There was a moment of pain, a rupturing shudder, blackness, and Distance saying, *Periwinkle, open your eyes right now!*

She blinked, and she looked up at the concerned faces of Bellchime, Rockdream, Coral, and a bluish-silver dragon, her very own dragon, her kind and loving Distance.

"Waking Riversong was dangerous," said Coral.

Periwinkle sighed. "He did not even notice the rest of you."

"We kept giving you new dream bodies," said Bellchime.

"Soon enough to keep me from most of the pain, but I had to strike back. He will remember this dream."

53.

The next morning, Bellchime spoke to the council about the dreamsending. What they decided was to send smoke messages toward Human Camp the moment Riversong was seen anywhere on Goblin Plain, and they danced a war dance to strengthen their spirit-beasts, so that Riversong would have trouble hearing their thoughts. Then the council ended, and Beartooth's wife Cicada sent message runners to neighboring camps telling the council's decision, and the chiefs and shamans began to leave.

After this, Periwinkle finally had time to visit with her parents.

And I finally have time to hunt, said Distance. *Who will come with me?*

"Do you need someone?" Bellchime asked.

I crave the taste of antelope.

"Take Rockdream then; I have no skill with the bow."

"Why not both of us?" asked Coral.

"Fine with me," said Rockdream.

Bellchime watched Distance take off, and saw Periwinkle sitting in the shade of the large oak with Tarragon and Black Rose, then noticed Froth and questioned him about some of the children they both had taught.

"Fine students, all of them," Froth said, "except the ones who are old enough to remember *your* flamboyant stories. I think I did not emphasize feelings enough to show them what it was like to be the people in whatever story I was telling. But I spent the last twenty-one years of my life in a gray half-lie, through no fault of my own, I must admit. Vividness frightens me. It is hard for me to know who I am, or who I have been."

"Could you say that the ice in your heart is melting, and it hurts?" asked Bellchime.

"Ouch," said Froth.

"One of the Newport exiles, an ex-priestess named Hope, said that about herself some time ago."

Froth snorted. "And here I come, innocently to Goblin Plain at Lord Tarragon's request, and I cause you more trouble than I ever did in four years of trying to kill you. Someone in the spirit world must have a grim sense of humor."

"It may be my fault as much as yours," said Bellchime. "Ever since I learned about Riversong attacking Newport, I wanted to someday use Distance to kill him. What storyteller would miss a chance to become hero of the age? But now that this may actually happen, it means little to me compared to what I have already done here on Goblin Plain. Riversong is one enemy. If he dies, that is that. But here I have brought peace to thousands of people, each different, many with hatreds as complex as any of Riversong's." Bellchime sighed. "It is too late to make peace with him now."

"It was always too late for that," said Froth.

"He said that he only made peace with those who won battles with him."

"The only way to win a battle with the likes of him is to kill him," said Froth.

"He must have made some sort of peace with Redmoon," said Bellchime.

"And he may have told you riddles and lies."

"If Redmoon defeated him at Moonport, then he conquered Newport—that makes sense, does it not?" asked Bellchime.

"Dragons are said to be like keepcats in two ways: Both purr, and both confound mating with fighting."

"Dragons do purr, but who has ever watched a pair of dragons mating?" asked Bellchime.

"Did I hear you talking about Riversong?" asked Periwinkle. "Come over to the shade of the oak before the noon sun gives you both headaches."

"We were making guesses about Redmoon mating him," said Bellchime.

"We were talking about steel arrows," said Periwinkle.

"She does not think Lord Wentletrap's tactics can be used again," said Tarragon.

"We have neither Wentletrap's smiths nor his ore supply."

"And even if we did, I am certain Riversong knows how Mugwort was killed," said Bellchime. "He attacked Newport in such a way that steel arrows were useless. He waylaid merchants and dragonbound them. He swooped down on ships in the fog and burned them to the waterline. He flew high above the city, beyond arrow range, and dropped large rocks and other heavy objects. He dreamsent dreams of fear and death. He listened to the thoughts of warriors on foggy nights and burned whatever part of the city was least well guarded."

"Uncommonly cautious, for a dragon," said Tarragon.

"How else would you expect a dragon to behave these days?" asked Bellchime. "From the moment of binding, both dragonling and bound human are marked for death in the eyes of almost everyone. Only cautious dragons live to reach majesty."

"Could one be cautious enough to pretend to love people?" asked Black Rose.

"Distance could not lie to me without me noticing contortions behind her thought," said Periwinkle.

"Can you hit a moving target from Distance's neck in flight?" asked Tarragon.

"Of course, and so can Rockdream. Distance has a taste for antelope, and shooting from the air is the only practical way to kill one. They run and dodge as fast as unicorns."

"If you had steel arrows—"

"Father, it took hundreds of arrows to kill Mugwort. One archer aloft shooting Riversong is like mosquitoes biting a condor."

"If you hit his other eye—"

"That, of all things, he will guard most against," said Bellchime.

54.

At the foot of the Gray Hills, across the river, Distance spotted a herd of auroch and antelope, which immediately sensed that the dragon was hunting and began to run.

"That one?" asked Rockdream, notching his bow and watching the crazed zigzag flight of one antelope.

Let me try first, said Distance, and she swooped down at where the antelope had been and pulled back the ribs of one wing to turn sharply to one side. To the dragon's surprise the antelope turned the same way, then was caught between her forepaws and lifted into the air.

Distance bit the neck of the squirming screaming antelope, dropped its body, and flapped to a landing beside it.

"Good job," said Coral, while she and Rockdream dismounted, though her stomach was uneasy from the sudden maneuvers. The dragon was already scratching a wide swath of bare ground around the carcass. Eagerly she tore large chunks of meat from its hind legs and flamed them inside her mouth, slobbering the hot juices.

"She is hungry," said Coral.

Distance ate its guts and the meat from its forelegs and back no less eagerly. *Eating this fast animal will make me faster*, she said in a moment of thought between bites. Suddenly she raised her head and looked toward the afternoon sun and bellowed.

"Do you see something?" asked Rockdream.

Not yet, said Distance, and she tore out the antelope's heart, flamed, chewed, and swallowed it.

"Do you sense something?" asked Coral.

55.

On the eastern horizon, the beginning of a smoke message became a thick cloud of continuous smoke. Periwinkle and Bellchime ran into camp, followed by Black Rose, Tarragon, and Froth.

"Riversong burned Bonedance's Camp. I am almost certain of it," said Bellchime.

Beartooth was already gathering his warriors and ordering everyone else to scatter into the tall grass.

"No!" shouted Bellchime. "The river!"

For an instant everyone hesitated. Beartooth looked at Bellchime, then agreed with him and repeated, "The river! But scatter!" Froth began running toward the river with Muffin, Sedge, and the other human servants, but Tarragon grabbed his arm from behind and pulled him short.

"Too late for you to hide," he said. "Riversong is too interested in you."

"I am the one he wants now," said Periwinkle.

"I would guess Riversong flew around to the east some

roundabout way to surprise us and attacked the next camp east when he realized they were sending messages," said Tarragon.

Periwinkle took a deep breath and screamed, "DISTANCE!"

"That got her," said Bellchime. "I sense her coming."

"Is a dragon's hearing that acute?" asked Tarragon.

"From miles away, all the dragon hears is strong emotions," said Bellchime, "unless she is asleep or unoccupied. The scream was just a focus of power."

56.

Will you mount me? Riversong attacks Beartooth's Camp!

Coral jumped on the dragon's neck at once. Rockdream closed his quiver in such a way that only the three red arrows were in reach and climbed on behind Coral, telling Distance that those arrows would not burn. Distance jumped into flight, flapping her wings higher and higher until she could see the peaks of the far-off Silver Mountains above the eastern horizon. Thick smoke rose from Bonedance's Camp, and the tiny copper-green form of a dragon moved low over the grass toward Beartooth's Camp.

Distance reached out lightly to touch Coral's mind. She was always in close tune. Rockdream? There he was, both eager and reluctant to merge. She welcomed him, saying, *You must know what I do when I do it*, and in the middle of this thought she folded her wings for a sudden dive. They were startled, but linked well enough with her to stay securely mounted.

57.

A bellow shook Beartooth's camp, and there was Riversong, vast and copper-green in the shimmering sunlight, flying straight towards them from the east. Bellchime's body trembled, and a breeze began blowing at his back as the warriors raised their spearthrowers.

Now! Riversong swooped down to shoot a blast of flame at the tents and goblin warriors, the warriors let fly a volley of spears, and a sudden hurricane wind swept the flames back into Riversong's face, knocking over one of the burning tents and throwing a few goblins off their feet. Riversong scooped his wings forward to let the blast of wind sweep him upward and back, over most of the confusion of spears and fire. Many of the spearshafts burned up, and a few spearheads clattered uselessly against the dragon's tail.

Riversong turned and beat his wings heavily crosswind, trying to circle camp to put the wind in his favor, but the wind quickly died down. Bellchime's body shook again and a breeze began blowing in the other direction. Riversong promptly folded his wings and landed with a boom that shook the ground, then began walking toward camp.

Can you knock me off my feet with your wind, wizard? asked Riversong.

Beartooth led a charge of spearthrowing goblins, and was burned by Riversong's fire despite Bellchime's wind, but not before throwing a spear that by some chance struck between the scales of the dragon's armored belly. Riversong howled and threw blasts of flame in every direction, while trying to dislodge the spear with his forepaw. At last it fell out, a small wound, but sore.

More goblins rushed him, throwing spears. He breathed a hard blast of fire that sputtered and flickered and went out, then ran headlong into camp, trampling tents, goblins, and anything else that did not move quickly out of his path. His body was covered with scratches from the spears, but there was no serious damage, and now his enemies had no more buildings to hide behind. He bent his neck down to eat a trampled goblin, squinting his good eye to protect it from attack.

"He has no more flame!" screamed Periwinkle, rushing with drawn sword toward the huge dragon. His blast of breath was hot and foul but did not catch fire. He stood tall on his legs, which raised his belly out of reach, and his head was high as a tower. *Will you cut my feet, little warrior?* he said, but Periwinkle knew the speech of dragons well enough to know that Riversong was genuinely afraid of her. His right eye was clouded and blind, his snout scorched, his belly wounded. She watched his forelegs and neck for any sign of movement. A dragon that size is powerful beyond imagining, but limited in reaction speed.

A sharp pain suddenly hit Riversong's left hind foot when Tarragon swung his sword to cut through ankle scales and tendon. Riversong raised his leg, jerking the embedded sword from Tarragon's hands, bellowed in pain, and almost stumbled, twisted his head around to snap at Tarragon then turned his blind eye toward Periwinkle, who was about to dash forward to hack at another foot when she heard Distance bellow.

Riversong flapped his gigantic wings and screamed when he jumped into flight because the motion drove the sword deeper into his ankle. His feet almost bumped ground twice before he finally began to rise. He shook his hind leg and the sword fell out, red with scalding hot blood. It hit the ground and broke in two. Only then did Periwinkle realize to her horror that the body she had saved from Riversong's jaws was Drakey the high shaman.

Distance dove toward Riversong, very much aware both that the big dragon's fire was gone and that he was already wounded. He twisted out of her way and flapped his wings to gain altitude. Then, deciding that it was better to attack than to flee, he swooped at her. She dodged to one side and swung a claw at his wing, making a deep and painful scratch, but the force of his backstroke knocked her spinning.

Coral clung tightly to Distance's neck, and Rockdream grabbed at her clothes to stay mounted. The leather began to rip, but he managed to balance himself, and Distance regained control of her flight just in time to dodge Riversong's dive.

"I lost my bow," Rockdream said, "not that it was that much good to us."

"Just stay with me," said Coral, hearing Rockdream mostly through Distance's mind. She felt herself slipping into trance, felt her own Great Father Condor doing battle in this game of swoop and snatch. Rockdream's fangcat wanted weapons, wanted a good tussle on the ground with fangs and claws, where there was no fear of falling.

It was as if Coral could see Riversong's movements in slow motion, Distance's twists and turns. It seemed to take several seconds for her own eyes to blink, or for her heart to slowly squeeze the blood through her arteries.

Faces seemed to drift through the sky while Distance flapped slowly to dodge Riversong's graceful dive. There was Drakey, Beartooth, several goblins she did not know, all newly dead. Riversong killed Drakey and Beartooth? He must die! And when she thought that thought, she saw the faces of her own parents, killed by Riversong when he dropped a stone on the Newport Market four springs ago. And there was the face of old Lord Herring, grandson of Wentletrap, and last lord of Newport. What was Riversong doing? He seemed confused, seemed to be trying to attack the faces in the sky.

Coral wondered whether the faces might actually be clouds, and if so, could she coax lightning from them? Under her legs, Distance's shoulders throbbed in a slow-motion shudder. From the face of—ah—Froth's wife, Limpet, who Coral recognized from the dreamsending, came a jagged streak of light that struck the wing muscles of Riversong's back.

Coral shook her head, wondering where all the stormclouds came from. The air around her skin felt dry and tingly. Riversong flew quickly toward them with sparkles all over his scales. Below were hills and valleys covered with dense forest.

Suddenly Distance made a steep dive into a valley and flew low over the treetops there. When Riversong swooped down to follow, a bolt of lightning connected him momentarily to a hilltop tree, splitting the tree and stunning the big dragon. He came to himself just as his body crashed into trees at the bottom of the valley.

The ribs of his wings were cracked, his front legs were twisted and broken among splintered trees, moving his neck was horribly painful, and blood trickled out through the partly healed cut in his blind eye. He opened his mouth to bellow but made only a hoarse cough. His mental voice screamed, *Kill me! Kill me! Kill me!*

Distance circled overhead. Except where Riversong's body had smashed the trees, the forest was too thick for even a dragon her size to land.

"Kill you with what?" asked Coral.

You have the power, witch.

"To make lightning strike the bottom of a valley? I do not think so. Besides, the other lightning bolt only stunned you."

I am too small to bite through your neck bones, said Distance.

Coral was perplexed. Here, of all things she least expected, was the biggest dragon east of the sea, lying helpless and broken and begging her to kill him, and she could not think of a way to do it.

Scratch and tear! Make me bleed to death!

No! said Distance angrily. *He is trying to make us feel his body's pain, but I am blocking him. He wants to lure me close to kill me before he dies.*

"Then let us leave him there as he is," said Rockdream.

"No, Distance," said Coral. "Give me a few moments more." She slid into trance again and made prayers to all the spirit-beasts. Although she felt a trace of late afternoon wind on her face as

Distance continued to circle, most of her awareness was in a garden, a grove of blossoming rose trees surrounding a fountain much like one she knew in Newport.

Riversong, as a dragonling about the size of a dog, was perched on the edge of the fountain. Coral reached to scratch him behind the ears, as she often scratched Distance.

"I am sorry that your life went where it did," she said, "but does it not feel good to be here?"

Where am I? asked Riversong.

"The rose garden of Newport. It is yours as well as mine, you know. You can stay here if you like. There are sweet fishes in the fountain for you to eat, and roses for you to smell."

I would like to stay here. Can you stay with me?

"I will stay until you go to sleep. You can sleep right under that rose tree. It is perfectly safe here, and warm. Smell the roses. They will help you go to sleep. They will help you dream beautiful dreams."

She sat beside the little green dragon while he curled up to sleep beneath the rose tree, and said, "You will sleep, sleep as long as you need to, and when you wake up, you will have a much better life. I know all about these things. I am a witch. Goodbye, Riversong."

Coral shook her head, sobbing freely, her hands against Distance's warm blue scaly neck. Riversong's vast broken body lay still, barely breathing; his mind was unconscious, in trance.

Coral, I love you, said Distance as she flew over the ridge and away from the reddening clouds in the west.

"So do I," said Rockdream.

"And I love both of you," said Coral. "But where are we? I guess somewhere in the Emerald Hills, but where is Goblin Plain?"

We will get there, said Distance. *Do we return to Beartooth's Camp?*

"To whatever is left of it," said Rockdream.

58.

The chaos left behind at Beartooth's Camp was not so bad as it first appeared. Beartooth, Drakey, and four other warriors were dead, but most of the others who had faced Riversong were unhurt. The tents were all flattened, but only about half of them were burned or torn, and goblins were hard at work re-erecting the others.

"You are not responsible for my husband's death," Cicada angrily told Bellchime. "Beartooth fought Riversong on the ground, as he said he would do, as we all did. I lead this camp until a new chief is chosen. How can I serve you?"

Bellchime said, "Send messengers. Find out how it is at Bonedance's Camp, and whether Riversong attacked any other camps, and tell everyone—" Bellchime found it hard to say the words, "who is alive and who is dead."

Cicada clasped Bellchime's hands and looked openly at him with her dark brown eyes watering. "You grieve for my husband. This is good. I grieve also." After a long minute of silent sharing, she half-smiled and said, "I will send runners to Bonedance's Camp and Gorge's Camp, and I will send smoke messages saying, 'High chief lives. Beartooth's Camp, now,' to ease the minds of the people in other camps."

Bellchime considered this for a moment, then said, "That would be good."

The work of rebuilding the camp continued till sundown. A messenger came from Bonedance's Camp just when everyone present was starting a council circle.

The messenger said, "We heard a bellowlike thunder and saw the big dragon flying from the east. We started a smoke message. He made several low passes over camp, breathing fire. We stopped shouting war-cries and ran to the river. The dragon was already flying from our camp toward this camp. Our camp was burned down. The grass was burning. We crossed the river. You can still see the smoke from here. But we do not weep. None of our people were killed, though some have burns, and already our warriors hunt mammoth for food and tents. We will trade for our grain this winter."

Bellchime said, "As you know, Beartooth and Drakey are dead. We are sitting this council to choose Beartooth's successor. Glowfly the shamaness made a chant about the day's battle, which she will sing afterward."

People spoke around the circle, mentioning a few names, but the first choice of most was the warrior Gray Lizard, who was a close friend of Beartooth, and had been the goblin ambassador to Upriver. He sat in the center of the circle, a man of about thirty summers, his hair black and long and wavy behind his pointed ears.

Cicada said, "I, Cicada, accept Gray Lizard as my chief," and everyone else in the circle repeated this formula with their own names, except the humans and the messenger from Bonedance's Camp, who each said, "I accept Gray Lizard as chief of this camp."

Gray Lizard said, "We have much to discuss, but first Glowfly should sing her chant."

Glowfly stood up, nodded her head, and immediately began to sing, with a stirring dramatic voice, about High Chief Bellchime's spirit wind and Riversong's fire; about the bravery of Chief Beartooth and High Shaman Drakey; about Periwinkle—the one warrior Riversong feared because she cut his eye—how she stopped the dragon from eating Drakey's body and kept his attention, while her father, High Chief Tarragon from the far north, cut his ankle-tendon; and about Distance, who led the great dragon far away, swooping and scratching at him. "Here my song ends, and may it please the heroes it celebrates," she chanted.

Tarragon said, "I suppose history will know me as Tarragon the ankle-chopper," and Froth stifled a laugh.

Gray Lizard said, "I scoffed at the human stories about Riversong as much as Strong Bull did, but now I know they are true. Where is he now, I wonder?"

Bellchime said, "I sense that Distance is alive, unhurt, and far away. Sooner or later, Riversong must land, if he has not landed already. Once he does he will be unable to take off again, for he has no firegas in his flight bladder and a hamstrung hind foot. We can sleep easily tonight."

"I want a guard of at least six," said Gray Lizard. "The smell of blood in this camp may attract fangcats or wolves."

The circle broke into groups of friends talking, then the goblins crowded into the available tents to sleep. Periwinkle and Bellchime shared a tent with Gray Lizard's family, and Tarragon's retinue slept aboard the *Pook-of-the-Silver*.

59.

Periwinkle and Bellchime both woke in the dark to the gentle inner prodding of Distance's voice, dressed quickly and quietly, stepped around a sleeping goblin's covers, and went outside. A light mist was falling. They walked past dark forms of tents toward the council ground, where they heard Coral talking to a guard.

"Is it you?" Coral asked, hugging them both.

"What happened?" asked Bellchime.

"We left Riversong all but dead," said Coral. "He fell from the sky and broke most of his bones. I put him in a very heavy trance to stop the pain. We had no way to kill him. He died while we were flying back. I caught the echo's echo of his presence, and it had the clarity of death."

I sensed this also, said Distance. *Riversong is dead*.

"Your news is good beyond belief," said Bellchime. "How did you do it?"

Coral hesitated, then said, "I do not want anyone to fear me. It was not just me, but a sky full of dead people's faces. The face of Froth's wife, Limpet, struck Riversong with lightning at my urging. He looked sparkly after that, until Distance led him close to the ridge, then lightning went from Riversong to the tree. He was stunned and crashed in the valley."

"No one will fear you," said Rockdream. "You are a first woman on Goblin Plain, where shamans are respected. Everyone already knows you can make lightning strike."

The goblin guard said to Coral, "Humans fear power because they do not know their own spirit-beasts. You are a brave and powerful goblin, like Beartooth or Drakey or Periwinkle."

━━14━━

THE HOARD

60.

The next day at noon, after Distance had killed and eaten an auroch calf, she said to her four bound humans, *Now we will fly to the place where Riversong died.*

"I wish you were big enough to take all four of us," said Periwinkle.

"You and Coral go," said Bellchime. "Make certain Riversong is dead, then cut off his largest tooth with your sword. I do not think anyone will dispute our claim to the hoard of Newport if we move swiftly and wisely enough, but we should take proof of our kill. Rockdream and I will go toward Newport in Tarragon's boat, with as many warriors as we can manage. Meet us in Spirit Swamp this evening."'

"I hope Redmoon does not dispute our claim to the hoard," said Periwinkle.

We killed Riversong, said Distance. *We can kill Redmoon.*

"I hope we do not need to," said Coral.

The dragon considered this for a moment, then said, *So do I.*

Rockdream said, "If there is trouble, Periwinkle is a better fighter than I am."

"Do not belittle yourself, husband, just because you dropped your bow," said Coral. "You would not be chief if you were not a good warrior."

"I do not deny that, but she is better on dragonback, and you are the finest shaman on Goblin Plain."

Coral kissed him. "If we do not meet you by dark, go to sleep as quickly as you can, and I will send you a dream message."

Bellchime kissed Periwinkle. "See you tonight," he said, and she climbed onto the dragon's shoulders.

Coral mounted in front of Periwinkle, and Distance flapped her wings and rose overhead, leaving Bellchime and Rockdream talking about how many goblins they would need to give the *Pook-of-the-Silver* a full crew.

Distance flew a straight course over Goblin Plain and north of Spirit Swamp till she reached the valley where Riversong fell. Condors and crows scattered in flight from Riversong's vast broken body. Distance circled to a landing amid the smashed trees.

"It is hard to believe he was as big as this," said Coral, dismounting and walking around the body toward the head. The scavenger birds had eaten some skin and meat from Riversong's wounds, but most of his hide was too tough to pierce. His eyes were both gone, and Coral leaned over to pull down his eyelids. She turned away when Periwinkle drew her sword.

"I cannot get his mouth open," Periwinkle said.

"Sister, this is unspeakably crude," Coral said, turning to face Periwinkle. "Riversong is a dragon, not some animal we have killed for meat. If we take this trophy we are no better than your great-grandfather who cut off goblin heads and stuck them on poles."

Periwinkle sheathed her sword, looked into Coral's moist eyes, and the two women hugged each other, crying.

Coral said, "We will leave his body for the condors and wolves and worms since we cannot bury it."

The women walked back to Distance, climbed on her shoulders, and she jumped into flight. When she turned to fly south, she saw the bright green land near the Moon River. What seemed to be a condor against the sky cast a shadow much too far away.

She knows I am here, said Distance, and turned to fly toward what could only be Redmoon.

"What are you doing?" asked Periwinkle.

Distance roared as loud as she could, and even though Redmoon was still miles away, they heard her answering bellow. *If we win a battle with her now, no more of our people will have to die*, Distance said.

Minute by minute, second by second, the rust-colored dragon drew closer. If she was smaller than Riversong, she was not much smaller. When she came within ten times her length from Distance, the smaller dragon flew to one side, circling to maintain the gap between them.

The big dragon spoke: *I am Redmoon. Riversong is dead. You killed him*.

"I killed him," said Coral, and for some reason her spirit condor did not resist when Redmoon invaded her mind, vicious as a keepcat with suckling mice. Coral did not scream or cry when Redmoon's laughter raped the memories. Suddenly Redmoon stopped.

You are very deep, she said, and Coral knew she was reacting to the rose garden. *You touch things I do not want to remember*.

When Redmoon tried to invade Periwinkle's mind, the spirit fangcat slashed and tore.

You are like a dragon, said Redmoon. *Your love makes you fierce*.

The dragons circled each other, now higher, now lower. If Redmoon changed direction to lunge at Distance, the smaller dragon flapped to change direction, making a new circle.

You are fortunate in your choice of humans, said Redmoon.

I have others, said Distance.

Again, Redmoon flew at Distance, and again, Distance made a new circle. So far, despite Redmoon's anger, this was more a contest of skill than a battle, but Riversong had been wound-maddened from almost the beginning.

You blinded Riversong with your sword!

"I did not want to fight him at all," said Periwinkle.

With her trance eye, Coral noticed strands of silver light in front of both dragons, which changed direction before the dragons did themselves. Redmoon's strands kept twisting behind Distance, particularly to Periwinkle and her sword. The strand turned copper-colored, and this time when Redmoon lunged she belched flame. Distance folded her wings, dived, flapped back up to Redmoon's level, and continued the circle.

You do nothing but respond to me, said Redmoon. *I cannot anticipate you*.

Nor could Riversong, said Distance.

I will do the same, she said, and both dragons did nothing but circle each other for several minutes.

From the depths of her trance, Coral began telling a story, using both dragons to magnify her voice. "I was standing in front of my home when the dragon came, with three people riding her. I had four warriors with me, whose faces were so fierce I hardly recognized them. I gave the order to loose arrows. The dragon knew we were going to shoot and flew out of range. One of the women on her back sang a song about peace and the dragon made certain we heard it. I told them to land and right then we sat the peace circle."

"When I was a girl," Periwinkle said, "the man I wanted to marry when I grew up became dragonbound, and everybody wanted to kill him, and the dragon. I wanted to kill the dragon, to free him. The dragon offered to love me, and I accepted. She tried to turn us against each other, but our love was too great. We left the dragon alone in the forest while we got married in the church. When we came back to the dragon, she said she missed us."

Some goblins attacked us without warning, said Distance. *I was wounded in the thigh with a spear. We killed them all with fire and wind and sword. I was in a rage. My humans were upset that we had to kill them at all.*

By this time the strands of intention were looped into a continuous circle the dragons followed through the sky.

No, said Redmoon, making heavy wingstrokes to rise above the smaller dragon. *You cannot fight me with deceit.*

Distance flapped vigorously to match Redmoon's motions.

"What deceit?" asked Coral. "You know that everything we said is true."

His mind had twisted darknesses like no other, said Redmoon. *I left my hoard and searched until I found him. Our mating was like the passion of smashing a city. He was so inspired by it that he smashed another city.* Redmoon's dragon laughter was sharp with sadness. *Where will I ever know another like him?*

"You love him," said Periwinkle.

Why are you trying to love me? Redmoon demanded, bellowing wild flames and swooping at Distance, who flapped her wings to rise when Redmoon expected her to dive.

"Because we truly do not want to kill you," said Periwinkle. "We love Distance, and she could have become like you."

You think she will not? said Redmoon.

I will not kill them, said Distance. *I need them to live and be strong.*

Riversong attacked these women's people. You defend them like a hoard.

Yes, said Distance, and now the smaller dragon seemed fierce, and the majestic dragon in doubt.

Redmoon finally said, *I understand*, and made a rumble like the lowest note of a church organ, and her silver threads of intention arched across the sky toward the ruins of Moonport. *I will not fight you. You will go to Newport and claim the hoard. I will keep Moonport.* She swept back her vast wings to dive and flew swiftly away, over the lush green toward the river and the sea.

Coral said, "Give praise and thanks," and Periwinkle hugged her tightly.

"You were so right about respecting the body," said Periwinkle. "If I had taken that tooth, all the things we said to Redmoon would have been less true."

Distance flew south, toward Spirit Swamp and the Turtle River.

61.

The *Pook-of-the-Silver* stopped briefly at Human Camp. Bellchime only intended to organize a crew to help rebuild Bonedance's Camp, but ended up having to call a circle and tell the whole story of the battle at Beartooth's, and then Rockdream continued the story to Riversong's fall.

"We are going to Newport to claim the hoard," said Bellchime. "There may be enough to give every survivor of Newport a portion of cash, even those who stay wherever they are living now. We may decide to rebuild that city. There is much we do not know yet, and you can understand our need to hurry. I think we are at peace, and those of you from Upriver who planned to return there may do so now. Tell Lord Blackwood I will meet with him myself."

When the circle was breaking up, Bronzeberry asked Rockdream privately, "Is Froth aboard the boat? He was a close friend of mine in Moonport—"

"Froth is there; go see him if you want. We will be leaving soon and I have to—" and Rockdream went back to talking to Sharpstone and Feathergrass about leather and tent poles.

Bronzeberry was surprised to find herself running toward the river and paddling the smallest of the camp canoes through the slow clear water to the anchored riverboat.

"Who comes here?" called Captain Muffin.

"Bronzeberry of Moonport, now a warrior of Human Camp, with a personal concern. I come to see—"

"Bloody death!" said Froth. "I do not believe this."

"You know her?" asked Black Rose.

"No bloody death at all; I am alive and quite well," said Bronzeberry. "Stop gawking and lower me a rope."

"She was my wife's best friend in Moonport," Froth said, lowering the line.

"Quite a tub you got this time, Froth," she said, climbing over the rail.

"I am only part of the crew, alas. The *Pook* belongs to Lord Tarragon of Indigo. I am his storyteller. Blood! How did you escape? I was so certain you were killed, like all the others."

"I swam across the river and never looked back. I walked all the way across the Foggy Mountains to Newport, offered my service to Lord Herring, and continued to serve his son, Drill, after Newport fell. I was burned out of two cities by the same backstabbing dragon! How is that for luck? At least I survived both times. When Periwinkle came to Drill's Village in the Swamp, I left with her. Drill was dying, and Marten, his son, was doing nothing for our people, but Periwinkle was doing all she could. Now tell me what happened to you. Were you truly dragonbound to Riversong?"

"Forget all that," said Froth. "I cannot understand the pattern of my life. All I wanted to do was catch fish and enjoy my family. Riversong killed my family, then dragonbound me, without me ever suspecting this, and what use he made of me I do not know. Did he want me to kill dragonlings and wizards, or was that my own desire, or both? Sometimes I even think some higher power was using me all along to cause Riversong's death. Or am I looking for meaning in a life filled with accidents?" Froth studied Bronzeberry's concerned face. "I wish I was still the fishcatcher you once knew. You seem the same as ever, older and wiser, I suppose, but—"

"Say rather that I am restored," said Bronzeberry. "I had honor, but very little hope or heart left when Periwinkle found me."

"You are a very strong man," Black Rose said suddenly.

"Remember how you told me that Bellchime would be driven mad if we killed the dragon he was bound to for four years? Why, you were dragonbound to the worst dragon who ever burned a city for twenty years, and though the binding is broken, and the dragon is dead, you still have your mind. You are confused, but far from mad."

"Well, whoever the blood you are, I am glad to see you!" said Bronzeberry. "After twenty-one years, do I deserve a hug or what?" She put her arms around him and he returned her embrace.

When Bellchime and Rockdream returned to the boat, Bronzeberry said she wanted to go to Newport, and Black Rose urged Bellchime to agree to this. When the skiff and Bronzeberry's canoe were secured, Captain Muffin ordered the crew to pull anchor and set the sails.

62.

The first familiar sight Distance spotted as she flew south was the river of Sharp Bend Village, and realizing how far west they were already, she was eager to go to Newport to see the hoard.

"We should have thought of this when we arranged things," said Periwinkle.

"I promised Rockdream I would dreamsend him if we were delayed. That should be good enough," said Coral.

Distance flew southwest toward the gap in the Foggy Mountains where the Turtle River passed from Spirit Swamp to the coastal plain. Beyond the three keeps was farmland grown over with weeds, burnt timbers, and scattered stones. Ahead, Newport was a vague jumble of blocks, with the blue sea stretching beyond.

"I think my home was one of these," Coral said, when they flew near another group of rubble piles and burnt trees.

"Look, one orchard survived, I think," said Periwinkle.

"That was old Spineball's holding. I do not suppose I will ever see him again."

They passed over the outer wall of the city, which was broken in many places, especially the towers. The great inner wall was less damaged. In the inner city, many of the stone buildings still stood, though most had burned or broken roofs. The church was totally reduced to rubble.

The lesser towers of the castle itself were partially broken, the courtyard strewn with rocks and other debris. The great tower, five stories tall and ninety feet wide at the base, looked undamaged from the outside, except for the conical roof being torn, but through this hole it looked as though the ceiling and floors were burned away. Distance landed on the rim of the wall, which was twelve feet thick, and from here the tower was clearly gutted and empty. The shells and coral once spread in a thick layer over the ceiling to insulate the tower from dragon fire were mixed with the heap of burned wood at the bottom. The tower had been burned from below.

"This is the first time in my life I have ever been inside Newport Castle," said Coral. "Lord Herring did not allow witches to live inside the city walls, or to visit the castle. When Rockdream married me, he was demoted to gate guard. It was just as well, because not many of the castle warriors survived."

"Where do you think the treasure is?" asked Periwinkle.

The smell of Riversong is strong on this tower, said Distance. *This perch is where he watched and listened and sensed.*

"But where did he live?" asked Periwinkle.

"Rockdream would probably know, if he was here," said Coral, looking vacantly over the broken wall toward the sea, then down at a pile of rubble and burned timbers, where a large sheet of lead roofing still nailed to broken timbers lay on the ground.

There! said Distance, and immediately she jumped, flapping her ribbed wings down to the courtyard, where she lifted one corner of the piece of metal with her foreleg and sniffed. *Dismount so I can move this*, she said, and after the two women climbed down, she seized the corner in her mouth and began pulling. It moved some, but her teeth began ripping the lead and the taste was foul. She then tore a hole in the lead with her front claws and bent back the edges until it was large enough for her to crawl in. The two women followed.

Inside it was dark, almost too steep to stand on, and smelled strongly of dragon.

"We need a torch," Periwinkle said and went back outside to find a suitable piece of timber.

"Distance, come back up," said Coral. "We need a light."

I found the hoard, said Distance.

Periwinkle came back with a sizeable stick.

I will light your torch, said the dragon, climbing back to the entrance. She made a flicker of flame to see by, then blew a thin jet of fire to the end of the torch.

They were in a rough rounded tunnel in solid rock leading down to a large cave, which for Riversong must have made a tight, cozy den. The light from Periwinkle's torch made countless bright sparkles; the floor was spread deep with coins of gold, silver, and copper, mixed with gems and crystals, cups, and statuettes.

"I had no idea there was this much wealth in all of Newport," said Coral, picking up handfuls of heavy gold starmarks and sifting them through her fingers. "I wonder how deep this is."

Deep enough to sleep on forever, said Distance, sprawling on the coins and raking them with her claws while she purred.

"You will have your share to sleep on, but you cannot have it all," said Periwinkle.

"We will have to find or make Distance a cave or something to keep her share," said Coral. "Look at this crystal," she said, picking up a clear quartz the size of her hand.

"I found a silver brooch with a turquoise," said Periwinkle.

"If you see any stone that truly calls out to you, take it," said Coral. "But take only those, or you will only clutter your tent and your life with things you do not need, which someone else may want."

Periwinkle said, "This reminds me of the display of spirit gifts at midsummer, all this together, which different people will soon divide and take home."

The two women spent some time exploring the treasure; Coral took two quartz crystals, an emerald, a small ruby, and a moonstone; Periwinkle looked at the turquoise brooch and decided she did not want it, then stuck the torch into a heap of coins near Coral and sat down next to Distance, who was purring in her sleep. Did sleeping on gold give a dragon good dreams? She wondered, and noticed a silver flute next to the dragon's head.

She picked it up, placed her fingers over the holes, and blew into the end. The note was slightly thin and breathy, but Periwinkle was no flute player; in Bellchime's hands, this would sound incredibly sweet. It actually was not hard to play, and sounded nice in the echoing chamber. She blew single notes and phrases of melody, while she got up and walked around, experimenting to hear how the echoes changed in different parts of the cave.

"That was beautiful!" said Coral. "You found what called to you."

"I was thinking I would give it to Bellchime."

"I think it is supposed to be yours. Play some more."

"But I do not know what I am doing; I never learned the flute."

"You are learning more than quickly enough."

Periwinkle played some more and found most of one of her favorite melodies.

When Coral took the torch and went outside to pass water, she brought another torch down with her. "It is night outside," she said.

63.

In the depths of Spirit Swamp, the *Pook-of-the-Silver* made its way hour after hour down the wide winding waters of the Turtle River. This late in the summer, most of the trees stood high on mounds of mud and reeds—twisted willows with long dark leaves, or cypresses with knobby roots and branches smothered with lichen. Herons and cranes, wading in the river's edge, took flight at the boat's wind-speeded approach, sometimes in large flocks that flapped their wings like distant thunder. Occasionally they saw a river lizard swimming, with only its eyes and nosetip above the water's surface, and once they passed five large ones sunning on a mudbank.

At twilight when the frogs and insects blended their songs to a richly textured drone, a drakey flew across the river.

"This river is more than a mile wide in winter," Bronzeberry said to Froth.

"They should be here by now," Rockdream said to Bellchime. "Coral said she would send a dream tonight, but I do not know how she expects me to sleep when I am worried."

"The only feeling I get from Distance is one of joy and great peace," said Bellchime.

"Coral says death is like that."

"Stop doing this to yourself!" Bellchime said, then added with a supportive voice, "Try going below and praying to the Great Mother Cat for guidance and peace."

After Rockdream went below, Bellchime realized how worried he was himself. Staring ahead at the river, he offered a prayer to

Grandfather Condor. Around the next bend, he saw a golden crescent moon setting over distant trees, and there he saw a condor take wing—it was clearly a condor, not a young drakey. The condor circled the boat, then flew across the river and out of sight.

"Thank you, Father," said Bellchime.

The unseen frogs continued their racket, and a thin mist began to form at treetop level, dimming the stars. Captain Muffin ordered Froth to take command and went below; Bronzeberry, Tarragon, and Bellchime became Froth's night crew.

64.

Coral sat by herself in a corner of the treasure cave, listening to the slow rhythm of Distance purring, and stared into the fire of the torch, letting her own breathing settle into slowness, and searched the flames for her husband's face.

She closed her eyes and found it, but it was blurred and vague. Ah, there was his chest, rising and falling beneath some colorful silk clothing, and all she had to do was breath with the same rhythm and she would be able to see him sharply, to touch him and talk with him.

They were walking together through the bare stone streets of Newport as it was before Riversong came, toward one of the many garden squares. Rockdream was dressed in the fine dyed silks of a castle warrior, and she wore a simple brown skirt and blouse. She remembered that spring day, it was the second month of the 195th year, and Rockdream began to blur again. In this dream this is now, she forced herself to think. We are walking in the garden.

He spoke awkwardly. "Coral, I know what you are," he said, meaning he knew she was a witch, "but I love you even so."

She said, "You must love me because I am myself, not despite it." That was her answer then, and still a good answer now. She took his hand and sat beside him on a bench facing the fountain. "Your hand feels so solid. May I kiss you?" she said, which was not at all what she had said before, but an honest expression of how she felt now. His kiss felt breathtakingly real.

"Come with me," she said and led him more quickly than any real street of Newport ran, to the gate of the castle.

"You cannot go in there," said Rockdream.

It was true; the castle was whole, and Lord Herring's guards stood at the gate.

"Let us go to my mother's cottage then," she said. "She will not be there."

Again she took a short-cut only possible in dreams and sat beside him on a bed of straw covered with a brown blanket, kissing him again and slipping her hand beneath his shirt to caress his back. She loosened the fastenings of his shirt, and while he took it off she pulled her own blouse and undershirt over her head. He reached to touch her small bare breast, and she felt his hand there for a moment, then backed away and said, "Before we go any further, husband, I want you to remember our camp on Goblin Plain."

He hesitated a moment and said, "Of course," and the room they were about to make love in somehow became their tent. "That is right. You were going to—" he said, and began to blur.

"Do not think of that," she said, relieved that his hand was solid when he touched her breast again. She took both of his hands in her own and pressed them together. "I have something I want to show you, and then we can make love. Do you agree?"

"Of course," he said, and removed the rest of his clothes.

Coral took out the emerald and the ruby.

"Periwinkle and I went to Riversong's hoard today, and I got these," she said, putting the gems in his hand.

"I am glad," he said and handed them back to her. "Can we make love now?"

She took off her skirt and bloomers. He began to blur the moment he entered her, but she matched breaths with him and moved very slowly. "We went to Riversong's hoard," she repeated. He was still asleep, solid and real until the moment of his orgasm, when he suddenly disappeared.

Coral reached under her short leather dress to touch herself as she came out of trance and immediately shuddered waves.

Below deck on the *Pook-of-the-Silver*, Rockdream was surprised and disappointed to find her gone from his arms, but then he understood her message and was overjoyed, and pulled on his breeches and vest and climbed up to the deck to tell Bellchime the news.

65.

About midmorning the next day, Captain Muffin and her crew were tacking the *Pook-of-the-Silver* to keep it in the main channel, while taking advantage of a strong breeze. They were passing through open marshland when Rockdream sensed something, and ahead was a bluish-gray dragon flying swiftly toward them.

I come alone, to bring Bellchime and Rockdream to Newport, said Distance.

"She cannot possibly land on this boat," said Sedge.

"Why not?" asked Rockdream. "She weighs less than two horses. Her wingspan fools you."

"Only two horses?" said Muffin. "Why, we could almost load a mammoth on this boat. Furl the sails," she ordered, and when this was done, *Pook-of-the-Silver* slowed to a drift.

Distance stopped circling and flapped her wings to land as lightly as possible on the bow, but even so, the boat rocked as though battered by a great wave of the sea. Bellchime, who was just climbing out of the hold, was almost thrown off the ladder. The dragon took a step toward the main mast to balance herself better, and Rockdream mounted her shoulders.

"Do you want a ride to Newport or do you want to sleep?" he asked Bellchime, who was standing groggily.

"Give me a moment to wake myself up. I do want to go, but my head is full of cobwebs."

"Here," said Black Rose, handing him a cup of steeped peppermint and a chewy biscuit.

"Thank you," he said. The tea was cool enough to drink, and he sipped it between bites of biscuit and handed her back the cup. Still chewing the biscuit, he mounted the dragon behind Rockdream.

Distance spread her wings, flapped them several times, and jumped into flight, giving the *Pook-of-the-Silver* a sudden lurch that made Sedge and one of the goblins stumble and fall.

"My sea legs are not what they used to be," Sedge said with some embarrassment.

"Well, I have sailed storms and floods with overloaded boats, but I never dreamed I would sail a dragon's roost," said Muffin.

66.

The river fell away beneath Distance's neck and forelegs. They passed over open marsh and dense groves of cypress, over the Sharp Bend Village river and the wide gap between the northern and southern Foggy Mountains.

The ruins of Newport upset Rockdream. "Ten thousand people once lived in this city, and perhaps a thousand live now," he said.

"The moment someone begins to rebuild Newport, many more survivors will reappear," said Bellchime. "But even so more have died than live." He sang the song that Coral made:

> Cry till our grief becomes love
> for friends both dead and living,
> renewing our joy in being alive
> and sharing this truth with each other.

"You ease my heart, brother," said Rockdream.

Distance flapped to a landing in the castle courtyard, where Periwinkle and Coral stood in front of a large piece of lead roofing with a hole torn in it.

"This was Riversong's door," Periwinkle said after the men dismounted. "We could not move it, so we broke in."

Coral struck a sparker and lit a silver lamp, both of which came from the hoard, and all four, and the dragon, ducked through the hole and walked down the large tunnel.

"Riversong dug this tunnel through solid rock," Rockdream said, feeling the clawmarks on the walls.

Digging is not hard, said Distance, and to demonstrate, she belched a blinding flame at the wall and struck the rock with her left forefoot, knocking out a chunk the size of a human head.

Bellchime and Rockdream were amazed by the hoard, and even more amazed by the story of the contest and truce with Redmoon.

When they discussed what they would do with the hoard, Bellchime wanted to set aside a share for Distance's hoard, a share to rebuild and repopulate Newport, as a city where humans and goblins could live together, and a share to Lord Blackwood of Upriver, with the provision that it be returned to the Newport refugees living there. This much the others agreed to, but then Bellchime wanted to claim the title and power of king, and to use this power to train the dragonbound.

"What just happened with Redmoon proves even more that if every dragon was bound to people who love her or him the way we love Distance, there would be no more dragon attacks," he said.

"Now you are wishing for the impossible," said Rockdream.

"If a camp of humans can live like goblins, is any change in custom truly impossible?"

"There are only about seventy of us. You want to change the customs of hundreds of thousands."

"Which is why I must be king," Bellchime said with a smile, putting the silver cup he was fingering on top of his head like a crown, which made Rockdream laugh.

Coral said, "If you have the power to be king, it does not matter whether you have the title. We have a claim to both Goblin Plain and Newport; and the people still in Spirit Swamp, except those of Drill's Village, all but acknowledge us as their lords and ladies."

"Who should we make the new Lord of Newport?" asked Bellchime.

"I disqualify Drill and Marten, even if either of them still lives," said Periwinkle, "and I suggest my father Tarragon. He is the only surviving person besides the four of us who had a direct hand in killing Riversong. Unless you want Newport," she said to Rockdream.

"I prefer my tent."

"We do not know Tarragon very well," said Coral, "but if Bellchime thinks he would be good—"

"Who would replace your father at the keep?" asked Bellchime.

"The city of Indigo, you mean," said Periwinkle.

"Oh. Right."

"Why, Heroncry, of course! He made the peace with the goblins."

67.

Having decided that, Periwinkle and Bellchime took Distance hunting, while Rockdream and Coral explored the castle. As might be expected, large animals were scarce near Riversong's den, but in the Foggy Mountain foothills they finally spotted a herd of wild pigs in the brush and killed two of these, one for Distance to eat and one to take back to Newport. Periwinkle and Bellchime dug up some of the tubers the pigs were rooting at, then saw some wild lettuce and other herbs and took some of these.

Meanwhile at the castle, Rockdream and Coral found a large stewpot among other useful things, and so it was that when the *Pook-of-the-Silver* dropped anchor among the wrecks in Newport Harbor, and the crew took the skiff and canoe ashore, they found a feast waiting for them in the castle courtyard.

Bellchime and Periwinkle showed off the hoard to everyone, then made their offer to Tarragon.

"A lord is vassal to no one but a king, Bellchime," said Black Rose.

"Let me tell you what laws I have in mind and see if they seem acceptable to you," said Bellchime, and Periwinkle and Coral clarified some points when Tarragon asked questions.

Tarragon said,

> Wiser than elves you must be,
> to bring your people peace,
> to give them long lives, and laws
> better than the laws of old,

paraphrasing "Good King Wintercress" from *The Oldest Book of Songs*.

"Do it, my lord," said Froth. "With just a few hundred of these coins, I could build you a fleet of ships that will pay for themselves in three years. We control the mouth of the river, and there will be trade as well as fishing."

"I like it," said Bronzeberry. "Froth the fishcatcher, merchant, storyteller, and wizard, becomes Froth the portmaster." She reached over to squeeze his hand, looking into his eyes very seriously for just a moment. She was too old to give him a child to replace the son he lost, but she could give him her love, if he would accept that. The next thing she knew, he was giving her a hug, not hesitantly as before, but with solid strength.

"I agree with Froth," Sedge was saying. "The city we are starting to build up in the mountains is nice, but compared with what we can do here, it is little."

"One question remains," said Tarragon. "What if someone survives from Wentletrap's dynasty?"

"The people of Newport depose them," said Coral. "We told the people of the four villages about Lord Herring's son and grandson, and they say that Drill and Marten abandoned their duties as lords, which we four fulfilled."

Periwinkle said, "Marten may have caused the death of his entire village with his fear of me. After all the work Coral and Rockdream and I did to stop the epidemic of swamp sickness, not to mention killing Riversong, I am not going to give the city of Newport to the fool who exiled me from its lands forever, for the crime of discovering his secret village and offering to save his father's life."

Bronzeberry said, "I served both Drill and Marten for three years, and call myself a fool for doing so. Drill is almost certainly dead, and Marten—if he lives, he will wait till the castle is rebuilt, then come striding up to the gate to proclaim himself Newport's rightful lord. By then, the people of Newport will know their rightful lord is you."

Bellchime said simply, "Are you the rightful lord of Newport? The decision is yours. We can choose someone else if you refuse."

"Refuse?" asked Tarragon. "Certainly not. Your majesties, you have hired yourselves a lord, and one of the best. What do we do next?"

—15—

A NEW TIME BEGINS

68.

"There they are," said Periwinkle, and just north of the Bear River was the riverboat of the Upriver ambassadors, sailing against the current.

Distance angled her wings and dove toward the boat, saying, *Lord Bellchime comes to tell you that Tarragon is Lord of Newport. We are going to see Lord Blackwood. Will one of you come with us?*

The ambassadors spoke with each other, and the woman named Yarrow agreed, and was taken ashore. While Periwinkle rigged the harness for her to sit on the dragon's hips, Yarrow said, "This will be something to tell my grandchildren, that I rode the dragon Distance with Bellchime and Periwinkle. Your deeds will be the matter of song and story long after I am dead and forgotten, maybe even long after Lord Blackwood is dead and forgotten, but do not tell him I said so."

Hour after hour they flew, crossing the Silver Mountains late in the afternoon, sighting Fallow's Keep just before sunset. Sometime after moonset they saw the glowing streetlights and windows of Upriver.

"Stay high till the guards accept us," said Bellchime.

Distance bellowed and belched a small flame, then said in a booming mental voice, *The dragon Distance brings Lord*

Bellchime and Lady Periwinkle of Goblin Plain, and Ambassador Yarrow of Upriver, to see Lord Blackwood. The dragon Riversong is dead. May we land in peace? After a moment, she said quietly to Bellchime and Periwinkle, *They seem stunned. Should I repeat my message?*

"Give them a few moments," said Bellchime.

Never mind. They are discussing and shouting. One of them is running inside. We can land.

She landed in the courtyard where warriors were gathering, and the three humans dismounted.

"I am Lord Bellchime of Goblin Plain, and this is Lady Periwinkle. We have come to speak with Lord Blackwood. Will he see us?"

"He welcomes you to Upriver Castle and offers you his finest guest room. What does your dragon require?"

A goat would be nice, said Distance.

"She flew all the way from Newport today and is hungry," explained Bellchime.

"Take care of it," Yarrow said to one of the lesser guards. "I will show them to their room," she said to the captain. "Come," she said and led Bellchime and Periwinkle through a maze of torchlit rooms and corridors, and up a flight of stairs to a guard.

"Ambassador Yarrow, Lord Bellchime, and Lady Periwinkle to see Lord Blackwood."

"But I thought—" the guard began, and Yarrow cut him off. "Is Lord Blackwood awake?"

"Yes, but— "

"Then we will see him."

"It is your head."

"Why do you say such a crude thing?" asked Bellchime. "I am certain my lord Blackwood is no more inclined to behead an ambassador bringing important news than I would be."

"Your pardon, Lord Bellchime," said the guard. "It is but a figure of speech for his displeasure."

"Then say so."

"Yes, my lord."

Periwinkle stifled a giggle, and they walked down the hall to another guard.

"Ambassador Yarrow, Lord Bellchime, and Lady Periwinkle to see Lord Blackwood," she said again.

"Send them in," said Lord Blackwood's voice, and the guard opened the door.

They stepped into a bedroom richly furnished, with intricate tapestries from west of the sea hanging on the wall, and Lord Blackwood dressed in a silk robe sitting in a large oaken bed.

"Just like young people to call at this hour," he said. "Come in, sit down. What is it that cannot wait till tomorrow morning?"

"Riversong is dead. I come to talk about the Newport Hoard."

And they talked about rebuilding that city. When Bellchime said he wanted to give the refugees who chose to remain in Upriver their fortunes back, Blackwood said, "That sounds most kind of you. Have you reasons besides kindness for doing this?"

"Kindness is our most important reason," said Periwinkle.

"Which may be unusual behavior for a lord," said Bellchime, "but—"

"Kindness is very lordlike," said Blackwood, "but distributing treasure must be done carefully, to avoid riots and disturbances."

"Exactly. However, we do have our price."

"Speak plainly. What do you want?"

"We want a peace that endures," said Bellchime. "Peace with goblins and peace with dragons."

"I suppose you want to instruct me on how to do this."

Bellchime and Periwinkle talked about Human Camp, and peace circles, and dancing with pooks, and how all these practices not only helped them end the war on Goblin Plain, but modified Distance's instincts.

Periwinkle said, "Distance phrased it very well when she said that love applied correctly is more powerful than power."

"I want to make it possible for other dragons to grow up with the same kind of love," said Bellchime.

"Interesting," said Blackwood.

"A dragonbound human is totally alone, except for the dragon," said Bellchime. "I had no friends except one girl on the edge of womanhood miles away who accepted my dreamsendings. Now what kind of child would a mother raise, who had comparable isolation and resentments, especially if the child was born with the soul of a fierce warrior or a black wizard? What would happen if dragonbound humans were not exiled or killed, but, instead, trained?"

"Hopefully not something like those goblins of the far south with the dragonbound priests and sacrifices," said Driftwood.

"I do not believe that story," said Yarrow.

Periwinkle said, "Distance will never eat any people at all, human, goblin, elf, or pook. If the laws and customs were changed, the dragonbound might seek us out."

"Why not require them to be trained?" said Yarrow.

"That would be possible since you are the only people in the world who could train them. It still amounts to exile, at least until the dragon is trained."

"A dragon is a good defense against other dragons," said Yarrow.

"Do you serve me or Bellchime?" asked Blackwood sharply.

"I serve you, my lord. I believe it is in your best interest and Upriver's to make this new law."

"Is that your price for sharing the treasure?"

"Yes," said Bellchime.

"Done," said Blackwood. "I will issue a proclamation tomorrow. Have we any more urgent business as rulers tonight?"

"No."

"I understand you were once a storyteller. This tired old man wants a good bedtime story. Tell me how Riversong died."

"With pleasure," said Bellchime.

69.

When Bellchime and Periwinkle came on foot to the harbor to buy a boat, to move Distance's share of the hoard to Goblin Plain, they found carpenters and sailors busy everywhere, making repairs on the fleet, and discovered that none were for sale.

"You heard the proclamation," said the portmaster, not knowing who Bellchime was. "We will be needing all our boats."

"Then I want to charter a boat to Newport."

"Perhaps I can do that, but what is your hurry? A charter will cost you ten starmarks, and in a month or less we will have passenger service for maybe as little as eight treemarks, less if you work your way. Are you outlaws or something? In those clothes you look almost like goblins."

"I am Lord Bellchime of Goblin Plain and I will gladly pay ten starmarks to charter a boat."

The portmaster squinted at Bellchime. "Truly? Blood! Lord Bellchime? I beg your pardon, my lord. I expected a lord in bright silk, or maybe dark sorcerer's robes, riding a great blue dragon."

"Of course the lord of the goblins would dress like a goblin," said Periwinkle.

The portmaster bargained at length about the price, trying to find some justification for raising it. Bellchime finally agreed to twelve starmarks if he could choose the captain and crew himself, because it was crucial that these be trustworthy people, and called Distance to the harbor to help him make these choices.

"She heard you?" asked the portmaster.

"She is at the castle and will be here in a minute," Bellchime said, and soon the dragon appeared overhead, and settled to the ground with a few flaps of wide ribbed wings. The sailors all stopped working, frozen between curiosity and fear.

You have never seen a dragon before, Distance said to the stunned portmaster, and stretching her head toward him, she said, *I like to be scratched behind the ears*.

"She is trying to be friendly," said Periwinkle.

The portmaster very hesitantly reached up to touch the dragon's head.

"Can we select a crew?" Bellchime asked Distance and the portmaster.

"I need a crew of fourteen for Newport and back!" he shouted. "Ten treemarks, and one starmark for the captain!"

"Stop living in the past!" one sailor-woman shouted derisively.

"We could not even get drunk on that!" shouted an older man.

"It is like this all over Upriver," the portmaster whispered to Bellchime and Periwinkle. "Too much work and no one to do it, so they all want higher wages. Do you see why I must charge so much?"

It was not till he shouted, "Fifteen treemarks! Anyone for Newport?" that any sailors gathered to volunteer.

Guided by Distance, Bellchime and Periwinkle made their selection, and chose the young woman who had shouted first to be captain, which brought some applause and cheers of "Captain Maggot!"

By this time, word had somehow spread through the city that Lord Bellchime the Hero-Conqueror was at the docks with his dragon, and a small crowd of people gathered, some to ask questions about Newport or Riversong or the treasure, but many just to gawk at the dragon. Before long, five armed guards on horseback rode through the market to the dock area, politely asking Bellchime and Periwinkle whether they wished to grant these people an audience, and suggesting that the castle might be a more appropriate place.

"We do not mean to go against your custom," Bellchime said, "but we plan to fly to Indigo as soon as I finish chartering this boat, and these people want to see me. Distance would know if there was any danger to us or chance of riot."

Your fear creates the unease you come to prevent, Distance said to the warriors.

"You have half an hour," said the leader. "For more than that, you must have Lord Blackwood's permission, and we will watch."

Many of the hundred or so people who had gathered were Newport refugees, and this exchange gave some of them one more reason to seek a new life somewhere else. Twenty decided to take Bellchime's charter to Goblin Plain or Newport.

"That is packing them in like slaves," said Captain Maggot, "but if they are willing to row, I will take them all."

"We rowed here from Newport, and we can row back," said one man.

Bellchime thanked everybody for coming to see him, and promised to hold a formal audience the next time he came to Upriver.

"We sail at noon," Maggot said to the prospective passengers, most of whom hurried away with the rest of the crowd, except six who had no possessions to fetch.

"I hope Lord Blackwood will not be displeased about this scene," Bellchime said to the portmaster.

"You have a way with malcontents," he replied. "If anything, he will be glad you took some away. There was a small riot the last full moon about people not getting paid on time and going hungry, and some of the guards are uneasy about crowds. Lord Blackwood tried to make it possible for the city to absorb everyone who came here, but he could not do it, and here you show up with the promise of a treasure. The warriors were worried about your intentions, I think."

"We should give Captain Maggot her instructions and be off," said Periwinkle.

70.

From Upriver to Indigo was perhaps two hours' flight, over hills and valleys carpeted with the lush forests of late summer. The towers and walls of the castle and keep looked diminutive to Periwinkle now, after the vast ruins of Newport, and even the sizeable castle of Upriver. Several newly completed and partially built houses enlarged the village in the center of the farmkeep, and the new farmland stretched beyond the junction of the roads to Hammer's Keep and Slot's Keep.

"Hardly a city," Periwinkle said into Bellchime's ear.

"Upriver went from this size to a city of one thousand in less than ten years," said Bellchime.

"And caused a war by doing so."

"Humans and goblins respect each other more than in those days," said Bellchime.

"If we were king and queen, and if both Heroncry and Stormbringer lived under our peace—"

"It is their choice," said Bellchime. "So far they seem to have made a fine peace without us."

Distance circled over the castle, bellowing and announcing the coming of Lord Bellchime and Lady Periwinkle of Goblin Plain, and before she even mentioned the death of Riversong, Heroncry told them to land in the courtyard.

"Blood! I am glad to see you alive and well," he said to Periwinkle when Distance landed. "You also, Bellchime. I was so glad to hear Lord Blackwood's news of you, garbled though it probably was. Did he and Tarragon make peace with you?"

"Yes, yes," said Periwinkle, "but there is much more news than that. Riversong is dead, my parents are the new lord and lady of Newport, and you, Heroncry, are the new lord of Indigo."

"Bloody death!" he bellowed, and Distance turned her head to look at him. "I hardly have enough time to go hunting even as a substitute lord, let alone—oh, all right, I will do it. Blood!"

"As a lord, you may be responsible for the lives and prosperity of your people, but no one is saying you must keep to your castle," said Bellchime.

"Huh. Well, Tarragon certainly did not. So how did all of this happen? Riversong dead? You must be the richest people east of the sea. Be careful."

When she began to explain their plans for the hoard, Periwinkle felt somewhat nervous, realizing that the seven other warriors with Heroncry, who had all watched her grow up, might be thinking of her as a rash young woman who would benefit from another year of lessons; but she forced herself to remember that she was now little less than a queen, and soon saw that even old Turner responded well to her authority.

When Bellchime told in summary the events surrounding Riversong's death, Heroncry was shocked and concerned by the implications of Froth's dragonbinding to Riversong.

"I am glad you survived breaking this curse in good mind. Poor man! I knew he was suffering, but never guessed why. Who would think a man who hated dragons was dragonbound? But is it well to spread this story? If it were common knowledge that a person could be an agent for the likes of Riversong without even knowing it, what a climate of suspicion that could create!"

"I never thought of that," said Bellchime, "but you cannot long hide the truth."

"I wonder why Riversong did it," said Periwinkle. "What could a dragon possibly learn from a man who never came near him again?"

"The one thing he did learn—" said Bellchime. "That a sorcerer lived who was strong and subtle enough to detect and break such a dragonbinding."

"Or else he expected one who hated dragons so much to join any warrior who tried to put together a force like Wentletrap's, thus making the army easier for him to sense," suggested Heroncry.

By this time, Distance was sprawled comfortably in the sun against the base of one of the towers, and Heroncry invited Periwinkle and Bellchime to stay for dinner, then led them into the pleasantly cool common room in the southeast tower.

"We had not planned to stay so long," Bellchime said.

"Come, Lord Bellchime, if you and I are lords, we must greet each other properly. Forest and the other warriors are out hunting and should bring us back a real feast. He thinks he knows where he can find a great elk. That is where Mandrake is, by the way," he said to Periwinkle. "The boat you chartered will not reach Newport until at least four days from now, and from your tale I know you can fly there in two. I will have the heralds proclaim a banquet when the hunters return, and you can tell your story in grand style to everyone in the keep—I mean, the city."

"Mandrake would be hurt if I missed him," said Periwinkle, "and someday he will be the lord of Newport."

71.

About an hour later the horns blew, announcing the return of the hunters, a procession of horseriders, leading two more horses pulling the carcass of a great elk in a narrow hunting cart. They stopped short of the castle gate because the outer guards had told them about the dragon, but Heroncry met them himself, assuring them that there was nothing to fear.

"Where is Periwinkle?" asked Mandrake.

"Right here," she said while the warriors led the horses through the gate into the courtyard.

He rushed up to her and hugged her. "Oh, I knew you were right! I knew it all along. But I was scared that maybe Froth was right, until Heroncry came back from Upriver with the news. I wanted to go with Father and Mother to see you, but they said no. We killed the biggest elk. Come look at it."

She walked with Mandrake toward the two horses with the cart. "That is a big one," she said. It was a male, and the antlers spread a full eight feet from tip to tip.

"That was my arrow," said Mandrake, pointing to a wound in the neck.

"If you are not going to help unload, get out of the way!" said Forest.

"We will both help," said Periwinkle, joining the men and women who made ready to pull the ropes to maneuver the cart into the great hall.

When they finally had it lowered into the roasting pit, Mandrake said, "I think I have to help skin and gut."

"Go spend some time with your sister," said Forest. "I am not that much of a beast that I cannot understand your need."

Mandrake and Periwinkle walked back out into the courtyard and toward the dragon.

"It is good that you stayed here," said Periwinkle. "You are not yet strong enough to be tested in battle against the likes of Riversong."

"Riversong!"

Periwinkle raised her hand over her head and said, "His head was this long from skull to snout, and he came within—" she drew her sword and gestured with it, "—that close. I slashed his eye. It was about as big as a plate. If he had been just a foot closer, I might have killed him, but he might have killed me. It does not matter, for he is dead now."

"Where did you get that sword?" asked Mandrake.

"Lord Herring's son gave it to the warrior Canticle, who was killed in the war, and Canticle's father sold it to me in the Upriver market the day after we got married."

"Herring was the last Lord of Newport, right? Is Bellchime Lord of Newport now?"

"Newport is part of our realm, but we made Father the Lord of Newport. He will not be coming back here."

"You could take me there with you, on your dragon," said Mandrake.

My name is Distance, said the dragon, opening her eye to look at the boy. *You may scratch behind my ears if you like.*

Mandrake was startled by the soundless words, but reached to touch the unfamiliar texture of the dragon's warm scales.

"I cannot take you with me this time," Periwinkle said. "I must take someone else, if he is still alive."

"Who?"

"An old, old man named Gar."

"Crazy Gar? Why do you want him? Heroncry says—"

"Never mind what Heroncry says. This is not his concern, and I see that it is also not yours."

Mandrake sighed.

This one is bored. He envies your deeds, said Distance.

Periwinkle shook her head slowly. "Oh, Mandrake! I would have been a very happy woman if Bellchime had never become dragonbound, if he had remained the keep's storyteller, if we had married here and lived together in my tower room for the rest of our lives. We were chosen to do these deeds by the Great Spirit, the Lord of Light and Darkness if you prefer, and I thank this power that Bellchime and I have proven capable and fortunate, because our happiness has been balanced on a sword's tip all too often. Do not ask to look death and destiny in the face. People who become involved in great deeds are more often than not tormented, as Froth was tormented."

"What do you mean?"

"Froth was dragonbound for twenty years to the dragon who killed his wife and son, and did not know this, and when Distance broke the binding, I was there beside him, and he knew me, as the same spirit who once wore the body of his wife, now completely committed to someone else, and unable to do anything beyond friendship to ease his pain."

Mandrake did not know what to say.

"I could have felt tormented by the things that happened to me, but I chose the way of love instead."

"I think I know what you mean," said Mandrake. "So tell me what happened the night you left the castle. You told the outer guard, 'May a mountain mammoth knock down your tower!' and rode Mother's horse into the snowy night, and then what happened? I want to know everything."

"Already that is more than I remember, but I will do my best," she said, sitting down on the ground next to Distance. "I left the road to try to make my own trail in a spruce grove, but ended up back on the road. The second time I urged the horse onto a unicorn's trail— " and she continued, for over an hour, telling him briefly about every interesting event.

Then Mandrake talked about his own life, how he was hunting with Forest and Heroncry, and learning swordplay, and Froth was teaching him calligraphy. Soon he was giving Periwinkle castle gossip: Heroncry's wife was living with a warrior at Slot's Keep, and Heroncry now spent most of his nights alone, and said he liked it better that way.

"Who will be Lord of Indigo when he dies, if he never has children?" asked Mandrake.

"There is always someone suited to the job," said Periwinkle. "Every dynasty sooner or later comes to nothing. Wentletrap's dynasty did. Come, if you are going to tell me about people's love affairs, at least tell me about your own."

Mandrake made a comical scowl. "All the girls say I am not old enough, or they are not old enough, or something, and the one I really liked, Stonewater from the farm, says she likes Jasper better, and besides a future lord should marry a warrior, she said. I think she thinks I am too serious a person. Do you think so?"

Periwinkle shook her head and said, "Stonewater has always liked Jasper, since before she even had breasts."

"I guess it takes me longer than you to notice these things."

"You will learn," said Periwinkle.

72.

Everyone in the village and castle came to the feast. When it was over and there was nothing left of that roast elk but soup bones, Bellchime told the story of Riversong's death in spellbinding words, but Mandrake told Periwinkle, "I liked the way you told it better. You can really understand a lot more when it starts with you leaving the castle. Of course if Bellchime told the story of that many things with vividness and detail, it would take many evenings, like the way he used to tell the story of Wentletrap and Pip. This story deserves the same. Someone should write it all down. I will, if Bellchime does not have the time."

Periwinkle and Bellchime climbed the tower stairs to her old bedroom, now a guest room.

"This became my room about a year after you disappeared," she told him. "This is where I was when you sent all those dreamsendings. Not quite," she added when she stepped inside. "Someone moved the bed." She felt the feather mattress. "In fact, this is a new bed. Well, everything else has changed." She unlaced the embroidered bodice of her dress. "Which reminds me—" and she told him about Mandrake's offer to write down their story.

"I said something like that to Froth, after the first battle, that killing Riversong meant little compared to what we had already done on Goblin Plain. Mandrake is right, the whole story is important, and if he transcribes it, the understanding he may gain will make him a better lord, when his time comes."

"Enough high-chief stuff for tonight, as Wedge would say," she said, pulling the dress over her head and putting her arms around him to unlace his vest. "Your wife wants to make love."

73.

The morning sun was still golden when Distance flew over the swift twisting waters of the Indigo River to the springs. Near this, in a small fenced clearing still mostly in the shade, was a small wooden hut. Distance said, *I think no one is here, but this one's thoughts are very quiet*.

"Oh, please let him be alive," said Periwinkle.

"He is probably out hunting," said Bellchime. "We should check the house."

Distance flapped to a landing and Periwinkle knocked on the door, calling Gar's name. When there was no answer, she opened the door and was relieved to see that everything looked much as it had last winter, but saddened by the sight of the skull of the wolf, Gar's former companion, above the hearth.

"Shall we look for him or wait?" asked Periwinkle.

"This early? He cannot have gone far."

"I think he is at the springs," Periwinkle said and ran off into the woods. In moments she saw him, trudging with a pail of water back toward his house.

"Slow down," he barked, not seeming surprised at all.

"Remember me? Periwinkle? The young war-woman? I promised I would bring you a knife and a crystal the next time I saw you. Let me help you carry that."

Gar shook his head. "Gar needs to know he can carry water himself."

"Bellchime and the dragon are waiting in your yard."

"You have the Great Mother Cat on your dress."

"I am also half a goblin now," she said. "My body is human, but my spirit is goblin. Bellchime is high chief of Goblin Plain, and we live there in a tent. This is what I really want to do, to take you there with us, to live in our camp, with friends and people, as the honored elder you deserve to be."

Gar set down his bucket, tears filling his eyes. "Gar does not know what to say. This is too good to believe, that Gar has lived long enough to see a new time begin."

"Spirit Father, I cannot leave you here to die alone," she said, and the old man hugged her, his body feeling both frail and strong to the young warrior.

"It is good that you wear the mother cat near your heart," he said.

"You are not afraid of cliffs or high places, are you?" she asked.

"You want Gar to ride your dragon? Gar is not afraid. Gar goes higher than that in the spirit world, and his hands are strong. He can hold on tight."

They walked together back to the clearing, Gar carrying his bucket all the way.

"He will come with us!" Periwinkle said to Bellchime and Distance.

Gar put his hands on his hips and looked at them both with a comic parody of frustration. "Give the old man time to pack his things," he growled, then burst into a cackling grin.

74.

It was long before dark by the time Distance flapped to a landing beside the new totem pole at Human Camp, where they were met by Coral, who asked how it went with Lord Blackwood.

"Perfectly," said Bellchime. "He agreed to distribute the treasure and gave us the new dragon law. And we also met with Lord Heroncry of Indigo." He paused. "Right now I want you to meet the shaman Gar, from Indigo Springs. Gar, this is the shamaness Coral, who killed the dragon Riversong."

"With much help from my friends," she said.

Periwinkle was untying the packs from Distance's back.

"Gar had no friends, no people, before today," he said.

His pain is deep. Do your best to make him welcome, said Distance.

Coral said, "We have plenty of dinner left over—steamed grain with bits of auroch meat, and a big piece of leg for Distance."

Good, said the dragon, walking carefully between the tents to the central cookfire.

"Other than that, you likely need a place to sleep."

"He can stay in our tent, till we make him one of his own," said Periwinkle.

"Gar can make his own tent," he said.

"If you prefer," said Periwinkle.

Bellchime said, "I do not want to seem impatient, but we must go to Newport tomorrow, to meet the treasure boat, so the sooner we can eat and go to sleep, the better."

"The boat just passed camp an hour ago. It will not reach Newport tomorrow," said Coral.

Periwinkle made an exaggerated sigh of relief. "Good. I need a day off from long flights and difficult discussions."

"So many people and situations to consider!" said Bellchime.

"A new time may be beginning, but the details will keep us busy all our lives."

"We will have plenty of help," said Coral, serving them each portions of grain and meat. Distance was already tearing bites from the leg. "Eat well. We can let tomorrow begin when we wake up."

APPENDIX ONE

PEOPLE AND DRAGONS

1.

The humans East of the Sea almost all came from the Middle Kingdom, West of the Sea, and consequently all spoke the same language. They varied somewhat in appearance, having skin sometimes as pale-pinkish as elves, sometimes as swarthy as the lighter goblins. Most had brown or black hair, but some had blonde or red. Their eyes were blue, gray, or light brown, their ears rounded.

In the first century after Windsong's founding of Turtleport, the humans had one religion, but two variant sects, each a heresy to the other, about whether the members of the Holy Family were separate gods and goddesses, or names for different aspects of the one true god, the Lord of Light and Darkness. In Periwinkle's time, the beginning of the third century, this dispute was no longer important, and humans would pray to whatever deity or name seemed most effective.

This shaded into witchcraft. Only priests and priestesses of the church were supposed to call upon or use the effective powers. In theory, their devotion, celibacy, and discipline prevented them from misusing these powers. In practice, most humans who needed these powers wanted them for a purpose that the church considered misuse, such as attracting a lover, advancing one's position, or sometimes even healing the sick.

Thus there were wizards and witches who used the effective powers for their own benefit, or that of whoever wished to hire them. These were the people most likely to attract dragonlings, with the usually dire consequences described in the story. In many cities witchcraft was illegal, in some it was tolerated as long as the wizards or witches lived ouside the city walls and did their work in a quiet way. Newport and Upriver were more liberal about this than most other cities.

Most humans lived in walled cities or keeps, or else in villages protected by these. Men and women were equally likely to take any occupation, and though there were more men warriors and blacksmiths than women, no one would think it unusual for a woman to be either of these. Farming was the most common occupation, followed by fishcatching. Other humans were builders, smiths, miners, potters, priests, merchants, storytellers, and warriors. Only a few practiced sorcery.

Scholars were mostly storytellers, priests, and sorcerers. Writing was pictographic, one symbol per word. Most artisans, merchants, and warriors also knew how to read and write.

The government of all cities was by a lord or lady, or both, and the warriors who protected the land and the people, not only from dragons or invading armies, but from anything else that threatened their lives and well-being. In times of poor harvest, a lord would buy his people food, or send his warriors out hunting. For the most part these people did not abuse their power, because of their deep belief in honor, which was not an established code, but a question to be asked and explored: Is this honorable? What would be the most honorable?

One logical consequence of this questioning was the partial breakdown of class barriers. A farmer's daughter could become a warrior, and a warrior's son could marry a fishcatcher, or become one.

Wizards and witches could not accept the discipline of the church, but many, like Coral, applied the question of honor to their own work.

To the Church, honor was not enough, precisely because it was used by people the church mistrusted, such as wizards or courtesans, to justify their own lives. Using religion to do this was heresy, no longer a punishable crime by itself, but often used as an incentive to urge lords and judges to find the heretic guilty of other crimes.

In Periwinkle's time, honor was a deeper part of most humans' lives than formal religion.

2.

The goblins were native to this continent, as far as they knew. They were all black- or brown-haired, and darker-skinned, with large, deep-brown eyes, pointed ears, broad noses, and fat lips. They claimed these traits gave them sharper senses and made them better hunters than humans. In the northwestern lands they had a tribal culture, more nomadic in some places than others, but always living in conical leather tents. Among goblins, men were hunters and warriors, and women did the work of the camp, an arrangement humans, especially human women, thought peculiar and unfair.

Goblins did not use cloth, or domesticate animals, but lived by hunting and gathering, and dressed in leather and fur. Many of their tools and utensils were by this time traded from humans, and some tribes and regions, such as Goblin Plain, adopted the human language because it was widely understood. Other than this they kept their own culture.

Their religion and magic were one; a shaman was both wizard and priest. They visualized the effective powers as spirit beasts. It may be noticed that the Oak Lake and Goblin Plain goblins have slightly different beliefs about these. To the Oak Lake people, they are clan spirits, inherited from parents, real or adopted; but to the Goblin Plain people, they are guardians who belong to each individual from birth, regardless of descent, and even humans, who as a rule know nothing about these things, have them. This belief is probably closer to the truth.

3.

Elves do not appear in this story, but they tend to be taller and thinner than other people. They have very pale skin, large blue eyes, narrow noses, pointed ears, and white hair, even as children.

Their wisdom and knowledge are legendary, and they are reputed to live forever, or at least much longer than other people, but according to Pip the Elf, wife of the first Lord of Newport, this is untrue, or does not mean what other people think it means.

Elves, goblins, and humans seldom intermarried at the time of this story, but any combination was fertile.

4.

Pooks are a people apart, no larger than cats or monkeys, and completely covered with fur, which may be any shade of yellow, brown, or black. They live in holes, play music on small pipes made of reeds, and seem to be as skilled at hearing thoughts as any priest, shaman, or dragon. They are seldom seen doing anything but dancing. They are supposed to eat wild fruit, nuts, tubers, and mushrooms, which they store in their holes and defend with curses of bad luck, but this is hearsay.

5.

Dragons and drakeys are lizards that have taken ribbed wings beyond gliding to true powered flight, and indeed exceed the size and weight of all other flying creatures. A large male drakey may weigh as much as a human, having a wingspan of nearly twenty feet, but dragons grow much larger than mammoths.

Dragons breathe fire and drakeys do not, but both have flight bladders filled with firegas, which is lighter than air. Dragons must have some mechanism preventing them from backfiring and blowing themselves up, and one preventing them from belching so much flame that they no longer have enough firegas to fly, but the nature of these mechanisms is unknown.

Drakeys are no more than animals, probably as intelligent as most predatory birds or mammals. Indeed the large brains of drakeys and dragons give their heads an unreptilian look.

Dragons are intelligent enough to use language, and some believe they are more intelligent than people, but their fierceness makes comparison hard. Of their telepathy and other mental abilities, little need be added here. Dragonbinding is probably necessary because dragons are too fierce to raise their own young. It may have originated as a hunting tool for young dragonlings, when small and awkward on land, and its use as a learning process was a natural side-effect of this, when dragonlings bound humans or other peoples, or even the more intelligent animals. But this is speculation.

APPENDIX TWO

CHRONOLOGY

At the time of this story, humans east of the sea numbered their years from Windsong the Mariner's last voyage and the founding of Turtleport, and their days from the spring equinox, this being day 1, and throughout the year to 368, or 367 on short years. The first day of summer is traditionally the 80th day, the summer solstice is the 93rd day, and Midsummer's Day is the 120th day. The fall equinox is the 185th day. The beginning of winter is the 260th day, the winter solstice is the 277th day, and Midwinter's Day is the 300th day.

The week has eight days, each named for one of the Holy Family, except for the eighth, which would be named for the Nameless Mother, if she had a name, but is instead called Market Day.

The date of Periwinkle and Bellchime's marriage, and the date Tarragon became fourth Lord of Newport, are both recorded, and from these the others may be approximated.

Year

  1. Windsong the Mariner founds Turtleport.
 10. Coveport founded.
 14. Settling of the Valley begins. Some trouble with goblins.
 22. Midcoast founded.
 28. Death of Windsong.

30. First Goblin War begins.
33. Isle of Hod settled. Noted as a place of pirates.
38. Goblin chiefs sit a peace circle with the lords of Coveport, Midcoast, and Turtleport. The region around Turtleport and the entire Valley of Two Rivers is opened to human settlement; other lands are to remain goblin.
44. Dragonbound wizard Bracken kills his dragon and ruins the weather around the Isle of Hod.
50. Rockport founded.
52. About then Auroch becomes dragonbound to Mugwort.
57. About then Auroch dies, and Mugwort flees.
62. Mugwort attacks and destroys Turtleport.
66. War of the Valley begins; humans fight humans.
71. Humans break the peace circle by founding Moonport.
72. Humans win the Moon Valley War.
89. Wentletrap born in Rockport.
98. Tipspear born in Rockport.
107. Upriver founded, as a keep.
117. Goblins attack Upriver.
120. Tipspear founds a keep on the Indigo River. Other keeps founded. Continuous war with goblins. About this time, Gar is born.
123. Wentletrap, after winning the Upriver War, gathers a private army, kills Mugwort, and founds Newport.
124. Wentletrap and Pip's daughter, Blackberry, born.
130. Stonewort born, son of Tipspear.
137. About this time Drakey is born on Goblin Plain.
141. Blackberry's son, the future Lord Herring, born.
144. Wentletrap and Pip leave Newport, never to be seen again, and Blackberry's husband, Stock, becomes second Lord of Newport.
157. Froth born in Moonport.
159. Tipspear dies; Stonewort becomes keepholder.
162. Heroncry born at Stonewort's Keep.
166. Black Rose born, daughter of Stonewort.
168. Tarragon born at what will become Slot's Keep.
169. Drill born, fourth son of Herring and great-grandson of Wentletrap.
170. About this time Beartooth is born on Goblin Plain.
172. Hope born in Newport. About then Riversong dragonbinds Moth.

177. About then Riversong kills Moth. Coral born in Newport.
178. Froth marries Limpet in Moonport. Rockdream born in Newport.
179. Bellchime born in Midcoast.
180. Herring becomes third Lord of Newport.
181. Oak Lake goblins attack Stonewort's Keep, killing his older children.
182. Riversong destroys Moonport, killing Froth's wife and son. Froth moves to Midcoast. Stonewort's campaign
183. Stonewort makes truce with Oak Lake goblins. Black Rose marries Tarragon.
186. Froth moves to Rockport.
187. Periwinkle born. About this time Gar is driven from Copper Mountain and moves to Indigo Springs.
190. Froth becomes a merchant. Marten born, son of Drill.
191. Mandrake born.
193. Stonewort dies; Tarragon becomes keepholder. Bellchime apprenticed to Rush, Tarragon's storyteller.
194. Froth meets Taproot while on business trip to Upriver, and becomes his apprentice.
195. Tarragon and Periwinkle meet Upriver's Lord Blackwood. Taproot becomes dragonbound. Coral marries Rockdream.
196. Froth kills Taproot and the dragonling, moves to Upriver. Rush dies, and Bellchime succeeds him as storyteller.
198. Bellchime dragonbound in Upriver. Two dragons, later identified as Redmoon and Riversong, are seen by a foreign ship captain sailing for Newport. Wedge born to Rockdream and Coral. Froth becomes Tarragon's storyteller.
199. Riversong besieges and destroys Newport in the spring, killing Lord Herring and most of his family. General Canticle tries to build a large settlement of refugees on Goblin Plain. Others build small villages in Spirit Swamp.
200. The Goblin Plain War begins. Spirit Swamp villages afflicted with swamp sickness. Bellchime visits Upriver, disguised as a priest.
201. Late in the summer, General Canticle is killed. Strong Bull wins many battles with Newport humans. Some escape to Upriver, some are driven back to Spirit Swamp.
202. Froth captured by Trout while looking for Bellchime. Coral heals Wedge of swamp sickness, with the help of her

spirit condor. Rockdream and Coral sit the peace circle with Strong Bull and Drakey, and found Human Camp.

202nd year, 364th day. Full moon. Bellchime summons Periwinkle.

367th day. They are married in Upriver.

368th day. Last day. They move to bears' cave.

203rd year, 57th day. Distance breathes first flame.

61st day.	Death of Strong Bull.
62nd day.	Peace circle in Human Camp.
68th day.	New moon. High chief trial.
76th day.	Contact with Driftwood's Village.
97th day.	New moon; completion of trade with four villages.
111th day.	Midsummer Moon Council
112th day.	Contact with Lord Drill's Village.
142nd day.	Heroncry and Froth meet with Lord Blackwood.
152nd day.	First battle with Riversong.
155th day.	Battle at Beartooth's Camp.
157th day.	Tarragon becomes fourth Lord of Newport.
159th day.	Meeting with Heroncry and Mandrake.

INDEX OF NAMES

Almost every place mentioned in the story is found on the map, except—places west of the sea; Swordwall, which is on the coast far north of Rockport; Southport and the Isle of Hod, which are both far south of Turtleport; and the Goblin Empire, which is twice as far south as that. The Mortarstone River, unlabeled for lack of space, flows from Cat's Tooth Pass to Fallow's Keep.

The list of names that follows briefly identifies every character mentioned in the story:

BRINE, human man, Driftwood's Village priest.

BRONZEBERRY, human woman, Drill's Village warrior.

CANTICLE, human man, Newport warrior killed in Goblin Plain war.

CATSCLAW, goblin man, Goblin Plain high-chief candidate.

CICADA, goblin woman, Beartooth's wife.

CONCH, human man, Drill's Village warrior.

CORAL, human woman, Human Camp shamaness, married to Rockdream.

CRICKET, goblin woman, Redfox's wife.

CUMIN, human man, Upriver priest.

DISTANCE, female dragon, bound to Bellchime.

DRAKEY, goblin man, Goblin Plain high shaman.

DREAMLEAF, 3rd c. before Windsong, elf man, west of the sea.

DRILL, human man, Herring's son, Spirit Swamp village master.

DRUM, goblin man, Redfox's Camp shaman.

DRIFTWOOD, human man, Spirit Swamp village master.

EASTWOOD, human boy, Tarragon's Keep farmer's son.

ELKHORN, goblin man, Goblin Plain chief, high-chief candidate.

ENDIVE, human woman, Newport exile in Upriver.

FALLOW, human man, Keepholder.

FEATHER, human woman, Blue River Inn barmaid, Upriver.

FEATHERGRASS, human man, Human Camp warrior.

FILAREE, human woman, Sleep and Spirits barmaid, Upriver.

FLATFISH, human man at Human Camp, married to Swanfeather.

FOREST, human man, Tarragon's Keep warrior.

FROTH, human man, Tarragon's Keep storyteller, ex-fishcatcher.

GABLE, human man, Sleep and Spirits innkeeper, Upriver.

GAR, half-human, half-goblin man, shaman at Indigo Springs.

GLOWFLY, goblin woman, Beartooth's Camp shamaness.

GORGE, goblin man, Goblin Plain chief.

GRAY LIZARD, goblin man, Beartooth's Camp warrior.

GREENSPEAR, human man, Tarragon's Keep warrior, recently died.

HAMMER, human man, keepholder.

HERONCRY, human man, Tarragon's Keep warrior.

HERRING, human man, third lord of Newport, Wentletrap's grandson.

HOPE, human woman, former priestess from Newport.

IRIS, human woman, Newport exile, Upriver guard.

IRONWEED, human man at Human Camp, married to Stone-water.

JASPER, human boy, Tarragon's Keep.

JAY, human girl, Human Camp.

LEAN WOLF, goblin man from Spincloud's Camp, married to Lightstep.

LIGHTSTEP, goblin woman from Elkhorn's Camp, married to Lean Wolf.

LIMPET, human woman, Froth's wife in Moonport, killed by Riversong.

LIMPET, human woman, Human Camp.

MAGGOT, human woman, Upriver sailor and boat captain.

MALLOW, human woman, priestess at Lord Drill's village.

MANDRAKE, human boy, Periwinkle's brother.

MARTEN, human boy, Drill's son.

MOTH, late 2nd c. human woman, witch dragonbound to Riversong.

MUFFIN, human woman, captain of the *Pook-of-the-Silver*.

MUGWORT, 1st c. male dragon, killed by Wentletrap's army.

OAKROOT, 2nd c. human man, Upriver sculptor.

PIP, early 2nd c. elf woman, Wentletrap's wife and advisor.

PIP, human woman, Newport exile in Upriver.

PERIWINKLE, human woman, Tarragon's Keep warrior

PERIWINKLE, pook woman, Little Dragonstone Mountain.

QUAGGA, goblin man, Goblin Plain chief, high-chief candidate.

REDBARK, goblin man, Goblin Plain chief, high-chief candidate.

REDFOX, goblin man, Oak Lake people chief.

REDMOON, female dragon, destroyed Southport, occupied Moonport.

RIPPLE, human girl, Birdwade's daughter.

RIVERSONG, male dragon, destroyed Moonport and Newport.

ROCKDREAM, human man, chief of Human Camp, married to Coral.

RUSH, human man, Tarragon's Keep storyteller before Bellchime.

SALMON, human woman, Human Camp shamaness, married to Bloodroot.

SEDGE, human man, Tarragon's Keep servant, ex-fishcatcher.

SHARPSTONE, human man, Driftwood's Village hunter.

SHELLFLY, goblin woman, Elkhorn's wife.

SILVERFISH, goblin woman, shamaness at Skyrock's Camp.

SKYROCK, goblin man, Goblin Plain Chief.

SLOT, human man, keepholder.

SPINCLOUD, goblin man, Goblin Plain chief, high-chief candidate.

SPINEBALL, human man, Newport farmer, presumed dead.

SPLIT HOOF, goblin man, Elkhorn's Camp shaman.

STOCK, 2nd c. human man, second lord of Newport, married Blackberry.

STONEWATER, human woman, Human Camp warrior, married Ironweed.

STONEWATER, human girl, Tarragon's Keep farmer's daughter.

STONEWORT, 2nd c. human man, keepholder, Black Rose's father.

STORMBRINGER, goblin man, Oak Lake high chief.

STORMCLOUD, goblin man, Goblin Plain high-chief candidate.

STOUT, human man, Blue River Inn innkeeper, Upriver.

STRONG BULL, goblin man, Goblin Plain high chief.

SUNDANCE, goblin man, Goblin Plain chief.

SWANFEATHER, human woman at Human Camp, married to Flatfish.

TAPROOT, human man, Silver Mountains wizard, killed by Froth.

TARRAGON, human man, keepholder, Periwinkle's father.

TIPSPEAR, early 2nd c. human man, keepfounder, Stonewort's father.

TOADSTOOL, goblin man, Redfox's Camp warrior.

TOMCOD, goblin man, Oak Lake high shaman.

TORCHFIRE, human woman, Hammer's Keep warrior.

TRILLIUM, human woman, Blue River Inn barmaid, Upriver.

TROUT, goblin man, Oak Lake people chief.

TURNER, human man, Tarragon's Keep warrior.

TUSK, goblin man, messenger from Gorge's Camp.

WEDGE, human boy, Rockdream and Coral's son.

WENTLETRAP, early 2nd c. human man, first lord of Newport, married to Pip.

WINDSONG, early 1st c. human woman, mariner, founded Turtleport.

WINTERCRESS, human man, legendary wizard-king.

YARROW, human woman, Upriver ambassador to Goblin Plain.

Stories
✠✠ of ✠✠
Swords and Sorcery

✠✠✠✠✠✠✠✠✠✠✠✠✠✠✠✠✠✠✠

✠✠✠✠✠✠✠✠✠✠✠✠✠✠✠✠✠✠✠

Please send the titles I've checked above. Mail orders to:

BERKLEY PUBLISHING GROUP
390 Murray Hill Pkwy., Dept. B
East Rutherford, NJ 07073

NAME _____

ADDRESS _____

CITY _____

STATE _____ ZIP _____

Please allow 6 weeks for delivery.
Prices are subject to change without notice.

POSTAGE & HANDLING:
$1.00 for one book, $.25 for each
additional. Do not exceed $3.50.

BOOK TOTAL	$_____
SHIPPING & HANDLING	$_____
APPLICABLE SALES TAX (CA, NJ, NY, PA)	$_____
TOTAL AMOUNT DUE PAYABLE IN US FUNDS. (No cash orders accepted.)	$_____

Fantasy from Ace
fanciful and fantastic!